LOAD THE DICE

LOAD THE DICE

MORIAH GEMEL

CONSENT.
an imprint of interlude press

CONTENTS

BLIND BET

BLIND BET

Eric's not sure how Andy convinced him to go to this thing. Gay hookup parties aren't exactly his normal scene—not for a long time, anyway. He prefers quiet piano bars and coffee shops. He prefers peace. The party scene was never peaceful for him. But they'd had a few shots of tequila at his place to pregame, and instead of going to a low-key gay bar, they're going to this party that Andy's latest girlfriend is attending. So Eric just walks along behind Andy, determinedly *not* imagining her falling off those sky-high heels, messing up her perfect pixie cut and perfect makeup on her perfect snub-nosed face and perfectly tailored pantsuit with no shirt underneath, even as they make their way up from the subway, and then a block to a trendy hotel in Manhattan.

"This is a classy gig, okay?" Andy says as they approach a set of elevators. "It's being thrown by some rich boy who's apparently tossing these shindigs all over the place, and only the hottest get in. So try not to be a twerp, okay?"

"Thanks, Andy," Eric grits out, quickly sobering as the elevator rises and his stomach drops. If Andy hadn't been his best friend for years, ever since he entered the scene, he might've told her to screw off. But more often than not, she has his best interests at heart, and always has in her own abrasive way.

The doors open to a foyer that's filled with stylishly dressed, beautiful people. Eric mentally thanks Andy for coaxing him into wearing one of his best outfits; if he'd shown up in jeans and T-shirt he would've been kicked out. But now he's here in black cigarette slacks, a tight, dark green waistcoat, and a starched white button-up with a textured black tie and a fancy silver-and-emerald tie clip that his mom and dad got him for his

-2-

last birthday. His hair is styled, he's put together, and he feels ready to face anything. Mostly.

A large man steps up to them when they enter. He's actually carrying a clipboard.

"Names?"

"We're not on that list, sweetheart," Andy says, smiling. "But go tell Leta that Andy is here with the promised man candy."

The man raises an eyebrow, but he turns and goes into the mass of people chatting and dancing and drinking their night away. Within moments, there's a squeal, and a curvy redhead with a great smile hurries forward and tugs Andy into a hug.

"Andy! You came!" she laughs. She looks over at Eric. "Oooh, man candy indeed! What is he?"

"Check the wrist," Andy says, and Eric narrows his eyes at the redhead suspiciously.

"Pardon?"

"Why do you think I told you to wear that?" Andy asks, pointing at Eric's leather cuff, positioned tightly on his left wrist. "It doesn't go with your outfit."

Eric hadn't questioned after the third tequila and didn't remember until now that he was even wearing it. He glances down and then grimaces. "What kind of party is this really, Andy?"

Andy pets Leta's hair and gives her temple a kiss. "I want you to go get me and my friend here drinks, pet," she tells Leta, her voice firm and commanding. "You know what I like. Man candy here will have a whiskey ginger."

Eric takes the opportunity of her distraction to look around. The room is all glass and chrome and black-and-white fabrics, set stiffly in straight lines perfectly parallel to the walls. It has no character, and Eric is overcome with a momentary fantasy of everyone in the room being robotic, just to match the weird perfection of the room.

When Leta's gone, Eric shakes his head to clear it of the image and turns on Andy, poking her hip hard and wishing it was enough to topple her. "Did you bring me to a scene party?"

Andy smiles at him sweetly. It doesn't match her face.

"What the hell, Andy?" he hisses. "You know I stopped doing this—"

"Only because your last boy toy was about as vanilla as a latte—"

"I only did it because of a boy toy in the first place."

"And you were never happier," Andy says evenly, staring him down, even brushing her short dark hair out of her eyes to give her a clear shot. "Even though *Stanley* was ten times more tolerable when you had him gagged as when you let his mouth flap. This is who you are, Eric. You shouldn't deny that, because there's nothing wrong with it. So look around, play the game, find a sub, and enjoy your whiskey—"

"I like a man who can take his whiskey."

Andy and Eric both turn to see the owner of the new voice, Eric with raised eyebrows and Andy with a subtle eye roll.

"Not your type, Pritchard," she says. "Maybe you should stop checking out his ass and check out his wrist instead."

"Pity," the man says. "I'd have liked to play with him."

Eric doesn't feel the least bit of attraction to this short, pale man, so he's not inclined to agree. He's about to open his mouth to say so, but Leta returns, drinks in hand. She hands Andy what looks like a brandy, and Eric takes his whiskey ginger and sips it carefully, testing the taste. But it tastes pretty damn good, so he takes a bigger mouthful. Then, since Andy and Leta are currently wrapped up in each other in a manner that Eric doesn't particularly want to watch, he turns to Pritchard.

What the hell kind of name is that?

"My friend here neglected to tell me just what game we might be playing," Eric says, clearing his throat. "I'm guessing this isn't just a simple party, if you have an entire floor rented out."

"Ian Pritchard never throws just a party," he says with a roll of his eyes, apparently his idea of a pleasantry. Ian—better than just Pritchard, anyway—continues, "This is for the New York elite to blow off some steam. My games are famous in the scene; I'm surprised you haven't heard of them."

"I've been out of the loop for a while," Eric says. He's already bored with this guy; his snobbery makes Eric want to claw his own eyes out. "Consider this my reintroduction."

"Lucky man, then," Ian says. "I invite only the finest subs. Only one newcomer here tonight, and I invited him special."

Ian points over to a dark man about their age, black hair in thick waves, wearing a tight ribbed sweater. He's got the best ass Eric's ever seen—high, tight, just a little bit round, as if it was made to fill out pants just right and then spill just a little bit out while peeling out of them—but that's about all he can see, the way the guy's facing.

"He went to my high school. Never could get him to go out with me—he was holding out for a Prince Charming."

"And now he's looking here?"

"Well, let's just say he thought he found a prince, but it turned out to be a frog. So I invited him here to try his hand at something new. If I could get away with it, I'd take him to a room right now, but the rules don't bend for anybody. Even me."

"So what are the rules?" Eric asks, wariness growing by the second as a sleek, modern grandfather clock strikes the hour, and the chatter starts to die away.

"You'll see," Ian says, with a sly look. "That was my cue."

He slips away just as Andy ambles up to Eric, wiping lipstick from the edge of her mouth. "Let the games begin," she murmurs, and Eric eyes her.

"You're not allowed to watch movies anymore," he says. "None."

"There's the Dom I know."

"Attention, friends," Ian calls. The party goes silent. "If I could ask you to separate, please. Doms on the left, subs on the right."

The room shifts. Eric, already on the left side of the room, stays where he is, watching with as much of an air of disinterest as he can. He notes Ian's scene-virgin heading uncertainly to the right, looking around as though waiting for someone to instruct him. Oh, yes, he's definitely a sub, with those wide, questioning eyes sharply tilted over his long, thin nose, that darkly tanned skin and dark hair—*god* he's gorgeous, actually—symmetrical and refined and fine-boned.

Eric blinks. No. He's not even sure he'll be playing; he shouldn't get ideas, especially ones that have him thinking up phrases like "wide, questioning eyes." And Andy is staring at the guy, too, and then back at Eric. *Great.* Eric directs his eyes up front.

"Perfect," Ian says. "Now, let's explain the rules."

He waves, and two of the waiters who had been circling with hors d'oeuvres set down their trays. Each one grabs two shiny bowls from a side table—one black and one white. It's impossible to see into them, but several people crane their heads anyway.

"The subs will approach one by one and select a card," Ian announces, gesturing to the waiter with the bowl on the sub side. "There will be a room number on the front of the card. The key you select will open that room and that room only. Once inside, you will find a kit with your instructions. Line up by gender—male identified take from the black, female identified from the white. And don't worry, everyone bats for the same team."

The subs line up. Eric notices the Virgin hesitantly sliding in at the end of the line. Then he catches sight of Andy sidling up to Leta and whispering something in her ear.

"What was that?" Eric asks, when Andy returns.

"Giving my sub permission to fool around with whoever gets her room number," Andy explains, but Eric gets the feeling she's lying from the way her eyes twinkle. "Naturally."

"Naturally," Eric agrees suspiciously. His eyes drift to Leta, who has dropped back to the end of her line and is saying something quietly to the Virgin, smiling broadly at him. They converse, but Eric can't read their lips from this distance. He's not entirely sure he likes what's going on, if Andy is the puppet master of it all. Not that there's anything he can do about it.

In the sub line, Leta and the Virgin both select their cards, and walk out together, chatting quietly. When they're gone, Ian turns to the Doms.

"What do you say we make 'em wait a little while?"

There's an appreciative chuckle, and Ian says something to the waiter, who puts the bowls down, and then sidles to the bar, chatting with another Dom and loudly ordering them drinks. Andy turns Eric to face her and grins at him.

"I know you had your eye on The Ass back there."

"The Ass? Really?" Eric says. "Even if I did, what does it matter? It's a game of chance."

"Everything's a game of chance," Andy says, "unless you load the dice."

Eric narrows his eyes. "What did you do?"

"Finish your drink."

Eric takes her suggestion, savoring the last burn of the liquor before setting his glass down on a table. "Andy—"

"You need to loosen up and shut up," Andy says, glaring. "I'm doing this because I care. You didn't even speak to that guy and you were looking at him like he was your perfect fucking prince. So have fun with him and make sure you slip him your number afterward, because he won't know who the hell you are."

Eric can't even ask what that means, because Ian is back up front, waving the waiter away from the bowls.

"Enough sweating for the subs," he says. "Come on, get your cards right off the table. No need for a show now. Your sub will be waiting for you. Safewords are standard, but the only other rule you get is that you have to leave the blindfold on. Keep 'em guessing."

Everyone lines up to go the bowls. Andy grabs Eric's arm and slows them down. Even Ian goes ahead of them; the only ones left in the room with them are the waiters and the bouncer.

The waiter stands close to the table, his hands on the edge of each bowl. Eric sticks his hand into the black one—

Nothing. But just as he starts to draw his hand back, a card drops onto the back of his hand.

He looks up, and the completely blank look he receives from the waiter is telling enough. He grabs the card and pulls his hand back out, as if nothing is amiss. He tries hard not to smile when he sees Andy circle the table and slip a bill in the back pocket of the waiter's ostentatious uniform.

"You're welcome," she says when Eric looks at his card, a black number seven on its face. They walk into the hallway behind the tables. "Now... I'm going to go see my girlfriend. I suggest you start planning what you're gonna do to your brand new toy."

She slips into Room 2 with a wink, leaving Eric alone in the hall. He walks up until he sees his number, and then pauses.

Once he goes through, that's it. He'll be a Dom again; he'll have to take care of a sub. And not just any sub, someone brand-new to the lifestyle. He'll be someone's *first* Dom. That's a lot of responsibility. Yes, he is incredibly attracted to the man on the other side of the door. It was an instant draw, the likes of which Eric's never experienced, and he can't seem to shake the fluttering nerves that flit from his stomach to his fingertips. The lack of control is worrying, and he doesn't want to be feeling it when he needs to be in top form. If anything, it's a sign of how out of practice he is.

He was in the scene for several years, acting as a Dominant in both relationships and hookups. But he left. He stopped, because he never found fulfillment with anyone in the scene. And yet, he's never found fulfillment outside of it, either. This became clear with his last failed relationship, the one that pulled him out of the scene to begin with. He's always wanted it all to match up—the perfect guy who's also the perfect sub—but life hasn't worked out that way. And now, Eric's not that person anymore. He can't hope for that perfect matchup anymore—he's had his heart broken by hoping too much. He's learned to be careful and weigh his options. To stay logical. To stay calm.

So he can go in and do his best for this guy, let himself have a hookup and take whatever consequences come of it, good or bad. Or he can leave now, stay in this zone of comfort he's retreated to and leave this poor, beautiful sub sitting there, abandoned.

He unlocks the door.

The room is sleek and comfortable. And, apparently, fully stocked. At the foot of the bed is a black gift box, and Eric's certain that it holds supplies and toys.

He's sitting on the edge of the bed, his ankles crossed and his hands in his lap. His head is hanging down and he's chewing at his lip. When Eric walks in, the sub's head lifts and turns. His eyes are covered with a black cloth.

"Hello?" His voice is pretty, smooth and pleasant, though a bit timid.

Eric smiles. "Hello. What's your name?"

The sub smiles faintly. "Uh, James Kader. Jamie, actually."

"Hello, Jamie. I'm Eric Yates."

"Hi, Eric," Jamie says. "Um, is there... something else I should call you?"

"You can just call me by my name," Eric replies. "Unless the inspiration should strike you otherwise."

"Okay. Um."

"Are you okay, Jamie?" Eric asks, unable to hold it back anymore. "I heard that you were new to this–"

Jamie laughs. "Yeah. I—I think Ian wanted to get me for himself. But he didn't, so I couldn't complain. I would, if he did. I mean. I don't want to gossip or speak badly, just—"

"You can always complain, Jamie," Eric insists. He sits down on the bed next to Jamie, and Jamie turns his head, tensing a bit. "You know that, don't you? You can safeword at any time. Even if you want to do it right now. If you aren't comfortable with this situation, it is perfectly okay to say so."

Jamie takes a deep breath. "I do want to do this," he says. "I... I did some research after the first time Ian tried to get me to come to one of these. It sounded fun, but I was in a relationship at the time, and my boyfriend wasn't comfortable with it. But...we're not together anymore. So I thought I'd seize the opportunity."

"Try something a little wild, huh?" Eric teases.

Jamie laughs. "Yeah. I guess I went kinda far on that, huh?"

"There are few places beyond this, I think."

A deep sigh, and then, "Might as well make it count, then."

Jamie's smile is beautiful. Eric wishes he could see Jamie's eyes.

"Do you—do you want to keep that blindfold on?" he asks. "I know the rules say you have to, but it's just us in here." Jamie fidgets, and Eric instantly adds, "Whatever you want is fine."

"I think I'd like to keep it," Jamie says. "I just...I feel like I *should* follow the rules. If I'm going to be a sub, I should learn to obey, right?"

Eric studies Jamie. "It doesn't always work like that, but I see where you're coming from," Eric says. "Just promise me, if you do end up wanting to turn this into a regular thing for you, that you'll talk to an experienced sub? If you just take advice from Doms, especially ones who want you for themselves, they could easily take advantage."

"Do you know Ian well?"

"No," Eric replies, nervous that he might have offended. "Just met him tonight. Would he not do that?"

"No, he would," Jamie says with absolute certainty. "I just wondered if you were that good at guessing or if you knew the whole time."

"He's not exactly a hard read," Eric replies, relieved.

"No. He's not very subtle." Jamie rubs his palms on his pants, and Eric reaches out instinctively, gripping his near wrist.

"Don't," he says gently. "It's okay to be nervous. But don't ruin your pants; that would be a shame. They look too good on you."

"Sorry," he says meekly, and Eric squeezes his wrist reassuringly before releasing him.

"It's okay," he laughs. "Nothing to be sorry for." He stands, and steps in front of Jamie, lifting his chin so that their faces are pointed at each other, even if they can't make eye contact.

"Are you willing to submit to me, Jamie?"

Jamie shivers, his mouth dropping open a bit at Eric's tone. Eric's shifting into Dominant mode now, drawing his body up taller, wider, lifting his chin and letting the power he keeps in reserve flow through him. He's not holding back now—he's completely in charge and he wants to make sure Jamie can feel it, even if he can't see a thing.

"Yes," Jamie whispers, with barely a breath.

"And do you understand that, if at any time you don't feel safe, if you feel we're not acting sanely or if you stop consenting, that you have every right to stop play?" That's the core tenet of BDSM. SSC: Safe, Sane, and Consensual. If play isn't all of those things, it's not okay unless expressly agreed upon ahead of time—and that's crossing into hardcore territory that isn't for beginners. It's best if they stick to the basics for now.

Jamie nods his head and agrees again, faintly and barely coherent. But it's enough.

"Good." Eric leans down and kisses him, light and teasing, barely brushing their lips. Jamie whimpers and opens his mouth in invitation, but Eric doesn't take it.

"You have to earn that, Jamie," he says, pulling back. Jamie inhales shakily, and Eric hums, pleased. "Don't worry, it's your first time. We'll go easy." Eric steps back, pushing the box out of the way with his foot. "I want you on your knees."

Jamie instantly drops down, hitting the floor with a muted thud. Eric almost winces in sympathy, but Jamie seems completely fine.

"Good boy," he praises, and Jamie smiles, bright and happy. Eric smiles back, glad Jamie can't see him. He can give in a little bit, not keep a perfect demeanor. "Now. I want you to get undressed; while you're doing it, I want you to tell me your safewords and limits."

"Red to stop," Jamie begins, quickly undressing, shuffling around to get everything off. "Yellow to pause. Green to continue. My limits are on the card on the top of the stuff in the box."

Eric raises an eyebrow, a little miffed that Jamie didn't just answer his question, but he checks out the box first, allowing Jamie to wiggle out of his pants and underwear in silence. There's a card inside, with typed instructions on the top.

State your limits for tonight's Dom, and write requests on the other side of this card.

Jamie's limits are pretty standard. He doesn't want any of the really hard kinks—no unnecessary fluids or intense roleplaying or extensive pain play. Eric's both surprised and actually pleased that, under soft limits, he's written *deep throating* and *bottoming*. However, he does have *spanking/flogging* on his list of wants, as well as *teasing/edging* and *dirty talk*.

"Would you like to be the one doing the dirty talk, or do you prefer to hear it?" Eric asks.

"I—I don't know," Jamie admits. "I've never really done it before either way. I just think... it would be nice. I... I fantasize about it."

And that's when Eric gets the perfect idea. He looks down at Jamie, kneeling, naked, half-hard. So pretty—his waist is trim, his shoulders broad, and he's got a spread of dark hair over his torso that Eric wants to explore at length. In fact, he wants to explore all of Jamie's body. But that will happen in time.

He crouches in front of Jamie and grips his chin. "Thank you for being honest with me," he says. "And thank you for being honest on your card. It took courage to write that you don't want to bottom or deep throat."

"I'm sorry," Jamie blurts. "I know I should be okay with it—"

"There is no should, Jamie," Eric interrupts. He smiles at himself; he's using Jamie's name a lot, and it feels a little silly, but he hopes it serves the purpose of calming the sub rather than just feeling good on his tongue. Like the rest of him will... "I don't need you to deep throat me and I don't need you to bottom for me. Any Dom that demands that isn't worth the title. This is about what's okay for *both* of us. Do you understand?"

"Yes," Jamie breathes, apparently relieved. Eric leans forward and kisses him.

It's full-on this time. He doesn't hold back, kissing hard, taking over and sucking Jamie's top lip into his mouth. He takes Jamie's face in his hands and hums in pleasure when Jamie grabs his face as well. He likes his subs to be able to do things, to trust him to put them in their place if they misstep. Too many subs are scared to do anything, and too many Doms are prone to mistreatment. Eric likes that Jamie feels comfortable enough to do things he likes rather than trying to make it all about Eric before he knows what Eric really wants.

"Was that okay?" Jamie pants, when Eric pulls back. And there it is: "I'm sorry, I—"

"Whatever you've read, Jamie?" Eric says. "Forget it. Do the things you want to do. If you go wrong, I will tell you."

Jamie smiles. "Thank you, sir."

Eric bites his lip at the title, and gives Jamie another hard kiss. He's so turned on at this point, so ready. "That sounds so good. I think we'll try having you talk tonight."

Jamie nods, his body trembling, fully hard now, his cock sticking out between his legs, curving up. Eric wants to touch it, but he's got a plan and he'll see it through. It'll only make things better.

"Stand up, and lie down on the bed, face down. Is there anywhere on your body that my mouth would be unwelcome?"

Jamie scrambles up eagerly and spins, feeling his way to the bed and crawling onto it with no attempt at grace whatsoever. Eric almost laughs, his heart swelling—it's adorable and sexy, the way Jamie doesn't even care if he's being alluring. He's just so ready, so turned on. Eric presses the heel of his hand into his own hard-on, biting his lip as Jamie settles down, spread before him, muscles of his back on display, tapering to his stunning ass and down to strong thighs.

Eric wants *all* of it.

"No," Jamie says.

"Hmm?"

"No, there's nowhere... unwelcome. You can put your mouth everywhere, *please*—"

Eric rocks into his hand, unable to stop himself from doing just that little bit. Jamie sounds so *desperate*. He can only hope he doesn't sound the same, simply replying, "Okay. I will."

He crawls onto the bed and straddles Jamie's thighs, his clothed body barely touching Jamie's, and Jamie whimpers. "Are you still wearing all your clothes?" he asks breathlessly, and Eric leans down and kisses the top of his spine, letting him feel the fabric of his clothes over his bare body.

"Yes, I am," Eric says, and Jamie rocks down into the bed.

"Oh *god*, that's so hot."

Eric chuckles and then sits back up, making sure to keep as little contact as he can.

"I want you to tell me about your fantasies," Eric says. "For every fantasy you tell me, I will explore one part of your body with my mouth and hands. The more details you give, the more I will pay attention to the spot I'm on." This gives Jamie just a little bit of control and lets Eric know the kinds of touches he likes best. Jamie can decide if he wants to keep Eric somewhere or move on—it'll keep him on his toes, and Eric has one more trick up his sleeve to ensure it.

"But if you stop talking," he adds, "and you don't move on to the next fantasy, or tell me more about the one you're on, you will be punished. Is that understood?"

Jamie whimpers again, nodding.

"I need an answer, Jamie."

"Yes, sir."

Eric kisses the top of his spine again. "Good boy. Number the fantasies as you go. You may begin."

Jamie takes a deep breath, and Eric pulls back and listens carefully. If tonight goes well, he wants to remember what he hears.

"One," Jamie begins, and Eric immediately starts kissing up Jamie's left arm, caressing it gently in his hands. "I have a fantasy that I'm tied up. Two." Eric almost laughs. Apparently Jamie's arms do nothing for him, so he decides to challenge Jamie, moving to his other arm. "I have a fantasy that I'm spanked by different... um, objects I guess. Three."

Eric moves to his back, kissing down his spine, and Jamie starts speaking slower, drawing it out. Eric grins against his skin, kneading the muscles all the way down to just above his ass and listens closely as he tries not to get too lost in Jamie's warm skin and hard body, just a little bit smaller than Eric's own.

"I—I have a fantasy that I'm in a dark room, alone. And someone starts speaking, but I can't see him, he isn't even in the room. But he's watching me and tells me how to touch myself. He talks me through it. I have this fantasy all the time—I imagine it's happening when I'm at home in bed. He tells me to stroke my chest, and my hips and my ass, and doesn't let me touch my cock until I'm ready to beg. And then he makes me take it slow. Four."

Eric knows Jamie expects him to go to his ass, so he slips down and starts playing with his legs, starting at the calves and working up to his thighs.

"Unh. I have a fantasy that my Dom treats me like a slave. Five." Eric moves to the other leg, immediately sucking a mark into the back of Jamie's thigh. "I—I have a f-fantasy that—oh—that my Dom drops hot wax all over me. Six."

He almost squeals the number, because Eric's hands are gripping his ass, feeling the muscle and the fat and the skin in his hands, squeezing and spreading and massaging. His hips back up, and Eric can't help but wonder why he doesn't like bottoming if he seems so eager to be touched, to be *rimmed* here. Maybe he doesn't get it—

"Please—please put your mouth on me—"

Or maybe he does. Eric hums lightly. "You aren't telling me your fantasy," he says. "Remember what I said?"

"I'm sorry, I have a fant—"

Smack.

"Oh, *fuck*—"

"One smack for each time you are punished. Meaning next time, you'll get two. Then three, then four and so on. Continue now."

"I—I have a—oh, Eric—"

Smack. Smack. His hands comes down on Jamie's ass, first one side, then the other, making Jamie's cheeks bounce and redden. He doesn't hold back—but Jamie seems to like the sting, moaning and rocking back and forth, feet scrabbling on the bed for some kind of leverage.

"Your fantasy, Jamie," Eric prompts. His mouth hovers, impatient.

"I have a fantasy that I'm kneeling," Jamie groans. Eric immediately dives in, kissing his hole, dirty and wet, tongue and lips and thumbs pulling his cheeks apart. "I'm—I'm kneeling and I'm tied up. And I can't move at all, I'm totally bound. And my Dom makes me watch as he fucks someone else, makes them beg and call him Master, makes them come again and again and again and I can't come at all—"

"You want the other sub to bottom?" Eric asks, pulling back to breathe, stroking over the skin of his hole lightly, not even hinting at penetration, but keeping him stimulated. He pulls in all the breath he can between words, catching himself up to reality from the deep focus he'd fallen into, that special place where nothing exists but his sub's pleasure. "Is that what you're saying?"

Jamie seems to realize why Eric's asking, because he immediately explains, "I don't want to *never* bottom. I just—I only want to do it with someone I'm... I'm in a claim with. A relationship. I don't want to bottom with someone I don't trust completely. It's...it's really vulnerable, and the one time I did it during a hookup, I felt awful afterward. It's just too much, with a stranger—"

"I understand, it's okay," Eric soothes, kissing him again, drawing out more moans. "But you don't have a problem with topping a stranger?"

"Not if they're okay with it," Jamie gets out, between quick breaths. "It's not as scary for me, I guess. Not as—as intense."

"That's okay," Eric says. "Continue."

"I—I want my Dom to fuck that sub," Jamie says, breath coming faster as Eric licks him hard, voice hitching and growing less controlled as he's worked over. "I want him to talk about how the sub feels and how good they are. I want to be desperate for my Dom to fuck me instead. And then, when the sub can't take any more, my Dom lets them go, and they get to watch as my Dom fucks me, and it's so much better, and we know each other, and we come together and don't even notice when the other sub leaves. Seven."

Eric pulls back, wiping his mouth on his arm quickly before urging Jamie to turn over, hungrily looking over his body as it moves and positions for him, just how he wants it. He skips the arms and legs this time, eager to keep going, and instead starts leaving hickeys on Jamie's chest as he speaks.

"I have a fantasy that my Dom makes me come in my pants in a public place, like a restaurant. He puts a vibrator inside me and he keeps making it go higher and higher until I just come all over myself, all inside my pants, and then he keeps it going, makes me keep feeling it till I have to leave the table. And—and he times me. However long I last… that's how long I get to worship him that night. Eight."

Eric slips down and he ignores Jamie's cock, going for his balls instead. "You've got some pretty detailed fantasies," Eric says, lips brushing against the soft, wrinkled skin. "I think you've wanted this for a long time. Wanted this longer than you might ever admit. I wonder just *how* long." With a chuckle, Eric sucks one testicle gently into his mouth.

"I—oh, I—I—I can't—"

Eric pulls back, lifts Jamie's legs up toward his shoulders, and exposes his ass. He lays three smacks across it, relishing Jamie's cries before dropping him back down and gasping, "Continue," before he goes back to sucking Jamie's balls back into his mouth.

"I—I have a fantasy," he says, trying again though his thighs tremble and his stomach clenches above Eric's head. Eric sympathizes, in his own way. He feels shaky with adrenaline and arousal himself, though it's the rush of control and not of the release of it that is driving him wild— as calm as he may keep himself on the outside while taking in Jamie's admissions. "A fantasy. That. Um. That my Dom lets me fuck him from behind, but he tells me exactly how to move and won't let me come till he has two or three times. Nine."

Eric grins at Jamie's desperation and slithers up, starting to worship his neck and face instead. Jamie all but sobs, body rocking up for friction as Eric kisses his cheek and drags his nails down his neck.

"I have a fantasy," Jamie continues, his voice high and thready now, "that my Dom ties me up and spanks me. Paddles me, flogs me. I don't care. I just... he hits me, he marks up my back and legs and ass. And... and he ignores my safeword. He pushes me, and he won't let me tell him to stop. He just keeps going." Eric kisses him so, so gently, lips dragging over his cheeks, kissing over his eyes beneath the blindfold, his nose, his forehead, his soft, plump lips between words. "And then, when he's ready, he comes all over my bruises and then makes me come just by talking to me. I—I don't even know what he'd say, I just want his voice to make me come while I can't even move. Ten."

Eric lifts off of Jamie, not speaking a word, and Jamie starts to babble as soon as contact is broken.

"Please, sir, please I've been good," he says, and Eric moves quickly to the box, finding what he's looking for as quietly as possible. "Please let me come. Or you come. Something, I need someone to come, please, sir—"

As fast as he can, before Jamie can figure out what's going on, Eric rips open the foil and pulls out the condom, rolling it down onto Jamie's straining cock. Jamie moans so loudly, Eric is sure anyone around them could hear it. But the sound bounces off the walls, rings in Eric's ears, and it's perfect. Jamie has been so good.

"Give me the best fantasy you've got," Eric demands and then sucks Jamie's dick between his lips.

"I have a fantasy," Jamie says and he can barely get the words out now, he's breathing so hard and fast. Eric looks up, and Jamie's hands are in his own hair, his legs are flexing and stretching on either side of Eric's body, his stomach muscles are jumping and he must be so close. Eric sucks him hard, bobbing his head and stroking the base of Jamie's cock in tandem, flicking his tongue along the underside, moaning—god, he needs to get laid more often, he's missed the feeling of a man in his mouth, on his skin, inside his body, and he can't get enough with this alone. "I want my Dom to...to blindfold me and make me—make me lie down and talk about my fantasies, while he—while he touches me, and kisses me, and—*unh, unh!*—sucks me, oh god. And I can't even see him but I know he's there and that he wants me, and then I want him to fuck me while he's still fully clothed, oh *fuck*—"

Eric barely registers that Jamie is suddenly coming in the condom, hot and fast against the roof of Eric's mouth, only latex between him and the taste he really wants. He sucks hard a few more times, letting Jamie buck and writhe and cry out at the approach to oversensitivity, and then pulls off.

He needs to come himself—he was paying such close attention to Jamie, he could almost forget the tightness of his own cock against his pants, but it's in full focus now and he's about to come right inside them, and that would make an awkward walk home.

"I said I wouldn't fuck you tonight," Eric groans, unbuckling his belt and undoing his pants, tugging his cock out, hand flying over it while the other massages Jamie's thigh. "And I won't. But god, do I want to—"

"Eric, oh my god—"

"Wanted to fuck you the whole time," Eric murmurs, his arm starting to burn. He's going to come *so hard.* His groin tenses up, the rest of his body following as he strains toward release. "Wanted you bouncing on my cock, wanted you falling apart around me. You'd feel so good, Jamie, wouldn't you? Would you feel good for me?"

Jamie reaches forward, sitting up to put his hands on Eric, grabbing his hips and feeling the way he fucks his hand in lieu of watching. "Yes, Eric, I'd do anything, anything you wanted—"

"You were such a good boy, Jamie," Eric gets out, heat pooling, and Jamie's got to know Eric's about to mark him up. "Would've let you top me if we had more time—so good for me, such a good sub—oh, oh, Jamie!"

Jamie lunges up to kiss him, off center, but Eric corrects it just as he comes, muffling wild cries in Jamie's mouth. He shoots come all over Jamie's neck and collarbone, trickling down over his chest and then slowing to just cover his own hand. He catches his breath, drawing out his orgasm with a few slow strokes.

"Can I—can I taste?" Jamie asks. "I—I want to taste it; can I sir? Can I taste it?"

"You do?" Eric blurts, a little sex-stupid. "You don't even know what I look like—you want to taste my come?"

"I want it," Jamie nods. "I trust you—I do—"

"Not this time, baby," Eric says. Jamie pouts, but Eric's sure about this decision. "Before you trust me, I want you to be able to see me, get to know me. I don't want you making decisions you'll regret when you're vulnerable from a scene, okay?"

Jamie's breath hitches, and the way his face moves, Eric's nervous that he's crying. But he lets out a wet-sounding laugh instead. "See? I can trust you."

Eric feels a rush of warmth for Jamie, so he leans down and kisses him, pulling the decorative kerchief from his breast pocket to wipe the come from his hand and Jamie's torso. It's a sacrifice, of course, but he's willing to make it so that he doesn't have to go search for tissues or a washcloth. Now, he can just hold Jamie.

"Um—can I request something?"

"Of course."

Jamie's hands flutter over where they've been rubbing at Eric's hips. "Could you—could you maybe take your clothes off and—and hold me?" he asks, obviously anxious. "I—I just want to feel your skin. You don't have to—"

"Jamie, that's a wonderful idea," Eric interrupts, kissing him again reassuringly. "Just give me one second to undress and I'll be right back."

He shuffles off the bed and undresses, tossing his clothes over a chair. He crawls back on the bed, naked, and curls Jamie into his arms, stroking his back and hair as Jamie buries his face in Eric's neck, the blindfold slightly damp on his skin.

"Thank you," Jamie says, so sincere and sweet. It must have been intense for him, doing this for the first time, letting go in a way that regular, vanilla sex doesn't encourage. And it was intense for Eric, too—he got so easily wrapped up in Jamie, and it struck a deep chord in him that had lately gone silent. Eric feels a surge of fondness for Jamie, feels close to him, as though there's something special here. He *likes* Jamie, and Jamie seems to like him. This doesn't feel like sex for the sake of sex—this feels like something deeper, if only from the way Eric's heart starts to ache in his chest, eased only when he kisses Jamie's temple and holds him, skin to skin.

"Thank *you.*"

They say nothing else. Eric just holds Jamie, touching him, palms warm and slow on Jamie's light brown skin, gentle kisses pressed to his forehead, nose in sweaty hair that smells faintly of pepper.

This is exactly what Eric's been missing—it's true, this is who he is. He wants to take care of a wonderful man like Jamie, make him feel things he didn't know he could feel, show him how the scene could be *so much*, could provide things for Jamie that vanilla sex couldn't. Because BDSM can go beyond that—it's not just sex, it's a whole experience. If Jamie's enjoyed this first time, felt this first time so strongly, what could he feel with more? And Eric wants to feel that in return, wants to be able to give that to someone and have someone who wants to give in return. He wants someone to trust him and care for him and dream up new things to experience with him. And someone who fits the bill is right here, now, not even knowing what Eric looks like. But they're playing a game with the understanding that they're to part without truly meeting. He's not sure if he wants to praise or berate Andy for pulling this off. She really did give him such a perfect entrée back into the life he loves, but one that he can't really keep.

And then, in the midst of Eric's pressing thoughts, Jamie's breathing evens out and his body goes limp and heavy. Eric kisses him one last time.

"I mean it," he whispers, though Jamie is deep in sleep and can't hear a thing. "Thank you."

He slips away, letting Jamie hug a pillow, and covers him with a spare blanket so he doesn't get cold.

And then he breaks the rules completely.

This is a hookup party. But this was not a hookup, and Eric knows it. He thinks Jamie knows it, too. After all, Jamie was the one to describe what Eric was doing as his perfect fantasy, to describe *Eric* as his perfect fantasy.

Eric has to take the chance. He's already this deep—he'll never forgive himself if he lets it go.

Jamie's phone is in his pants. Eric opens it—thankfully Jamie doesn't have a locking screen—and puts his number into Jamie's contacts. Then he finds Jamie's number, and puts it in his own phone before setting the phone on the bedside table, on full volume and vibrate, just in case.

He picks up his clothes and is sorting them, when he catches his own eye in the mirror above the dresser. He's definitely not an ugly guy—he's tall, maybe too thin, maybe too blond. He gets stubble too quickly and he's got a serious case of sad puppy eyes. He'd charitably call his nose strong. But he possesses his body entirely, confidently. That's something the scene gave him—absolute mastery over his body, a knowledge of its edges and its capabilities and how far it can truly go in terms of pleasure both given and received. He's powerful, inside and out; he's done some amazing things with this body and hopes to do more. Would Jamie like it, seeing it instead of just feeling it? Would he appreciate it in spite of the moles, the pinkness of his skin, the weird proportions of his height and lengthy limbs? Would he love it because of those things, if given the chance, the way Eric would love Jamie's clearly developed muscles, his deep, smooth coloring, his aesthetically perfect proportions?

He's done what he can to see if any of these questions can be answered. He's given Jamie and himself an opening to wiggle through, to see if either of them wants more. He's put himself forward, and he can't do anything else now. So he dresses, and tiptoes out.

A few people mill around in the foyer, having drinks and talking casually, obviously sated and relaxed from their activities. Eric doesn't look at their wrists—and he can't tell who's a Dom or sub, can't tell who was affected by this evening. Probably nobody. They're used to it. And that's fine for them, but something churns in his gut at the thought that he might have to do this sort of thing for a while before he finds someone, if Jamie doesn't join him in his minor rebellion.

He waits until he's down in the lobby before he texts Andy, letting her know he's on his way home. Then he texts Jamie:

Thank you so much for tonight. I know Ian has rules about us not seeing each other, but I have a rule about wanting to look into my sub's eyes. If you'd rather follow my rules, and keep the fantasies going, let me know.

He pockets his phone and begins the walk home, thoughts in a whirl. He'd pushed this part of him away, this fulfillment in exercising Dominance. He wanted to find a man who was interested in the long term, a man who was compatible with him on as many levels as possible, a man who could be his fairytale prince. He was far more likely to find him outside of the BDSM scene, where everyone was divided into groups and sometimes had rigid expectations that could so rarely be met. Eric had been willing to work with regular old run-of-the-mill sexual compatibility for the chance to meet someone who was compatible with him in other ways as well, who didn't just want him for the sex and the Dominance. But this experience with Jamie—it's as if a crack has been made in the dam holding back his desires, keeping it a still pool rather than the wild rush that it is with BDSM. Jamie and he are, at this first glance, well matched. They don't know each other, but the spark is undeniable. Is that enough? Can Eric go back to that life, already having found someone to enter it with?

No, he can't get his hopes up like that. Fairytales are just stories, and they don't happen to people who like to use whips and chains for what Eric likes to use them for. It's just so hard to hold back hope for a man he doesn't even know, on the off chance they might have more outside of the bedroom, that there might be a fantasy kingdom somewhere in the vast array of fantasies Jamie gave him earlier that night. He has to try to let that go.

He doesn't have to try for long. His phone buzzes in his pocket, and he pulls it out so fast he's almost embarrassed at his own neediness. But he has to know.

Jamie: Yes, sir.

Eric smiles. It's a start.

HOLDOUT MAN

HOLDOUT MAN

Eric's not much of a gambling man. He doesn't play poker; he doesn't watch races or sports; he doesn't go to casinos and play the slots. And he also doesn't gamble with himself, much of the time.

Jamie is certainly changing that.

Whenever Eric dated before, he'd take his time. If he was being pursued, he'd wait until the moment was right before he returned the interest. If he was pursuing, he'd take it easy, wait until he was sure before making moves. He'd grown into this; he was far different from the fumbling, nervous wreck he'd been in his unsuccessful high school love life. He always made absolutely certain, because getting hurt is not on Eric Yates's agenda, and he's experienced it far too much despite that, thank you very much.

Eric can't get a read on Jamie, though. He's not entirely sure who's pursuing, or if they're both pursuing each other, or if neither of them are. The only contact they've had since the night three weeks ago when they met (and fucked, so beautifully and deeply, despite no eye contact or penetration whatsoever) has been via text and three or four vaguely nerve-wracking phone calls. It feels as if Eric's in high school again, fumbling again, totally unsure of how to properly date a man, or at least move forward toward dating. He's interested; he's certain Jamie's interested, but they keep circling the subject. They flirt and then retreat, side-stepping any inquiries, each in turn.

It's exhausting, and Eric's a bit miffed at his own behavior. He's a Dom, and just because he's only now getting back into the lifestyle, that does not mean he can act as if he's inexperienced. He needs to stay powerful, reclaim his Dom instincts, especially with Jamie discovering his submissive instincts.

They talk about that, too. A lot. Jamie has a sub he's talking to—Leta, Andy's girlfriend, who's been a sub as long as she's been sexually active. Jamie's been discovering certain things about himself and the scene, but he has a lot of smart questions about boundaries and limits and aftercare that only a Dom can really answer. And Eric is more than happy to provide them, even if he ends up unbearably needy for a sub (Jamie, for example) to dominate afterward; just talking about it riles him up, like a man suddenly desperately thirsty after his first drink of water in ages. He just doesn't want to stop Domming Jamie.

So when Jamie finally asks him out for coffee, Eric accepts with absolute relief that Jamie made the first move. It's important to Eric that a sub set up the boundaries before the Dom takes over, and being the one to ask him out gives Jamie the upper hand. Let him control the circumstances in which he hands over control—he's vulnerable enough as it is.

It's also the first time he'll see Eric, and Eric wants him to be ready. He's so terrified of Jamie's reaction, even though he knows objectively that there's nothing to worry about. He's confident in his looks, and Jamie already likes what bits he's experienced. Jamie's text arrives during his lunch break from the flower shop where he works the day of their date.

Jamie: So how will we find each other? Should we wear roses?

Eric finds this so endearing that he finds himself giggling and blushing before he can stop himself.

Eric: Roses are out of style. What's a fancy flower I can buy on the way over?
Jamie: Romance is out of style? Call me gauche.
Jamie: Why don't we just pick a flower ourselves? I'm pretty sure no one else will be carrying a flower into a coffee shop.
Eric: Ok, but if there's a sudden meeting of floral enthusiasts, we're screwed.

Jamie sends back a simple *lol* and Eric tucks away his phone. He'll never make it through the day if they continue talking.

* * *

Eric picks up a stem of crimson amaryllis with three flowers clustered at the top. It caught his eye, and the woman behind the counter had cooed when he asked for it. Cooing is good, flower-wise, and it clued him in to how good a choice it probably is—Eric's a copy editor, he deals in words and rules and red pen and finite things. Flowers are so...*flowery*. The rules are different.

His nerves sing all the way to the subway station by the coffee shop Jamie had picked. But once he comes out of the subway and starts walking the final block and a half, he settles, his shoulders relaxing, his strides longer. He and Jamie connected. They *still* connect, even when their bodies aren't a part of the equation. They'll connect now.

When Eric enters, he looks around casually for Jamie. He finds him sitting at a table for two next to the window, already staring at him, his mouth hanging open a little bit, his eyes searching. Eric smiles at him and starts forward. As soon as he does, Jamie's face breaks into a huge smile, which Eric can't help but return.

"Eric?"

Eric nods, and Jamie is instantly up, approaching eagerly until they're less than a foot apart and about to collide, at which point he freezes, hands swinging awkwardly as though he were going in for a hug and decided against it.

Eric bites his lip and contains his laughter. "Jamie, you can hug me."

Jamie laughs and relaxes, dropping his head for a moment. "I'm sorry, there's really no precedent for this."

"There isn't. So don't apologize."

Jamie smiles up at him, sweet and fond. "I won't."

And then he hugs Eric. His arms wrap around Eric's waist, and Eric immediately wraps around Jamie's shoulders, his nose pressing against Jamie's temple as Jamie's head goes into his neck, nuzzling gently. It feels intimate and familiar in a way it shouldn't, not with how little they know each other. But it does feel *right*.

Eric pulls back. He can't trust that feeling. His instincts are going out of control, the way his body folds over Jamie's, the way he feels protective and strong around the smaller man, with his sweet smile and his wide, pleading eyes.

"Let's sit. I'll go get my coffee, and—"

"Oh, I—I already got you one," Jamie says uncertainly. "I didn't get here too early, so it should be just cooled down enough by now. The coffee here is scalding; you have to wait forever for it to be safe—"

"Jamie, thank you," Eric interrupts gently. He resists the urge to caress Jamie's cheek. "Do you have magical coffee-order guessing powers or did you get me a regular?"

Jamie looks at Eric with a smile. "You... kind of told me your order the other day. You like coconut flavor in it, right?"

"Oh, yeah."

He leads the way back to the table. Eric sets his flower down in the center of the table with the one Jamie bought, and instantly cocks his head questioningly at it.

"Jamie?" he asks, settling into his seat. "What on earth is that?"

Jamie looks proud of himself as he seats himself across from Eric, leaning forward eagerly. "It's an anthurium," he explains. "It's... it's like an alternative to roses. It's... supposed to be romantic."

He becomes less and less energetic about it as he speaks, watching as Eric picks up the flower and studies it.

"It's a heart," Eric says.

"Yes."

"With... "

"That's called a spadix."

"You got me a heart. With a penis."

Jamie snorts and bursts out laughing again, and Eric notices his head dropping to hide it.

"I didn't... I just—oh god, I just wanted to get you something unique, and we just got these into the shop, and I thought it was interesting—"

"It's perfect, Jamie," Eric says, unable to stop grinning. "Can I take it home with me, or will your boss notice it missing?"

"I got the okay. But only if I can take yours," Jamie replies, pulling up the amaryllis and gently touching one of the beautiful flowers.

"Deal."

They sip their coffees for a few minutes, smiling across the table and exchanging small talk like any awkward date ever. And then, Jamie opens and shuts his mouth several times, sighing and shaking his head. Eric sets his coffee down carefully.

"I get the feeling you have something to say, but have no idea how to say it."

Jamie blinks at him and then smiles in awe. "I think the problem is actually that I know exactly what I want to say," he corrects softly. "I'm just not sure how you'd take it if I said it."

Eric reaches over and takes one of Jamie's hands in his own. Jamie immediately warms and softens and he locks eyes with Eric just as Eric wants him to.

"I'll make you another deal," Eric says. "Or an exchange of promises. If you promise to be completely honest with me and say what you need to say, I will promise to hear you out and try to understand before I react. And I promise whatever extreme reaction is in your head right now isn't going to happen—no disgust, no storming out. This place is way too crowded; I'd never do it without knocking into somebody—"

Jamie laughs, and Eric just stares at him, probably with a dopey smile on his own face. This man is precious and sexy and sweet, and trying so, so hard. Eric wants nothing more than to be kind to him in all ways—to be a kind friend, a kind lover, a kind Dom. Jamie deserves that. In fact, they both might deserve it.

"Okay, I'll tell you," Jamie says. He takes a deep breath. "Just... let me get it out? I... I tried to plan this, but I have no idea—"

"It's okay, Jamie," Eric assures. "Go ahead, and you let me know when you're done."

Eric settles back a little bit, sipping his coffee casually, looking at Jamie calmly and trying not to seem too expectant. If Jamie needs time, he'll give him time. And Jamie smiles gratefully at him for it.

"Okay. I want you to know that... that you changed my life. What you did for me, how you... how you treated me, when we were... um, together. At the party. I don't think I would have been able to do more with this... part of myself, if it—if it hadn't been you."

He shakes his head and runs his hand through his wavy hair, the other still held quietly in Eric's.

"I can't imagine, I just—what if I had gotten Ian? Or someone else who just wanted to hook up once and never again? I think I might've... might've been too... too... um, I don't know exactly how to say this."

"Take your time."

Jamie finishes off his own coffee, and then looks over at Eric. "May I please get you another coffee? I can go up and get it, maybe think—"

"Of course. Thank you. Why don't you get yourself a snack, too? Something nice."

"I'll get something for both of us," Jamie suggests, and Eric nods, grinning. And then Jamie's gone, taking their cups to the trash before getting in line, fidgeting and bouncing on his toes. When he realizes he's staring, Eric turns back around and stares at the empty chair instead. Giving Jamie time to think probably doesn't involve making him feel uncomfortable and watched.

Eric thinks he knows what Jamie is trying to say, but he wants to be sure. He's under the impression that Jamie is thanking him for being a good Dom, for looking out for the sub first and not pushing things for his own benefit. He had the same feelings himself that night and many times since—he was lucky, getting Jamie. If he had had a casual hookup, he would've felt cheap. Not because of anything inherently wrong with hooking up, god knows he's done it himself before, but it's never really sat well with him. He wants something more, to feel worth something to somebody, more than just a body. And Jamie made him feel like that. He's continuing to make him feel like that, by trusting him, by wanting to be around him, even if only as a friend for now.

Jamie slides back into the seat, pushes the coffee forward and sets a plate with two biscotti on it at the center of the table. Eric removes the lid of his cup and almost has to duck back from the cloud of steam.

"I told you they make it too hot here," Jamie says ruefully. "Sorry."

"Not a problem," Eric assures. "We'll just have to be here for a little longer. Unless that's a problem for you?" he teases gently. Jamie laughs again.

"Not at all." He bites his lip. "Do you mind if I—continue?"

"Go ahead," Eric grants. Jamie nods.

"I think what I was trying to say is that… I'm really happy it was you that night. You treated me like a person, even though I'm a sub. I was scared of not feeling like that. Like… feeling like *less than* whoever I was with. The only person I know in the—the scene, is Ian. And—I'm sure you can imagine—"

"I can," Eric agrees wryly.

"Well. I was convinced that by taking the chance, by going to the party, I'd get him. I thought he'd rig it. And I… I didn't want it, but I didn't know how else to go somewhere where these—these feelings mean something. He's the only in I have."

"Not anymore," Eric reassures. "You have Leta now. And me."

"That's what I'm saying," Jamie agrees earnestly. "And I'm so glad it's you, because you make me… feel things. And I'm. Um, I'm learning, I guess? I'm figuring things out better now, now that I have a—a focus. Oh, god, I don't mean to sound, like… creepy, or anything, I just—"

"It's okay. You don't sound creepy. Say what's in your head, Jamie, don't worry about how I'll take it."

Jamie looks at him intensely for a moment.

"I have no idea if this is normal. I just want to… to fall on my knees, whenever you talk to me. We don't even have to be on the phone, just a text, and I just… I want to go back to that night, and do more, and feel more. And I have… no idea if that's at all normal—"

"Jamie, can I say something? Before you finish? It's important."

Jamie just nods, licking his lips in a way that Eric can't help but watch.

"Whatever you are feeling?" Eric says sincerely. "Is okay. Don't worry about normal or what other people think or feel. Your feelings are real. It's how you handle the feelings that makes a difference. And talking to me about them—I really appreciate it. And if you want to continue, I want to hear what you have to say."

Jamie's face twists as if he's got too many emotions to contain at that moment, but he settles on a smile and takes a shaky breath.

"Thank you."

Eric just smiles at him, and then sips his coffee, still a little too hot, but cooled enough not to scald him. When Jamie still hasn't spoken, he takes a biscotti and dips it, nibbling at the end, waiting patiently for whatever Jamie wants to say.

"I guess the point is that I want to... to see you. Like this, but also... like before. I want to show you how grateful I am for the things you've made me comfortable enough to explore. I've... talked a lot to Leta. You know what we've talked about, obviously, and... I want to explore these things with someone I... I like. And trust. And... you already know all my fantasies."

Eric smiles at Jamie softly.

"Are you asking me if you can be my sub?"

Jamie blushes and goes bashful and shy, and Eric's chest aches. It's not the all-encompassing love forever after he craves, but he really likes Jamie, and they're compatible, and Jamie is asking him to explore this new world with him. He would be a fool to turn this down, and he has no intention of being a fool.

"I... I guess I am. I'm sorry if that's too forward—"

"Do you know what I loved most about our first meeting? About all that happened?" Eric asks. Jamie shakes his head. "That you were comfortable doing things. Some subs... a lot of subs, actually... they make it all about the Dom. They don't do *anything* out of fear of doing things wrong. And I understand that, with how a lot of Doms are, but... I want someone who is my equal, not my inferior. I want someone who isn't afraid to kiss me how they want to kiss me, how I want to be kissed. And you did that."

Jamie's eyes go dark and wide, his lips part to pull in breath and he reaches over and grabs Eric's hand. Eric strokes over Jamie's knuckles with his thumb as Jamie bites his lip and then speaks.

"I would... like to be your sub. I don't know if there's a... a thing we should do? A... I'm not sure—"

"How about this?" Eric suggests. "Let's finish our coffee, and go for a walk and talk a little more. And then I'll walk you to the subway station, and say goodnight and make sure I know exactly when I'm going to see you again."

"I—oh, okay."

"Say what you're thinking, Jamie."

"I was hoping... you'd come home with me."

Eric wants to, so badly. But Eric doesn't gamble.

"How about we set a later date?" Eric suggests. "Just get to know each other a little better before we throw ourselves into the scene. I know it's mainly sexual, but we should at least like each other outside of that and we've mostly been talking about the scene since we met. Let's... be friends, first."

"Okay, friends. I... can be okay with that," Jamie agrees, face falling a little bit. "Can we...still talk about the scene, sometimes? I'm still curious, and—"

"Of course," Eric says. "I'd never take that away from you. Let's just keep the sexual part of it for a later date."

Jamie nods. "Okay."

* * *

They take new coffees on their walk, to warm them in the chill of the night air. How it got to be dark out that fast, Eric has no idea—as far as he can tell, they'd barely scratched the surface before they decided to grab another drink and head out, lest it get too late. And they'd walked up and down the blocks, ambling along easily.

Finally, Eric stops Jamie at the subway station.

"Do you take this, or are you within walking distance?"

"Actually, we passed my building," Jamie says. "Twice."

Eric laughs. "I'm sorry. If I'd known, I would've said goodbye to you there."

"Never," Jamie says. "I'm familiar with the area, and I wanted to walk you here so I can make sure you get on the subway safely."

"That's very sweet, Jamie," Eric replies gratefully, charmed. "Thank you."

"You're welcome." Jamie throws away their empty cups in the trashcan nearby and then returns, taking Eric's hands in his own. "When can I see you again?"

Eric bites his lip and thinks.

"Well, I've got some meetings over the next couple of days, and that usually means catching up on work later, so I'll be busy till... Friday? Are you available?"

"I am," Jamie says. "Can I take you to dinner?"

That sounds a lot more like a date, and not just for friends. Maybe Jamie wants that after all. *Just go out with him,* Eric thinks. *You wanted this to go farther than just sex anyway.* "I'd love that, Jamie."

"Good." Jamie bows his head a little bit, like the most fantastic gentleman ever born, squeezing Eric's hands. "Friday. I'll pick you up at seven."

Jamie steps closer, and it hits Eric all at once that this is probably not the friend kind of date after all. The look in Jamie's eyes, brown like cognac, warm and just a bit golden, isn't the look you give a friend, no matter how much you're fucking. It's... sweeter than that. More intimate. More terrified, too. And Eric feels like squealing and dancing when Jamie's eyes move down from Eric's eyes and to his lips, because oh, shit, he might've misinterpreted what Jamie said about friends.

And so he can't help but smile into it as Jamie kisses him gently, a perfect, tingling, anticipatory, end-of-first-date kiss.

"Um... not friends, then?" Eric blurts out.

Jamie laughs. "Um. Sure. Friends. But... more, too? If you want to... try that?"

"Yeah," Eric agrees. "I can... I can try."

"Goodnight," Jamie whispers, pulling away. Whatever Eric did to get this karmic reward, it must have been big.

"Goodnight."

When he gets home, he slips into bed and imagines very vividly just how different the night could have been if he'd accepted Jamie's invitation home.

* * *

The date on Friday is wonderful, as are the dates on Saturday, Monday, and Wednesday and every date they can manage after that for another two weeks. But simmering under the surface is something more, something missing, something prickling and cracking at the edges of Eric's patience—for what, though, he's not totally certain. He's taking it slow. They're taking it slow.

Jamie ends their dates in a state of partially hidden agitation, and Eric is beginning to worry about just how much this really *is* about the sex. Their kisses are deeper, needier, and the whines in Jamie's throat are clipped short and desperate. On one date they'd just stayed in at Jamie's apartment, lying on the couch after dinner and making out like teenagers for far too long. And even then it hadn't been enough, evidently, for either of them.

The second time they spend an evening in, this time at Eric's apartment, Eric pulls back and brushes some of Jamie's hair off his forehead.

"What wrong?" Eric asks. And that's all it takes.

Jamie sits up and clenches his hands in the knees of his pants.

"I am going insane, Eric," he blurts out. "I'm having all these... feelings and needs, and you told me they were okay, but I don't know what to do with them. I just... I feel like I—"

He trails off, and Eric sits next to him and holds his hand.

"I stand by my promise," Eric says. "I will let you say whatever you need to say and I'll try to understand it before I respond."

Jamie shakes his head in exasperation.

"You—you gave me everything, Eric," he says. "You showed me who I really am and you did it in a single hour. What would you do to me with more? With weeks, months... with a lifetime? What could we do with each other?"

It's there. It's huge and it's fast, and Eric's not prepared to take this jump yet, not after just over a month of knowing each other. That's *ridiculous.*

"Jamie, I'm not sure—"

"You told me not to be ashamed of what I'm feeling, Eric. And what I'm feeling is... that I want to be around you. I want to be yours."

Jamie looks into his eyes and waits for his response.

Eric has always taken his time. Relationships that last need a foundation and work. Eric's never been in a rush before. But he can't deny that things with Jamie have only felt uncomfortable when he's put on the brakes. So are they only meant for a flash-in-the-pan romance? Rush through what they can get from each other, whirlwind their way through the fantasies Eric promised, give each other the intense love they can in that short time, and part with hearts broken? Because that's what Eric fears; that's what this feels like. It can't be that easy.

And Jamie is new to this. Eric is the only Dom he's had. Eric's worried that Jamie might have latched onto how Eric made him feel and equated the satisfaction of his needs with Eric alone, rather than as something other Doms could also provide. He thought he was doing what was best, giving Jamie and himself time to settle into their dynamic, make sure that wasn't the only thing between them.

But what can he do? Eric's feeling the same things as Jamie. He told Jamie not to be ashamed of his feelings—so maybe he should just take his own goddamn advice and take a chance, because his formula for love hasn't exactly worked up to now, and it's absolutely not working right this very second.

This whole thing is a gamble, a game. And you can't win a game without taking a few risks, right? The worst that could happen is complete and total heartbreak, Eric thinks. The best is forever. What's it gonna be?

"Stay tonight," Eric blurts out, and Jamie's eyes go wide.

"Are you—you're serious—"

"Of course I am," Eric insists. "You're right. I'm used to doing things a certain way. I'm careful. And I didn't want to mess this up."

"You couldn't," Jamie breathes, leaning in. "Nothing, nothing could mess this up—"

And then they're kissing furiously, and Jamie is pushing Eric down onto the couch, slotting between his legs, pushing in close to him. And soon enough, they're totally wrapped in each other, panting and catching breaths whenever they can before they lunge back in, unwilling to stop the slide and press of their lips and tongues and bodies, in all their combinations.

"Can we... like this?" Jamie asks. "Just—normal? Want to do so many things to you—"

"Unh, yes—"

"Come on," Jamie gasps, rolling them onto their sides and pressing their hips together. "Please—"

"Okay," Eric groans, gripping Jamie's arms and letting him kiss down his throat. "So show me what you want to do to me."

Jamie laughs, and complies.

They fuck right there on the couch. They suggest moving to the bed-room several times, but neither of them can pull away long enough to accomplish that. When Eric is laid on his back, naked, one leg rested along the back of the couch and the other spread out and bent off the couch, stroking himself when Jamie had stopped doing it for him, Jamie asks where the supplies are. He goes running to Eric's bedroom to get them—actually running, stark naked, cock hard in front of him. Eric laughs and covers his face and can't watch, as pleasant as the view probably is. He only looks again when Jamie lies back on top of him and lowers his already-lubed fingers, opening Eric too carefully before fucking him gloriously, grasping the couch and Eric's thigh for leverage, both of them sweating and loud and kissing messy and hard. Only when they've both come, hard and too fast and not nearly enough, do they stumble to the bedroom, vowing to clean up in the morning as they fall into bed and do it all again.

The next morning they wake and thrust tiredly into another orgasm. When they're lying on the bed afterward, drowsy and messy and gathering up the energy to shower, Jamie draws patterns with his fingers on Eric's chest next to where he'd laid his head.

"You told me to tell you honestly what I'm thinking."

Eric hums in agreement and looks down as best he can, waiting for Jamie to spit it out. Jamie draws a heart and lays a kiss inside it before he looks up.

"I want to do a scene with you."

Niggling doubt, the voice in his head, saying, *That's all he wants from you,* are ignored and pushed aside for a later time, when he's alone and can sort through things without Jamie looking at him. So Eric breathes in the scent of Jamie and the things they did together, and skips all the steps he's ever planned to take in a situation like this.

"Okay."

* * *

The next night, Eric goes to Jamie's apartment. He stands outside the door, shakes his head at his own probable stupidity and pulls out his phone.

Eric: *Are you home?*
Jamie: *Yes. Want to come over?*
Eric: *Don't ask questions. What are you doing right now?*
Jamie: *??? I just got out of the shower?*
Eric: *Unlock the front door. Then go lie down on your bed. Don't get dressed. Do what you would normally do when you're alone on your bed and naked.*
Jamie: *Oh my god.*

Eric hears Jamie walk up to the door and unlock it before moving away. Eric looks at the clock and gives it ten minutes. He leans against the wall next to the door and double-checks some things on his phone before checking the supplies he brought. He wants to make sure this goes well, no matter what happens and he has to be prepared ahead of time. He'll need to take care of Jamie tonight. He *wants* to.

Once the ten minutes pass, he very quietly slips into Jamie's apartment, locking the door behind him. Jamie's apartment is smaller than his own, but it's decorated with much more care. Everything matches perfectly in shades of brown and cream with deep red accents, and everything is evenly spaced and angled as if by a ruler. But it's warm and close and Eric can appreciate the aesthetic. He toes off his shoes and tiptoes to Jamie's room.

Jamie's done more than just lie down as he was told, and Eric's pleased, especially since he seems to have caught on to what they're doing—that, or got his hopes up. *Or he thinks this is the whole point of you two together. No, shut up.* The plush wing-back chair from Jamie's living room is now in the corner across from the door, the path between the door and the chair going right by the end of Jamie's bed. The lights are off, and Jamie has lit candles, which Eric finds both cheesy and romantic.

And Jamie is on the bed, sprawled out, gently stroking his own cock. He looks like gilded sex, his mouth parted, his eyes carefully closed. Eric stalks across the room as quietly as possible, so as not to ruin the fantasy that Jamie had told him that first night—the one that stuck strongest in his mind as something they could easily do, something he could easily fulfill for Jamie.

I have a fantasy that I'm in a dark room, alone. And someone starts speaking, but I can't see him, he isn't even in the room. But he's watching me and he tells me how to touch myself. He talks me through it—I have this fantasy all the time, I imagine it's happening when I'm at home in bed. He tells me to stroke my chest, and my hips and my ass, and he doesn't let me touch my cock until I'm ready to beg. And then he makes me take it slow.

Eric sits in the chair, settling in comfortably. He leans forward, elbows resting on his knees and he takes a deep breath.

"Stop touching your cock."

Jamie's eyes snap open, but stay trained on the ceiling, happy and awed and disbelieving. But he does what Eric says, moving both his hands to the bed beside his body.

"Touch your neck."

Jamie lifts one hand and strokes over his throat, fingers rasping faintly on his evening stubble.

"And your chest."

The other hand drags up, and Jamie lets his hands roam, pressing into muscles Eric knows are tense from a day of running around the city making flower deliveries and selling arrangements in the shop, all while questioning what he's doing with his life. Eric wants to give him some certainty, at least in this part of his life, even if Eric isn't certain at all.

"Go lower. Touch around your cock, but do not touch it directly."

Jamie's hips flex softly off the bed, rhythmically, even when he's not touching anything that could be affected by the rocking motion. It's as if he can't wait to feel the movement—behind his eyelids, he must be seeing something above him, something to fuck, the way his cock trembles and bobs and tenses with every lift off the bed, every writhe against the sheets, hands stroking his hips and thighs and drifting in to brush along the soft, thin skin of his groin. Even from where he sits, Eric can see the pre-come leaking from the ruddy tip of his cock.

"Spread your legs."

Jamie moans. His thighs flex; beautiful lines appear along them, strong and dark in the candlelight. It reveals the curve of his ass, which is spread enough that Eric can almost make out the pucker shadowed in the center. Eric wonders just how wide he can go.

"Wider."

Jamie licks his lips, nods faintly and then his hands flex and hover, unsure.

"Is there a problem?" Eric asks.

"I—I have to stop touching myself," Jamie says, voice low and faint. "I can't go wider without... um... help."

"I said wider," Eric insists. "I want to look."

Jamie's hips buck hard, his cock bouncing off his stomach, his hands grasped tightly into his sheets. He pants and whimpers, and when he calms, his hands continue to tremble as he reaches down and pulls his legs up.

Oh, fuck, he's gorgeous. Spread so wide his whole body has to go into it, sweat on his brow and down his neck and chest, over his deep tanned skin, he looks metallic, a paragon of every fantasy Eric's ever had, cast especially for him and presented of his own will. Eric wants to sink into him, mouth and cock and tongue and fingers, lube and sweat and echoing groans, flesh on flesh.

"Reach down. Touch yourself—but not your cock."

Jamie had been reaching to grip himself, apprehensive and most likely aching as much as Eric is, bulging against his pants as he is, with his legs crossed and binding him. But Jamie's mouth and eyes fall open in pleased shock, and his fingers bypass his first target to stroke below, dry and pressing, but the pleasure it's giving him is clear.

"Switch hands." Jamie does as he's told, and then Eric smiles. "Good boy. Touch that pretty cock for me."

"Thank you, sir," Jamie gasps, letting his legs fall to the side, the fingers of his left hand between his cheeks and the right circling his cock, jerking swiftly.

"Slow down," Eric commands. "You are not allowed to come yet. Wouldn't want to get there too fast, would we?"

Jamie almost sobs, but his hand slows to a crawl, hips bucking into his hand for a little more friction, but only at the pace Eric directs.

"You look so hot, Jamie," Eric says, watching every twitch and twist of Jamie's body, skin stretching over muscle, tight and sweaty and flushed. He isn't sure how much longer he can last, sitting here in the darkness, doing nothing—his hands and lips are burning with the phantom of the feeling Jamie will feel have when he finally gets to where Eric wants him to go. "So sexy for me."

Jamie stops stroking and squeezes the base of his cock, face scrunched, taking deep, steadying breaths.

"Are you close?" Eric asks. *Yes, please, be close, finally—*

Jamie opens his mouth several times before he just settles on whining and nodding his head. Eric uncrosses his legs and stands, grateful for Jamie's closed eyes as he approaches the bed and crawls up onto it, laying himself over Jamie, guiding his hands above his shoulders and pinning them down, with their fingers laced together.

"Do you mind," Eric whispers, mouth inches from Jamie's, pulling back to maintain the distance when Jamie tries to close it, "if we fulfill one of *my* fantasies?"

"Oh my god, yes, please, yes," Jamie babbles. "Want so much, Eric—"

"Where's your toy chest?"

In a tantalizing and somewhat awkward conversation, Jamie had shyly admitted he'd bought a chest and started filling it with various toys. They'd ended the conversation there, still tiptoeing around each other, but it had stayed in Eric's mind. He wants to know what Jamie purchased to put in his chest.

"Um... left side of the bed, under... underneath—"

Eric slips off the bed and crouches, then pulls out a small wooden chest about the size of a shoebox, but twice as long. It's good enough for basic equipment, but Eric makes a mental note to look for something better for the future, if their play advances.

There are several things inside—two dildos, one average sized and one quite large; a long, thin, curved vibrator; a few boxes of condoms and some lube; a little plastic case containing the aftercare supplies Eric had told him to pick up. Then Eric shivers in anticipation—Jamie picked up a crop.

The handle is long and faintly flexible, bending just enough when Eric tests it. It's wrapped up its length with cushioned leather, providing a comfortable grip that warms in Eric's hands. The crop itself is simple and supple, the leather cured soft and velvety. It'll provide quite a good snap, if Eric's any judge. And it's perfect.

The only thing missing from the box is something Eric thought to bring himself. He keeps hold of the crop, grabs a condom and one of the bottles of lube and puts the aftercare kit on the nightstand. Then he walks to his bag and pulls out two lengths of soft fabric, almost like short scarves. They're stretchy and soft. Eric smiles—it'll all work perfectly.

Eric goes back to the bed and lays out his selections next to Jamie. Jamie looks over and moans, fingers digging into his own thighs.

"Yes, please, Eric—"

"Safewords?"

"Red to stop, yellow to pause, green to go," Jamie recites quickly. "Please, Eric, need it—"

"Do you want to know what my fantasy is, Jamie?" Eric asks, stripping his clothes while Jamie watches, obviously enjoying the show.

"Yes," Jamie says, "yes, tell me—"

"My fantasy is to tie up my sub and flog him until the entire back of his body is covered in little red marks. I want to mark him up with little patterns, my patterns. And I want to make sure he knows he's mine. Are you mine tonight, Jamie?"

"Yes," Jamie whispers, arching his back, offering. "Yes, Eric. Eric I'm yours, always yours."

"Are you willing to let me prove it?"

"Yes, *god* yes, please do it to me, please—"

"Get on your stomach."

Jamie flips over easily and sticks his wrists up toward the headboard, face buried in the bed between his biceps. Eric, naked now, crawls up and straddles his lower back, leaning down to kiss over his arms lightly, dragging his lips to and from the veins that stick out, beating beneath the candlelit skin.

The first tie goes around Jamie's wrists, criss-crossing and wrapping around and tying off with a slipknot. The second loops around that and then ties to the headboard, with just enough give for Eric's purposes.

"So pretty," he comments, slipping off the bed again to look at his work. Jamie is stretched long, arms above his head, legs out straight, back expanding and falling with his deep breaths. "Are you ready?"

"Yes, Eric," Jamie says, lifting his head so his voice carries past the bed. "Yes, I'm yours—"

Eric grabs the crop. "I want you to count. When we hit ten, we'll take a short break. We'll keep going until I am satisfied. You are not allowed to come. Am I clear?"

"Yes, sir," Jamie breathes, and Eric smiles. Good—he's already starting to give in.

He stands at the foot of the bed, drawing the leather of the crop softly up the curve of the sole of Jamie's foot, teasing. Then he draws it back just a bit, and snaps his wrist down, landing a strike on the back of his leg, low above his ankle. Jamie gasps, his leg jerks and then he turns his head to the side.

"One," he exhales, eyes blinking as he adjusts to the sting. Eric leans down and kisses the spot lightly as the color rises, a sweet line that's slightly thicker on one end, a few inches long. This is a good beginner's crop—not too harsh, not too sharp. It'll sting and mark, but the leather is soft and thicker than some Eric's encountered. That softens the blow. Eric smiles.

"How did that feel?" he asks Jamie.

"G-good," Jamie replies. "It... it stings, but not much? It's a little deeper, I guess."

"Mmmm, good," Eric hums. "You should be glad you didn't buy a whip."

Jamie bites his lip and bucks his hips into the bed. Eric lays the crop warningly on Jamie's lower back, threatening a strike.

"None of that," Eric says. "I will be the one giving you pleasure now, and only when I say. There will be consequences if you cannot follow my directions. Do you understand?" When Jamie nods, Eric smiles again. "Good boy. Keep those hips still."

Before Jamie can settle in, Eric pulls back the crop and lays another mark, just above the one he just left, the crop turned just enough to lay it at a different angle. Jamie hisses and counts off, and Eric kisses the mark, enjoying how it darkens between when he leans down and straightens back up to strike again.

When they reach ten, Jamie is panting lightly, his toes flexing sporadically. Eric kisses the last mark, a light line just at the top of the back of Jamie's thigh, close to the crease where it meets his ass. The marks curve back and forth up Jamie's leg, rising like a vine from ankle to calf to knee to thigh, pretty and pink and throbbing.

"Ten," Jamie groans, and Eric lays the crop down.

"Such a good boy," Eric praises, and Jamie smiles and whispers his thanks. Eric spreads Jamie's legs a bit and kneels between them, stroking the outsides of his thighs, away from the marks. "I think you deserve a reward for taking this so well. Go ahead and rub yourself on the bed while I give you your reward, but stop me when you get close."

Eric pushes Jamie's legs up, patting him gently when he hisses at the stretching skin on the marked leg. His ass raises and he seems to anticipate what he's getting.

"Don't hold back those noises you make," Eric instructs. "I want to hear."

With that statement hovering between them, Eric leans down, spreading Jamie's ass with firm palms and spread, pressing fingers. He buries his face in the center, kissing hard at the puckered skin of his hole.

"Ooooh, fuck," Jamie gasps, hips rocking down, and Eric responds by sticking his tongue out to lave flat over him, broad and quick and firm.

Jamie continues to make the best moans and whimpers, and Eric gives everything he can, borrowing tricks he learned the first night they were together to draw out Jamie's pleasure to the snapping point. It takes longer than Eric expects, but it's only too soon when Jamie tenses and pulls away, blurting out, "Stop! Stop stop stop—"

Eric backs off, not even touching Jamie, allowing him to come down on his own. He does so slowly, finally settling and breathing evenly. Eric picks up the crop.

"Very good," he says. "Keep this up, and I'll let you come tonight."

Jamie needs another moment to calm after Eric says that, and Eric keeps it in mind, putting it on an ever-growing list that he'll write down at some point—perhaps to put in a contract, if they decide to make this about more than the fantasies, someday, *maybe*. And Jamie is such a good sub, so wonderful, so natural at this, Eric hopes they can do this as much as possible—

Eric pulls back his hand, and lets the crop flick in again. A mark raises on Jamie's other leg, followed by a wrecked "One."

At each set of ten, Eric pauses, giving Jamie a different reward. He turns Jamie onto his side and sucks his cock down, letting Jamie fuck his face deep, leaking pre-come into Eric's throat at an alarming rate—there's so much of it, filling his mouth with its musky taste. The next time, he fingers Jamie gently while dripping little drops of wax along his crack, just missing the marks he'd just cropped all over the fleshy meat of his cheeks. Then, at Jamie's frantic request, Eric fucks him with the handle of the crop, lubing it carefully before thrusting it in deeply, dragging it out at different angles, finally finding his mark when Jamie cries out and thrashes wildly. At that point, he steps back and lets it rest, sticking out of Jamie's hole like a tail, bobbing nicely when Eric flicks the crop, letting it rock into his prostate and stretch him all at once, vibrating harder as it wobbles to stillness. Eric worries for Jamie's voice when he does this, as well as his self-control. Jamie's cries are loud and harsh every time Eric does it, his body twisting and arching hard. Before Jamie calls it, Eric pulls the crop from him and wipes it down, petting Jamie's hair and kissing him deeply before he resumes his work.

"You are everything I've ever wanted," he whispers to Jamie, who is right on the edge of floating. God, and he must be in a state himself, saying things like this. "You're just for me, aren't you? Just mine."

"All yours," Jamie responds, his eyes shut, his mouth hanging open to gasp in breath.

"Okay," Eric says, grabbing the crop again. "Shall we continue?"

Three more times, they reach ten, marks swirling over Jamie's back and arms and down his ass and legs. The last set of ten are simply Eric adding finishing touches, filling in spaces that look too bare, too unmarked. And after the first two sets, Eric gives Jamie his rewards—first stroking Jamie's cock with the leather of the crop, teasing and tapping him slowly until he actually sobs for mercy, a plea which Eric ignores until he gets too close, and then kneeling next to Jamie so Jamie can suck him off while rubbing himself into the bed. This takes the edge from Eric's own rising desperation but also increases it because of the muffled moans and cries from Jamie's stuffed throat.

But when they finish, Jamie is a quivering wreck, and Eric spends a long time kissing him and rubbing him gently, calming him and soothing him, letting him drift for a little bit in a haze of need and endorphins and denial. Then, Eric slips behind him, lets him rest for a few minutes, Jamie twitching every few minutes when his cock throbs against the bed, whining and murmuring Eric's name.

Eric takes the lube and opens himself up, reaching back to spread himself with one, two, three fingers, only stopping when he's uncontrollably rocking back on his fingers, needing to come. And Jamie must be so much worse off, brought to the edge and denied so many times.

"Can you kneel up, Jamie?" Eric asks, coming forward, feeling strange with the slickness inside him. "Just a little bit."

Jamie nods and shuffles up, and Eric's glad of the length he gave Jamie on his restraint, because Jamie pulls it tight and uses it to hold himself up, and there's still enough room for Eric to slip in when it's time.

But first, he rips open a condom package and rolls the condom onto Jamie. When Jamie realizes what's going on, he takes a shaking breath and his eyes plead at Eric, heavy-lidded and quickly returning to sharp focus.

"Oh god, please," Jamie says. "Please let me fuck you—"

"If you're good," Eric promises, and Jamie thanks him frantically, his head throwing back, throat bobbing as he swallows air. Eric crawls up and slips beneath Jamie, face-down, straddling his legs and letting Jamie's restrained arms rest over one shoulder while he sets up. "Good boy. Now, just—help me get you inside—that's right—"

Eric reaches back and positions, sinking back as Jamie kneels, positioning his cock perfectly to breach him and slide in smoothly, so swollen and hard in the condom, slick with lube and hot inside Eric as he settles down onto his elbows, ass raised up to take Jamie just right.

"Do not move," Eric demands. "And do not come. If you get close, you are to tell me. If you move, if you come without permission, there will be consequences. Are you ready?"

Jamie's mouth opens and closes with a faint, wordless moan, and he just nods. Eric adjusts just a bit before he rocks back, taking Jamie to the hilt before pulling off and slamming back again. Jamie stays as still as he can, allowing Eric to fuck himself on his cock, head hanging and mouth open as he watches himself disappear into Eric's stretched ass, hot and tight and slick. Eric moans and keeps moving, pumping back and forth on Jamie's cock, angling himself until it's just right, crying out on every thrust that pierces the control he's kept. And Jamie just stares and gasps for breath, letting Eric use his body again and again, never complaining, never fumbling.

"I'm close," Eric grits out, his thighs burning, his cock bouncing hard against his stomach with the strength of his thrusts. "Can you hold off? Just a—a little more—"

"Yeah, yes," Jamie gasps. "Please, please come—"

Eric twists and reaches back, pulling the knot on Jamie's wrists, and the ties unravel.

"Now fuck me," he says, and then drops down as Jamie grabs his hips and gives it to him, pounding hard into him, drawing cries from his lips with every slap of his hips into Eric's ass.

"Yes, just like that—keep going," Eric babbles, letting himself go. "Yes, so close, just—fuck, fuck, fuck—"

He tenses, and then everything falls apart inside him, and he comes hard onto the bed, every spurt draining him of energy and strength until he's collapsed, loose and sated as Jamie continues to fuck him.

"You can come now, baby," Eric says. "You've been so good, come in me—"

"I—I can't," Jamie groans. "I—it's too much, I—"

He sobs and drops onto Eric, holding him tight and grinding in, kissing at the back of Eric's neck, biting and sucking and covering him, surrounding him, still fucking him in tight circles of his hips.

"I can't come, it's just... I can't, why—"

Eric stops his movements with a quick hand and then pulls off, and Jamie sobs in frustration again, folding over as Eric slips from beneath him.

"Can you lie on your back? Is it too much?" he asks. Jamie shakes his head and rolls over, spread-eagled and nearly crying with the force of his need, cock pulsing pearly beads but never giving him the release he needs. So Eric takes over, kneeling over him and settling back, holding Jamie's cock up so he can sink down onto it, pushing past his own sharp twinges of oversensitivity to grind gently on Jamie. He leans down, chest-to-chest, and kisses Jamie, hands stroking over his arms and neck and into his hair.

"You were so good for me, Jamie," Eric says. "You made my fantasy come true, and it was so much better than I ever thought. Thank you so much, so perfect for me—"

"Are you mine, too?"

Eric kisses Jamie softly, cupping his cheeks.

"Yes, I am," Eric replies, with total honesty.

Jamie nods, tears leaking from the corners of his eyes, his chest heaving for breath. "Please make me come," he requests. "Please, Eric—"

Eric rears up. He rises up on his knees and then comes back down with a hard slap, and then again, and again, until he's riding Jamie hard and fast, bouncing on his cock, every muscle burning. But Jamie is crying out, his voice louder and louder.

"Come, Jamie," Eric commands, putting every bit of Dominance he can into it. "Come, now."

Jamie does as he's told. His hips jerk up, lifting Eric straight off the bed, his back arching, his mouth open but totally silent for a long moment before he lets out a wild shout of Eric's name, sobbing his way down as his hips still, his body going lax.

When he settles, Eric draws off of him carefully, a little sore. He strokes Jamie's cheek and checks his breathing and pulse, which are slowing steadily as he rests, apparently either blacked out or just too overwhelmed to move, his eyelids shut and twitching faintly.

"My good boy," Eric praises, kissing his unresponsive lips tenderly. "Let me take care of you, baby. Let me be good for you."

He checks Jamie over, takes off the condom and throws it away. He puts their toys to the side for when they get around to washing them and grabs the aftercare kit, opening up the little plastic case. He pulls out the package of baby wipes and gives himself a quick cleaning before cleaning Jamie as well, softly stroking over the sweat of his body and the leftover come on his cock. Then, he turns Jamie gently onto his stomach, away from the mess they've made.

He pulls out the Lidocaine gel and goes over Jamie's crop marks, easing the sting and cooling him a little. Once he's finished, he grabs the little tube of arnica and applies it with gentle fingers, to help the bruising that might occur. It wasn't a hard flogging, but it still has a risk, and Eric wants to look out for his sub.

"Eric?"

Eric smiles and puts the kit away before sliding into bed with Jamie, carding his fingers through Jamie's hair.

"How are you feeling?"

"Mmm. Good. Sore. You?"

"Messy," Eric responds, a little goofily, but Jamie's busy floating in and out of subspace and doesn't seem to think it's funny. Oh well. "When you feel up to it, we'll take a shower, and I'll put some more arnica on your marks. Can you move for me, let me check if you hurt any muscles?"

Jamie nods and then moves with Eric's guidance. He doesn't appear to have strained anything, so Eric settles in, satisfied for now.

"Thank you," Jamie says, cuddling onto Eric, laying his body on Eric's chest, holding him tight, nuzzling his neck and leaving kisses where he can reach.

Eric grins, feeling a wash of emotion through him. His eyes prick, and he holds Jamie close.

"Thank you," he says. He waits several minutes, and then sighs. "I think... I might be falling in love with you. But it's too fast, Jamie, and I don't know if I trust it. I've never felt this before, not this soon. I'm just pretty sure we're both going to get hurt."

Jamie just breathes, contentedly asleep. It's a good enough answer for now.

CRYING CALL

CRYING CALL

The morning after their first scene as a couple, Eric wakes with morning breath, morning wood, and a heaping dose of morning-after awkwardness. Jamie is sprawled on his stomach next to him, one leg thrown over Eric's, grunting and knuckling his eyes. Eric grimaces and looks over.

"G'morning," Jamie rasps, a laugh touching the edges of the sentiment, a sleep smile on his face. Eric smiles back, shifting uncomfortably.

"Good morning," he replies. "Um. I'm gonna... go use the facilities, if you don't mind."

"Mmm, sure. Right across the hall."

Jamie seems completely unaffected by the unease Eric is feeling, slumping back down onto the bed with a grunt and a laugh as Eric slips out of bed and pulls on his briefs. He walks away self-consciously, but he lets himself smile when Jamie whistles appreciatively.

His bathroom's clean. Eric gives himself a quick wake-up routine, even going so far as to borrow a little mouthwash for the disgusting taste in his mouth. He's just considering whether or not he'll cross a line by just jumping into the shower, when the door opens and Jamie slides in.

"Hi," he says. "I was gonna wait to shower, but I can't. My back is really gross. Um... would you like to join me?"

Eric knows his eyes have gone wide and he blinks rapidly before he can help it. That's not an offer he's used to after a first night together—usually it's awkward goodbyes and a bit of a rush to get back to his place before work, or whatever else he's got going on. It's just awkward, wondering how domestic to be, how much is too much, when he's basically invading someone's space. Their relationship (however defined or undefined it is) is still new, and it's definitely a weird place to navigate.

And Jamie's just not letting him go about this the way he usually does. Instead, he's inviting Eric right in without a trace of self-consciousness or discomfort. So Eric feels he should at least be as mature as that and return the straightforwardness.

"Really?" he asks. "I mean... first morning after, I don't want to be in your way—"

"I asked, didn't I?" Jamie points out, smirking. Eric feels distinctly that he's being made fun of.

He sighs and rubs a hand over his face, smiling. "Um. I'm used to a lot more... politics with a new... um." He gestures between them and absolutely doesn't blame Jamie for the confusion on his face.

"Relationship?" Jamie suggests slowly, and Eric sighs again.

"Relationship," he corroborates. "I would love to shower with you, if it doesn't make you think I'm being overly clingy."

Jamie laughs and pulls him into a tight, warm hug. "It's a shower, Eric. You're not moving in."

No, but he is probably the most awkward person ever to exist, especially before he has caffeine in his veins. He feels himself blushing and shakes his head as he steps back. "Can we start over, without me being a total idiot?" he asks. "Good morning, Jamie, I was about to start a shower for us. How are you feeling?"

Jamie looks for a long moment as if he'd like nothing more than to not play along and give Eric a good teasing, but he shrugs and then leans up for a quick closed-mouth kiss. "Good morning, Eric. A shower sounds awesome. Get it going and I'll join in a second?"

"Sure thing," Eric says and he turns and fiddles with the controls for the cream-tiled shower, managing to nearly scald himself before he gets it to an acceptable temperature and steps in.

He lets the water take over for a minute, lets it relax and soothe him while Jamie does whatever he does to wake himself up and get a touch less gross on the other side of the shower curtain. By the time it flicks aside and Jamie hops in, Eric's feeling nice and warm and relaxed.

"Here, hop under," Eric says, stepping back. He feels himself slipping into his role as Dom, as caretaker. Aftercare doesn't just take place immediately after a scene, not if it's that intense, and he needs to check

Jamie for marks and any potential damage. "Let me get a look at your back."

Jamie turns and sighs as the water crashes over him, wetting his hair and sliding over the back of his neck. Eric slides his hands over Jamie's shoulders, taking a moment to appreciate the contrast in their skin colors—Jamie's dark, somewhere between tan and brown, even and smooth, a bit hirsute. The word *swarthy* comes to mind, and Eric traps the resulting giggle in his throat and looks down at himself. Eric is best described as pinkish, especially in the heat of the shower. He's got freckles and moles and he grooms his body hair only because it grows in patchy, as though he never quite finished puberty. He'd rather look deliberately, rather than accidentally, pre-pubescent.

But Jamie's back looks gorgeous. The marks are faded, and Eric can't see any bruising. He runs his hands over the warm skin, asking, "Any pain?"

Jamie shrugs. "I'm a little... I don't know. Tender?"

"You aren't bruised, so that should go away soon," Eric says. He crouches and runs his hands over the backs of Jamie's legs. It all seems good. "How do you feel overall?"

Jamie presses back into Eric as he stands again, and Eric obliges the hint, wrapping his arms around Jamie's body and holding him close, tucking his chin over Jamie's shoulder.

"I'm a little sore," Jamie says. "Like I worked out. Good sore. And... I'm still allowed to be totally honest, and you won't judge?"

"Of course," Eric promises. "Open door policy."

Jamie turns and kisses Eric languidly, humming. "Is that ever going to work both ways?"

Eric stiffens and feels instantly uncomfortable. But that's a fair question, and any relationship in the scene needs openness and honesty and communication. But Jamie seems to want something outside of the scene, too, and Eric can't deny that want as well. And it's a different want, something at odds with total openness that D/s requires. He feels too vulnerable with it; the risk of getting hurt is too big without clear boundaries around it.

Maybe that's the answer. Maybe they just need to set up boundaries for their relationship outside of the scene as well. Explicit ones, instead of the norm that Eric is used to, the unspoken rules of dating that are a comfort zone for him, a familiar alternative to premature vulnerability. Evidently nothing with Jamie is going to go as Eric expects.

"Yes," he says, finally, reaching for Jamie's shampoo. As he works it through Jamie's hair, he smiles. "But why don't you tell me what's on your mind now, and I'll open my door when we're all done with this?"

"I can live with that," Jamie says, letting the shampoo rinse from his hair. "Okay. So. Um. You know how, when we were talking about showering together, you thought I thought you were being clingy? Or... could be. Whatever we said," he finishes with a laugh.

"Yes."

"Okay. Well. I guess I'm feeling clingy? Like..." Jamie sighs and turns around, looking into Eric's eyes nervously. "You make me feel a lot, Eric. Not like a lot of different things. But a lot of each thing you make me feel. Does that... make sense?"

"Yes," Eric says. He tries not to tremble, tries not to give in to the urge to fall heedlessly. Logic is his ally, here. *Control.* He's the Dom. "A lot of that is... it's part of doing a scene."

"I feel it outside the scene, Eric."

"I know," Eric replies. *Honesty.* "Me too. But it's a lot stronger with... everything that this does to our minds and bodies. Neurochemicals and stuff."

"I never took a psych class. Or chemistry."

"Biology? No?" Eric laughs. "Oxytocin? The cuddle hormone?"

"Oh, yeah."

"Yeah. That. And others. Especially with pain play."

Jamie's eyes darken. "I, uh... I really liked that, by the way."

"I did too," Eric says. "You sounded... gorgeous. Looked gorgeous. Trusting me like that." Jamie kisses him deep, and in the water it's slick and weirdly tasteless and warm. Eric pulls back enough for a breath. "But if you liked it so much, we can talk about doing more. I believe it was one of your fantasies?"

"Yeah," Jamie breathes. "But... let's write those down or something. Later."

He presses against Eric, making clear his arousal, and Eric groans, pressing back. *That feels—really good—*

"Yeah, that's—that's a good ide-mmph."

* * *

The smell of brewing coffee mixes with the peppery scent of Jamie's shampoo still lingering in their damp hair in Jamie's cramped kitchen. Eric leans against the counter and watches with a little smile as Jamie opens a cupboard and pulls down two mugs from a perfectly matching line of them, all of their handles pointing in the same direction. His whole kitchen is like that—everything angles the same way, very carefully placed, very carefully clean. His whole apartment is like that, actually. Eric likes it—he's not the neatest himself, and this is a calmer atmosphere than his somewhat chaotic apartment.

"So," Jamie says, as the coffee maker spits out its last drips with a grinding, spluttering noise. "Open doors."

Eric laughs, barely more than a huff of breath, and steps up next to Jamie at the counter. Jamie hands him the first mug, and Eric reaches for sugar and starts to spoon it in.

"Okay. Um. I guess... this is all really new to me too, in a lot of ways," Eric says. "I've been in a lot of relationships over the years, and... they all follow a pattern, I guess."

"What pattern?"

"The usual?" Eric sips the coffee—it's pretty good, considering that the coffee maker looks as if it's been through a great deal of suffering in its day. "You know. Either... quick, sexual. Or slow and... and meaningful. You know? Nice dates, waiting, slow build. The movie romance."

"And... you think we're moving too quickly?" Jamie guesses.

"I guess that's part of it," Eric says, after a short pause. "I'm not—I don't—wow. I have... no idea how to say this."

"You've let me take my time," Jamie says. "Go ahead and take yours."

Eric smiles gratefully and leans over for a kiss. It tastes like coffee and sugar. "You're great."

"... But?"

"But nothing." Eric shrugs. "You're just great. And that's why I don't want to mess this up."

Jamie just watches Eric with his dark eyes and sips his coffee, patient, his shoulder gently pressed against Eric's arm.

"I guess I'm worried this is just sexual," Eric admits. "And we're thinking it's more because of the intensity of what we're doing. We did fall into things quickly, for me. And... you're still learning what you want. What you like."

"I like you," Jamie says quietly.

"I like you, too." Eric takes Jamie's hand gently. "I just want to know it's real before we go too far."

"What's too far?" Jamie asks frankly. "I mean... we've gone really, really far already."

"I mean emotionally," Eric says. "And yeah, we've gone pretty far there, too. But we're still... early, here. New. I guess... I just want to make sure we don't get in too deep without... I don't know, a ladder."

Jamie frowns and takes a deep breath. "Like... a contract?"

"No," Eric says quickly. "No, not yet. That would be too far. I just mean boundaries."

"Like what?"

"How about this," Eric suggests, fully turning to Jamie and pulling Jamie to face him. "We'll work on your fantasies. We'll hang out; we'll go on dates. We can fool around without the scene too if you want. But we won't promise anything... long-term, or permanent, until we finish your list of fantasies. When we do them all, we can... part ways. As friends, as strangers. Your choice. Or we can make a contract. And come up with some new fantasies together."

"So basically, you want to put a time limit on us," Jamie says, anger and disbelief creeping into his voice.

"No," Eric says. "Not like that. I want to give us a set time to make sure that this is as good as it feels right now."

"You don't trust me?"

"I don't trust me," Eric laughs. "Do you know how hard it is not to just say fuck it all and throw myself at you? Really unattractive."

Jamie bites his lip and steps into Eric's space, wrapping his arms around Eric's waist and laying his head on Eric's shoulder. "I find it really attractive."

"See?" Eric says, hugging Jamie close. "Told you so. Anyone else would be running and screaming."

They stand quietly in each other's arms, breathing. In. Out. In. Out. Chests tight together, and then relaxing away. Waves crashing into shore. Moon pulling a tide. Eric doesn't know which one of them is which.

"Okay," Jamie says eventually. "It's fair enough. We'll... do my fantasies. With some of yours thrown in," he adds, "because that worked out really well last night." Eric laughs, but Jamie looks up at him seriously. "But you cannot make all of this my choice. That's a lot of weight on me. I want to agree to do this together. Decisions and all."

"I kind of thought that's what I was doing just now, but okay," Eric says with a little shrug. "Both of us will agree to continue or not. We can talk it out and get a feel for it anytime, okay?"

"So the doors stay open then?"

"Wide, wide open," Eric says. Seeing that Jamie's eyes are still sad, still worried, Eric smiles. "Like I came home drunk and forgot to close the door and you're a burglar who comes in and steals my socks."

Jamie bursts out laughing. "Socks? Your socks?"

"I don't know what else you'd steal," Eric chuckles.

Jamie looks at him very calmly, and says, "I'd be going for your heart."

Eric freezes, and then blinks. That—that was— "That was the cheesiest thing I've ever heard."

Jamie slaps his arm. "You don't get to say a word. You think I'm a sock burglar."

* * *

I have a fantasy that I'm spanked by different... um, objects I guess.

Eric opens the door to his apartment the next weekend with that fantasy planned to a tee. It has to be written all over his face, the way Jamie's eyes go wide and his mouth draws into an open little circle.

"Eric?" he begins to ask. "What's—"

"Try again," Eric says. God, he hasn't felt this riled up in a while, this *needy* for a sub to Dominate *right that second*. Eric's always loved spanking, loves the feeling of a man beneath his hands, loves how intense it can get while still being fun and naughty and loves the way it looks and feels—and he just can't wait to try it out with Jamie, go deeper with it, show him all the things Eric knows how to do to make the pain feel good.

Jamie's eyes go even wider, and Eric stares right into them—deep ruddy brown with just a touch of gold near the irises, long curled lashes framing them, almond-shaped and tilted sharply, and Eric realizes he doesn't even know Jamie's heritage. He should ask sometime.

Jamie tries again, though, tentatively. "Sir?"

Eric pulls Jamie tight and kisses him hard, shutting the door behind him roughly. "That's it," he groans, barely pulling away to get the words out, diving back in and claiming Jamie as hard as he can with their clothes still firmly on.

"What—can I ask what we're doing?" Jamie throws his head back and lets Eric attack his neck, sucking and biting, his pulse hammering at the junction with his jaw. Eric presses his nose into it, *feels* it pulsing against him. He wants to feel that pulse everywhere, dig his fingertips into Jamie's skin till he can feel it in his chest, his hips, his ass, every artery and vein flickering against Eric's skin, close and hard and hot.

"I'll show you," Eric says instead. He grabs the skinny black tie of Jamie's work uniform and *tugs*, practically dragging Jamie down the short entry hall and into the living room. He stops Jamie abruptly and then circles around him, dropping the tie and grabbing his wrists, pulling them behind his back and pointing his whole body at the coffee table, which is cleared of its usual items, but full of another kind.

"What—are those?" Jamie asks, his voice high-pitched and breathy. "Are you going to—"

Eric laughs quietly. "Am I going to have to mask this as a punishment, or can we drop the pretense and just admit you want to be spanked?"

"Oh!" Jamie gasps. Eric holds his wrists tighter, pulls them back, forcing Jamie into a tighter posture. His hips jut out to compensate, and Eric peeks over his shoulder and hums happily when he sees Jamie's pants tenting just a bit. "Um—I like roleplay. That's... *exciting*."

"Mmmm, so what'd you do?" Eric asks playfully. The weight of silent expectation and pressure has been removed since their discussion the previous weekend, and he's been in an increasingly good mood since then, especially considering he and Jamie haven't seen each other in person all week. He *missed* Jamie, and texts and phone conversations, no matter how intimate or filthy they had gotten, weren't enough; he's really excited to see his boyfriend again. His *sub*.

"I—I don't know."

Eric *tssks*, pushes Jamie closer to the coffee table, letting his shins bump into it. "I think you do know."

It's not really fair to put Jamie on the spot like this, but Jamie doesn't seem to mind, and Eric kind of relishes it. After all, none of this is going to be fair—that's half the point. He's giving a fake punishment to his boyfriend for something he most likely didn't do, and most likely doesn't deserve corporeal punishment, not to the average person. But that's not what this game is about. It's about tilting the odds in his own favor, making Jamie submit to what he wants. He has an out clause if he wants—that's what safewords are for, to ensure consent. But Jamie wants to be forced to let go, and Eric's going to do it. Fair doesn't come into it. And neither of them want it to.

It's about giving both of them what they want. Jamie wants to explore what physical pain can do for him, what pleasure and release it can bring; he wants to surrender and let someone else take care of everything. Eric wants to give that to him, wants to hear and see his reactions, wants to feel as if he's taking care of Jamie. So maybe, after all, it is fair. In its own way, at least.

"I'm sorry, sir," Jamie says, and his voice is—different. Meek. Quiet. *Penitent*. "I'm sorry I stole from you."

Eric shifts the grip on Jamie's wrists to one hand and uses the other to reach around, grip Jamie's jaw, and turn him to face Eric, forcing eye contact. As expected, Jamie's eyes gleam wickedly. *Smartass.*

"Sorry's not good enough," Eric says firmly, falling into the role. He recalls, in the back of his mind, reading in a book somewhere about a tale of a magician giving a girl an egg with his heart in it, which she broke. He imagines Jamie, stealing that egg, and the risk of it smashing to pieces if not carefully handled, especially when it wasn't freely given. He instantly feels more stern, more authoritative, just a little bit more vindictive, having caught his thief. "Take off your tie, and kneel at the end of the table."

He releases Jamie, and he stands with legs apart, arms crossed, eyebrow raised, as his orders are carried out. Jamie slips the tie from his neck and kneels just how Eric wants him, at the end of the coffee table, facing in. He lays the tie down on the table before him, next to the first of the objects on the table, and Eric nods approvingly.

"Very good," he says. Jamie controls himself remarkably well, but Eric can see he's delighted in the settling of his shoulders, the straightening of his back, the crinkling at the corners of his eyes. "Do you know what I'm going to do with the objects laid out before you?"

Jamie looks at them carefully, his breath picking up as he takes them in. "I think so," he says finally. "You're—you're going to spank me with them."

"Mmm, yes," Eric says. "But only two of them. And you get to pick which two."

There are four. A plastic kitchen spatula, the kind without the slots, fresh bought for a whopping one dollar; a fancier wooden one with a much wider head and a nice thick handle, straight the whole way down; a mini plastic whiffle ball bat; and finally, Eric's favorite, and something that looks scary but is, in reality, probably the best option on the table, as well as the only one specifically designed for this—his leather paddle. It's got a short, thick handle, just wide enough for Eric's hand to get a really good grip, and then smooth leather wrapped around the hardwood for the full nine inches of its length. It can provide a deep bruising or a simple easy ache, or the soft leather can soothe stinging skin. Eric really hopes Jamie picks that one.

"The—the wooden spatula," Jamie says finally, clearing his throat. "And—and the leather."

Eric can't help himself. He strides forward and threads a hand into Jamie's hair and tilts his head back so he can lean down and kiss him hard. "Mmm, so glad you picked that one. Can't wait to use it on you."

"Please," Jamie whines, and Eric smiles.

"Undo your pants and push everything down to your knees," he instructs. "And then bend over the table. Make yourself comfortable." Jamie starts to do as he's told, and Eric moves the rejected implements to the couch with a careless toss, putting the wooden spatula and the paddle on the ground next to Jamie. Then, as Jamie shifts his pants and underwear down over his ass and bends over, he takes Jamie's tie and kneels next to him, positioning him. Arms facing inward, together, wrists to elbows, and winds the tie tightly around them.

"You are allowed three words besides your safewords, which you can use at any time. What are they?"

"Red to stop, yellow to pause, green to continue," Jamie recites. Eric knots off the tie and lets Jamie settle again, arms folded up beneath his chest, forehead on his joined hands.

"Very good," Eric says warmly. "The other words are 'please,' 'harder,' and 'yes.' If you have urgent cause to use any other words, use 'yellow,' do you understand?"

"Yes," Jamie says, breathing deeply, a faint smile on the edge of his mouth that Eric can see kneeling next to him.

Eric rubs a hand over his back in soothing circles, and the other he slides down, lifting the hem of Jamie's shirt so that it's up and out of the way. He caresses his ass with light brushes first, graduating to deep massages of the round flesh when Jamie relaxes. When Jamie is groaning, Eric lays a few light taps over the skin.

"How does this feel?"

"It—"

"You only have three words," Eric reminds him. "This is a punishment, remember? Thieves don't get to say whatever they want."

Jamie shudders, his breath gusting out of his mouth shakily. "Yes. Harder."

Eric obliges and taps harder, and Jamie's skin warms beneath his hand, pinks just a little bit. Perfect—he's receptive, relaxed, warming up nicely. Eric considers, rubbing his hand over the light flush, and decides it's time.

He looks at Jamie's face. His eyes are closed, his head is resting heavily, his mouth is open to pull in breath. He's *gorgeous*, so trusting, and that fills Eric with warmth from his core up to his chest, a smile breaking his face. He's got a responsibility now—Jamie's pleasure is in his hands, as well as his pain, and Eric feels proud to know how to give it and to have this man to give it to.

"Are you ready?" he asks. He intended to sound dark and foreboding, but he kind of just sounds like he's out of breath.

"Yes," Jamie moans, remaining completely relaxed. Good. He *wants* this, aches for it, needs it. It doesn't scare him, or if it does, not getting it scares him more. The slightest writhe of his hips, pushing his ass back and up, presenting, and Eric lifts the spatula and tests its grip carefully before snapping his forearm and wrist and letting the flat of it land sharp on the right cheek.

Jamie gasps, just a little bit, his body tensing at the short jolt of pain before it relaxes right back down. As soon as he's settled, Eric swats him again, this time on the left, just a little harder, and the next gasp is a little harder, a little deeper.

And there's no monotony as it continues. Each hit a little harder, the margin increasing when Jamie gasps out *harder*, moans, rocks back into the stinging left behind after the wood is pulled away. His ass turns red, the skin hot, and Jamie starts begging with the only words available to him.

"Please," he whimpers. "Harder. Please. Please. Please harder, please?"

He so obviously wants to say more, but Eric's got a role to play, and Jamie does, too, and they are both so obviously enjoying it. Jamie's affected, certainly, but Eric is sweating and hard in his pants. He's having trouble staying neutral and making it all about Jamie. He wants so badly to just toss it all away and take Jamie, right there over the coffee table, just shove his pants down and rut them together until they come. But this is a longer game, and Eric's going to play to the end.

"I don't think you're really being punished," Eric says slyly. "You seem to be enjoying this a little too much, huh?"

"Yes," Jamie says, peeking an eye open and looking over at Eric. His eye looks bright, almost feverish, and Eric rubs a soothing hand over his ass and sets the spatula down.

"Give me a color," Eric commands.

"Green," Jamie says immediately. "Green. Please green."

Eric laughs, and then lifts up the paddle. It's a good weight, light but thick, and it'll leave some wonderful marks.

"You realize you will most likely bruise?" Eric says. "It will hurt, and you'll be stiff and sore for a couple of days, no matter how well I take care of you after? You can use any words you want from now on."

"I know," Jamie says, and he sounds desperate. "I'm looking forward to that most—having you with me when you're gone, please—want it—"

"Okay," Eric concedes. Consent explicitly given, with the risks laid out, Eric tests the heft of the paddle and swings it in the air a few times, light little movements of his wrist, making sure he remembers the weight of it. "I will paddle you ten times. It will hit you across both sides of your ass. I'll be focusing there, and I will not hit you anywhere else. When we hit ten, I will untie you and we'll get you onto the couch so you can relax. Does that sound like what you want?"

"Yes," Jamie says, and that's it. Plans made, course of action laid out. Jamie nice and relaxed and not tensed up to make the hits hurt even more. Eric smacks the paddle across his ass, and counts himself, "One."

Jamie expels a breath loudly, tensing up and writhing. Eric murmurs soothingly, little nonsenses, using the paddle to rub softly, spreading out the deeper pain that this one elicits. The spatula was one thing—it was thin and light and delivered a sting, almost entirely surface. This goes deep, and Eric watches closely as he swats again, "Two," liking the way Jamie's ass ripples under the impact. This is a good sign—he's relaxed enough for the muscle to move rather than remain rigid, and only after the hit has landed and the pain ignites again does he tense up, quivering and moaning loudly.

"God—please," Jamie says. His eyes remain firmly shut, and Eric senses that he's starting to go under. His body and his mind are responding to the pain, responding to the scene, and Eric hits him again, saying "Three."

And then he pulls them back to their roleplay. "Are you sorry yet?" *Smack.* "Four."

Jamie cries out, and while Eric soothes the latest hit, he shakes and thrashes weakly, clenching his eyes tight. "Yes. Sorry. So sorry."

"Good," Eric says. *Smack.* "Five. Color?"

"Green," Jamie groans. "I can finish, please, let me—I'm good, I'm good—"

Smack. "Six."

Jamie's knees spread, and he drops, heavy, sobbing, still propped up by the table. Eric waits, lets him ride this through, lets the pain settle into the deep ache he knows Jamie has to be feeling. Jamie tenses and relaxes several times, waiting for the next hit, and finally, he opens his eyes.

"Please, Eric—" *Smack, smack.* Twice in quick succession. And Eric feels himself starting to come loose himself, feels himself starting to crack. *Just a few more until you shatter and your heart spills right onto the floor.*

"Seven, eight," Eric says. Jamie starts heaving for breath, quick and hard, and Eric hushes him gently. "It's okay. You're okay. Just two more."

"Yes," Jamie sobs. "Please do it. Please."

Smack. "Nine." And Jamie's ass is a deeper red, despite the fact that Eric isn't hitting him all that hard, is holding back. Jamie is crying, something knocked loose inside of him, some deeper pain that was brought out by the fake penance and the wrecking. But there's only one more, and then Eric can take care of Jamie how he wants to—wrap him up, whisper to him, hold him close and soothe him—

"Ten," he says, *smack.* And then the paddle is down, and Eric pulls the knot on the tie and unravels it. When it falls loose, Jamie is instantly in his arms, burrowing into his chest and crying openly.

"Are you okay, baby?" Eric asks, holding him in carefully but strongly and petting his hair.

Jamie just nods and sniffles, clutching Eric like a buoy. And when that metaphor buries itself in Eric's mind, he realizes he's keeping Jamie's from really sinking—he's soothing him, but he's keeping him from sub-space, holding him up like this, speaking to him, making him kneel uncomfortably.

"Come on, sweetheart, let's go to the couch, and you can lie down," Eric suggests. Jamie moves with him, but not on his own, so Eric has to guide him right to the couch. Luckily it's not far, and Jamie cooperates enough for Eric to undress him completely and lay him out on his stomach, his arms latching onto a pillow held beneath his head. Eric kneels next to him and rubs a hand up and down his back and stays quiet.

It takes a little while, but eventually Jamie sinks right down into sub-space. All it finally takes is Eric softly caressing the dark red skin over his buttocks and he sighs and calms, his breath only hitching occasionally. He's breathing deeply, he's apparently comfortable. So Eric tells him to wait, and receives only a faint murmur in response.

He returns as quickly as possible with a juice box, a tube of arnica cream, the bath running hot and slowly in the bathroom to give Eric time to ease Jamie back. He sets the juice box on the coffee table near Jamie's head and kneels by his hips, and begins applying the arnica cream thickly over him.

He's about halfway done with the second cheek when Jamie stirs and looks down.

"Hi," he rasps. A quick cough, and he tries again, this time his voice much clearer. "Hi."

"Hello," Eric says. "How are you feeling?"

"Ow," Jamie says, when Eric's hand returns with more cream. "Good though. Um. Embarrassed."

"Because of the crying?"

"Yeah." Jamie sniffles and wipes a hand over his eyes and cheeks. "Sor-ry... about that. I don't know why I did, I just..."

"I understand your embarrassment," Eric says, not wanting to invalidate Jamie's feelings, "but I don't think badly of you for it. I'm actually relieved you could let go like that. And proud of you." Jamie grins sheepishly, and Eric finishes up and caps the tube of cream. "I have a bath filling up for you, and I want you to drink that juice."

Jamie's eyebrows knit as he reaches for the juice box and studies it. "Why do I drink juice after, again?"

Eric smiles. "Rehydration. And restoring blood sugar. We're messing with brain chemicals here; when you go into subspace, or go near it, your brain does some funny things. It can act like you're doing drugs, kind of. You need to come back down from that place nice and easy, or you'll crash. Plus juice is delicious."

Jamie laughs and sticks the straw into the box, obediently sucking some of it down. "I can't have a sports drink? Much more manly."

Eric taps his side playfully, almost near his ass, and Jamie flinches, protesting, "Hey!" Eric just laughs and stands.

"Come on, bath," he says. "It's good for you. Ease the bruising and the soreness. Can you walk?"

"Yeah," Jamie says, and then, grabbing Eric's hands, carefully and clumsily stands up while trying not to let his ass touch anything. He almost overbalances, but he manages to right himself. "I am so sexy right now."

Eric laughs, but he kisses Jamie as sweetly as he can manage. "You kind of are, though."

Jamie follows in a kind of hobbling waddle to the bathroom, looking increasingly disgruntled. Eric tries so hard not to laugh, and he doesn't, but he's fairly certain Jamie can see it all over his face.

The bath makes up for it, though. The bathtub isn't big, not in this city and at the price he pays, but it's enough to cover Jamie to his waist as he sits back in it, and that's enough. It smells a little bit like lavender, the scent of the Epsom salts Eric had poured in. He turns the water off and lets Jamie just sit there, slightly slouched to put the weight on his hips rather than on the bruised flesh of his ass, but he seems content, so Eric just sits beside the tub and holds his hand.

"So I like that," Jamie says at length. "Not sure it's something I want all the time, though. It's a little... intense for everyday."

"You mean a full spanking, or pain play at all?"

"A full spanking," Jamie clarifies. "I mean... feel free to swat my ass whenever you like, that's great. But I don't... I don't know. I don't like that it made me so vulnerable, you know? Like..."

"The crying?" Eric asks. Jamie nods, looking uncomfortable. "Can I ask why it's so wrong that you cried?"

Jamie bites his lip and sighs. "My dad, I guess. I was never allowed to cry. He was... I don't know, stern. Anything that made me girly in his eyes was bad. I haven't... hm."

"You don't have to talk about it," Eric says. "But I'll hear it anytime you want."

"No, I know," Jamie says. "It's just shitty. I haven't seen my dad since I was... eleven? Yeah. Since I came out."

"That young?" Eric knows his eyes are too wide, but Jamie just shrugs.

"I knew," he says. "And he taught me to be honest, as well as to always 'be a man.' So I was honest. And since his version of Islam teaches that homosexuality is a sin punishable by death, he disowned me when I wouldn't repent. He dropped me off with my grandma—my mom's mom—and I've only gotten birthday cards with a really gross amount of money in them since. So at least there's that."

"I'm sorry," Eric says, not knowing what else to say. His own parents had been supportive.

"Well, I mean... it's been a long time. My grandma's awesome—I miss her a lot, she's back in D.C. Little Vietnamese woman, really ribald. You'd love her; she's wild. Uses her age and secondary English to say outrageous shit, it's really great."

Eric tilts his head and lays it on their hands. "I feel really white right now."

Jamie laughs and splashes him a little bit. "You *are* really white."

"So, no crying, then?" Eric asks.

Jamie looks at him long and hard. "I don't know. Maybe... maybe not until—*unless* we make things... more."

"I can live with that if you can," Eric says. "It's perfectly fair. We'll skip the heavy pain stuff until there's either a contract or you specifically ask for it. Okay?"

Jamie nods, and then smiles a little bit. "So... would a contract mean a collar?"

Eric almost chokes on his own spit. "Sorry?"

Jamie's grin is huge. "Leta mentioned collaring when we went out to lunch the other day. You know she and Andy are getting serious?"

That catches Eric off guard. "Like, Andy said so? Because Andy's... um, I love her, but she's flaky when it comes to relationships."

"There was talk of collaring, evidently," Jamie says. "I take it that's a huge step."

"Yeah, I guess," Eric says with a shrug. "I mean, not everyone does it. Those who do, there's a system sometimes, sometimes not. It's really individual, I guess. I don't want to make you wear a collar all the time, but I mean—if we get to that point, I'd be cool with getting you one, as part of a contract. You know... for private use."

The truth is, Eric's not looking for a lifestyle sub, someone who does nothing else. When he started as a Dom, it was for a boyfriend, and he took to it so naturally that he'd assumed something was right between them, and wanted a collar to signify that. But then the boyfriend moved on. That started a trend of men who never really managed to fit with Eric, and he hasn't wanted to use a collar since. He's played with men who dabble, men who play mostly in private, men who want to always crawl on their knees, live their lives in service of their Doms. In all of these, a collar is a symbol—important in the world of BDSM—and it can mean anything from a toy to use for one scene to something close to a wedding ring, depending on how deep in the lifestyle it's used. Jamie's not asking for it as a toy, and he's not asking for it as part of a lifestyle. He's asking for it as part of a relationship, something none of Eric's boyfriends have ever asked for. They either didn't want the permanence, or they didn't want the symbolic claiming, or they didn't want anything to do with the lifestyle at all. It just never *fit* with Eric's desire for some kind of perfect story.

Jamie's fitting pretty well, though.

"I think I'd like to try it out, anyway," Jamie says. "But uh... I'm getting cold right now, and a collar sounds awesome, but I'd rather have a sweater. Or a towel."

Eric pulls the plug on the tub and stands up, tugging a big fluffy towel off the rack. He helps Jamie up and out of the tub and dries him off himself, softly patting away the water and then pulling him to the bedroom and laying him on his stomach on the bed.

"Are you staying the night?" Eric asks, applying more cream.

Jamie looks back at him. "Am I invited?"

Eric gives him a look. "If I were really kicking you out, I think I'd be a little smoother than that. I wouldn't make you think I were inviting you to stay if I wanted you to go."

"I don't actually know what the hell you said," Jamie laughs, "but I need to tell you now that you're not the least bit smooth."

Eric gapes. "I am too."

"Oh, maybe when you're doing the Dom thing," Jamie says. "But when you're just Eric, normal, you're not smooth at all. You are a dirt road."

"I can't believe you just called me a dirt road," Eric says. Jamie laughs and rolls onto his side, tugging Eric up onto the bed.

"Shut up and cuddle me," Jamie says. "I'm in need of the cuddle hormone to make me feel better so I can blow you later."

Eric can't really protest that, so he just sighs and shakes his head and settles onto the bed, letting Jamie settle into his arms. As they relax, Eric runs a hand up and down Jamie's spine—like the spine of a book, he thinks. Lots of creases and cracks in him; he's been read a few times. You can see where people lingered. But Eric wants to look in the places that others skimmed, find the hidden beauty in him, not just the cover.

God, he's a sap sometimes.

"Want to order a pizza?" Eric asks.

"Mmkay."

Eric slides away and hops out of bed to go find his phone.

"I am sorry, by the way," Jamie says suddenly, a little sleepily.

"For what?"

"For being a thief," he explains with a wink. Eric wonders briefly if Jamie can possible read minds, but then Jamie shrugs and rolls gingerly onto his back and says, "I'll have you know that I know a great sock dealer, though."

"What?"

"A sock dealer," Jamie says. "Because I'm a sock burglar, remember? And you just punished me for stealing. I stole your socks. So you need more."

Eric laughs, and turns away to find his phone, hoping that Jamie's own laughter distracted him from seeing anything on Eric's face. Like Eric's loss of control in that second when he realized they thought Jamie had stolen different things.

An egg that contains his heart. Eric feels like an idiot sometimes. Jamie had been joking the whole time, and Eric can't expect any differently from him. Eric's the one who basically asked to keep it as casual as possible. He brought this on himself. So he'll just have to live with the damage and wait to see if it heals.

Crack.

FLOAT

FLOAT

The next item on their list (now a special list on his phone, accessible to him at any time) is one that Eric plans meticulously, with Jamie's input almost constantly arriving via text message.

> Jamie: *Are you sure we can't do it with just my friends?*
> Jamie: *What kind of underwear should I wear?*
> Jamie: *I think I'm going to wear tights under my jeans.*
> Jamie: *We're going to a restaurant with forks. I am not eating finger foods.*
> Jamie: *Do you have a vibrator picked out? I have suggestions*

Eric mostly just smiles at the texts and assures Jamie that he's got everything under control. That's not what Jamie wants to hear, of course, in his excited and trepidatious state, but it's what Eric's going to give him. That's how this particular game works. Jamie is not the least bit in control. And it's not so much that Jamie abandoning control this time—Eric is *stealing* it from him.

It's neither socks nor heart, but it'll do.

The dinner is planned a week ahead, two weeks after the spanking scene that got so intense. Eric finalizes the plans after an evening together in bed, totally vanilla. They're collapsed on the bed, sweaty, catching their breath, and Jamie struggles to remove the condom without making a mess, when Eric brings it up.

"So it's all set for next weekend," he says casually, dragging a tissue over his stomach to remove the come he'd splattered all over himself.

"I've got the vibrator, and reservations at a cool little place near the Park. Turkish food."

"You know I'm not Turkish, right?" Jamie says suspiciously.

"Yes," Eric laughs. "I'm pretty sure you mentioned your dad being Saudi at some point, and I do have a basic grasp of geography. But I happen to like the food there. It's one of my favorite places, and I want to see you writhing and desperate while I suck some meat off a kebob."

"Oh really?" Jamie asks, but it doesn't have any fire. He just looks kind of nervous.

"Mmm," Eric hums. "So. Us, Andy and Leta, your girlfriend from work, and Leta's friend Jeremy."

"Yeah, I think that's it," Jamie says.

"Okay. So the six of us at a tiny table in a sort of dark restaurant eating Turkish food, and you'll have a remote vibrator up your ass, which I will be controlling discreetly beneath the table. And I'll have a stopwatch, and I will time how long it takes for you to come, and then we come back here to my place because it's closer, and you do whatever you want to me for the same period of time. Does that all sound correct?"

"Am I allowed to wear my double layers?"

"Wear whatever you want," Eric says with a shrug. "I don't want to make you walk around with a wet spot or anything. Just want to see your face, see you try to hold off and hide it."

"That's a little sadistic," Jamie comments, curling into Eric's side and resting his head on Eric's shoulder.

"You'd think you'd figure that out when I'm in the middle of bruising you, but no—"

"That's not sadism," Jamie says. "You're not taking pleasure in my pain. You're taking pleasure in my pleasure, which just happens to be because of my pain."

Eric laughs loudly. "Because there's *such* a huge difference."

"There *is* a difference," Jamie protests, petulant. "Stop being difficult when I'm trying to make things easy for you."

"See?" Eric says slyly. "Sadist." And then he winces, yowling in pain, pulling away from Jamie's fingers, which are trying to pinch too hard around his nipple. "Ow, knock it off!"

* * *

That Friday comes quickly, and finds them walking to the restaurant from the subway station a few blocks away. They're holding hands, swinging between them gently, the metronome that keeps their step in time, keeps them in pace. It's almost picture perfect, but Jamie wears a faint grimace.

"Uncomfortable?" Eric asks.

"Well, yeah," Jamie says, his voice low. "I have a plug up my ass. And it's a lot bigger than I expected. I keep thinking people will know—"

"They won't," Eric assures. "You've got your tights on under those jeans, and you can't see anything under them. So no one will know. Not unless you *let* them know, which you are by making that face and waddling."

"I am not *waddling*," Jamie protests, but Eric just laughs and guides him to the entrance to the restaurant.

Owing to the time it took to prepare Jamie and get the vibrating plug in, they're a few minutes late, and their friends already have a table near the back right corner of the crowded, dark little restaurant, just past the door to the kitchen. They're talking quietly, but when Leta looks up and spies them, she throws her hands up and cries out happily.

"Yay! Eric and Jamie!"

They take the two free seats across from each other on the outside edge of the table, for which Eric is grateful—if things go as planned, they'll both be going to the bathroom a few times, and it'd be awkward if Jamie got up with a boner and a vibrating ass and tried to slide past someone. They would notice, which is not the point. The risk is the point, certainly; the fear of it is something that can release tension in Jamie just as much as the pain play can. Experiences that are normally negative can elicit positive responses—it's why people go on roller coasters and sky dive and work out until they feel the "burn." It makes people feel as if they've accomplished something special, as if they're stronger than what they've faced. It's not just about the adrenaline and the endorphins. It's about facing down something difficult and coming out on top. And in Eric's experience, both sub and Dom can get that out of a scene, even something casual and fun like this.

"And what took *you* so long?" Andy smirks, leaning her chin on her hand.

"Jamie couldn't decide what to wear," Eric says. He glances at the two other people at the other end of the table, opposite each other—Jeremy, a friend of Leta's, and Jamie's work friend Amanda, who waves to Jamie enthusiastically from Leta's other side as he sits very carefully down just across from Eric.

"You mean you couldn't decide what to *make* Jamie wear," Andy says, and Eric swiftly kicks her beneath the table. Amanda doesn't know the details of the unique relationship he and Eric have.

"I am not that much of a control freak; shut up," Eric protests—a little nervously, if truth be told. As a Dom, he can stand up to anyone and anything—from putting up with Ian at the party where he found Jamie, to easing Jamie through their first true meeting at the coffee shop, to paddling Jamie into a bruised oblivion. But he's hiding that side of himself, now, and while he still has to be a Dom for Jamie, with the vibrating plug sitting dormant in his ass as he looks over the menu, he also has to be his usual, slightly nerdy self.

"Your every bit of *existence* is about control," Andy says, almost skeptically. But she smiles, and Eric shakes his head and rolls his eyes.

"Did we do introductions?" he asks. "If I'm going to be a control freak, I might as well do it right."

Andy takes over. "I'm Andy Baker, that's Leta Baros, beyond her is Jeremy McMillan, this lady is Amanda something-or-other, friend of Jamie Kader over there, and you're Eric Yates. Can we order now?"

"What do you do, Eric?" Amanda asks, looking askance at Andy for a moment before turning her attention to him. "I got a lot out of Jamie, but not that."

Eric smiles at Jamie, who sheepishly refuses to make eye contact. "I'm a copy editor for a magazine I'm sure you've never even heard of. One day I'll bring all the greatest journalists to tears, but for now I scribble red marks in tabloid articles and celebrity gossip and the barest attempt at news."

"Control freak," Andy says triumphantly, waving a hand at him.

Eric looks over at Jamie, who is smiling up at him, and winks. Jamie sticks his tongue out playfully and then looks back down at the menu. "I don't know what to order. Eric, control freak me."

"Well, I'm getting the lamb shish kebabs," Eric says. "Do you want juice dripping all over you, or would you prefer something neater?"

Jamie's jaw tightens and works as he fights against either smiling or frowning. "Maybe something neater. I tend to make a big mess."

Eric almost snorts, but he holds it back. "I'd suggest the goat cheese salad or the kofta—like... Turkish meatballs. Really good, not as greasy as they make the kebabs here. You should escape unscathed."

"I should hope so," Jamie says blithely, smirking. At the sight of it, Eric feels the heat rising in his gut—it's time to wipe that smirk off his face.

"I need to use the bathroom," he says. He slides up out of his seat and smiles at Jamie. "Order for me, babe?"

The moment he slips into the bathroom, he pulls out the remote and counts down from five. When he reaches one, he turns it on to the lowest setting and starts the time on the stopwatch on his phone. Then he goes ahead and uses the bathroom—might as well. When he finishes up and heads back out, Jamie is sort of slumped in his seat, and Eric notices his ass tilted just enough to get the pressure off of the base of the plug.

"What'd I miss?" Eric asks, and Leta immediately starts filling him in on their conversation. But he's only partially interested—Jamie is smiling in a tight sort of way across from him, and when Eric reaches into his pocket and hits the button to increase the vibrations, he covers his mouth, looking as though he's considering something deeply, but Eric can see the beginnings of sweat on his brow. He leaves the vibrations at that level and joins the conversation.

When the food arrives, Eric checks his watch briefly—Jamie has lasted about twenty minutes so far. It's time to challenge him. As the waiter sets his plate down in front of him, Eric slips his hand into his pocket and turns up the vibrations once more, now on level three of five.

There's an instant reaction. Jamie jumps in his seat as though startled, and bites his lip. Eric looks at him, feigning ignorance and innocence as best he can. "What happened?"

"Just—um. Lost my depth perception for a second. Thought that plate was going to spill on me. Nothing major."

Amanda gives Jamie a little sympathetic pout, but everyone else at the table glances at Eric. He schools his face into neutrality and focuses on his food, feeling the eyes on him. When he looks up, Leta is ducking her head and shaking with laughter. Andy and Jeremy are exchanging looks, and Amanda just looks between them, confused.

"What's so funny—"

"Leta keeps telling this awful joke about depth perception that *no one* finds funny but her—"

"Hey, I thought it was funny," Jamie protests. He only sounds a little bit strained, though Eric can see the tightness in his shoulders and back. Eric knows the vibrations have to be shaking up his spine, hammering right near his prostate, sending sparks of pleasure through his groin and making him feel as if he's being stabbed with jolts of it. And he's sensitive all over down there—Eric's spent enough time there with his mouth to know that the vibrations must be doing insane things to the nerves, making him wish he had decent stimulation instead of the maddening, monotone buzz that's only getting harder rather than providing any friction or pressure where he needs it.

Eric turns the vibrations up again. Jamie gulps and shifts in his seat, closing his eyes and taking a deep breath before making an attempt to eat his food. Eric can see that he's having trouble paying attention, focusing on his breathing and the little bites of salad that he takes. Eric almost feels like laughing himself—he knows Jamie's feeling really good right now, but *really* trying not to show it. But then, it's pretty hot, too—he's got Jamie in the palm of his hand. If he wants Jamie to come, he can make that happen. He can turn the vibrations up all the way and be done with it, can casually put his feet in Jamie's lap and just *press*, can "accidentally" spill something on himself that needs help cleaning up and then tug Jamie to the bathroom for a quickie.

He can do all kinds of things, all of them so sexy and thrilling, and they're all *cheating* too. He only said he'd be turning up the vibrations, and he's not supposed to do it all at once—he has to give Jamie some kind of chance to make decent time. He's at half an hour now, and it's only increasing. But Eric is going lay himself out tonight, later, and let Jamie have his way with him, for however long Jamie lasts right now. Eric might take that little thrill in pushing Jamie's limits, but he wants Jamie to push him back. He wants to see what Jamie does when he gets the control for a while. Eric is definitely a Dom, but he doesn't live it like a lifestyle—it's a wonderful addition to how he lives. Sometimes, he's still just Eric, still just a guy, and he wants Jamie to take him apart.

He waits another five minutes, watching Jamie settle into this level, watching him gradually go from squirming with pleasure to stillness, and only when he starts to squirm uncomfortably does Eric flick up the vibrations to the final level.

Jamie swallows his bite of food hard and sits back, tense all over. Eric looks closely—he can see Jamie's stomach spasming under his shirt, rocking his torso just a little bit, and his hips beneath the table. He closes his eyes and *breathes*, and while all the people at their table who are in the scene have been casually ignoring any of Jamie's strange behavior, Amanda is not in the know, and the moment she notices, she speaks up.

"Oh my god, Jamie, are you okay?" she asks.

"I'm fine," Jamie says immediately, his voice a little hoarse. "I just feel a little sick, I think."

"Oh no, was it the food?"

"Not this food," Jamie replies, wiping his brow. "Maybe lunch. You know... just hitting me. I'm—um—"

He looks over at Eric and catches his eye. Part of the fantasy was coming right at the table, but it's possible he might want to safeword and doesn't know how. Eric thinks fast.

"You had peppers on that sandwich, right?" he asks. "I know the red peppers in your fridge were kind of old. Did you have the red, or green?"

He emphasizes the colors just a little bit, and Jamie gets it; he smiles and shakes his head.

"Green," he says, looking at Eric as though he just hung the moon in that moment, even through his sweat and shaking, which is currently Eric's fault. "Not a speck of red."

Amanda is going to ask more questions, though. So Eric shifts his chair further in, reaches over the table and takes Jamie's hand as obviously as he can while one foot lifts up, brushing Jamie's leg up to his crotch beneath the table, and hopefully still beneath the tablecloth.

"Do you want to go home?" Eric asks, and he squeezes Jamie's hand just as he presses down on Jamie's cock, ridiculously hard in his pants. Jamie's body shudders, and he breathes out in a single, long huff, his hips twitching beneath Eric's foot. He hastily removes it, trying not to shift too much in his seat, and then Jamie coughs quickly and opens his eyes.

"Um, I'm not feeling that bad," Jamie says. "Just... kind of had a hot flash or something. Do you want to at least box up our food first?"

"That's up to you, Jamie," Eric says, stroking Jamie's knuckles with his thumb. Jamie nods, smiling at Eric and waving over a waiter. And he's still not getting up from the table—the timer is still going. Jamie still wants to play.

Eric reaches into his pocket and turns the vibrations down to the very lowest level again, giving Jamie just enough time to relax into it before he shoots it back up to full blast. He does it three times in a row, watching Jamie's eyes widen and his face become increasingly panicked before he jumps up from his seat.

"I'll be right back. Eric, would you grab our food?"

"Sure," Eric says, and then Jamie's off to the bathroom across the restaurant. Eric turns back to the others, tries not to react to any of the looks on their faces—concern from Amanda, varying levels of amusement from the others—while he slips his hand into his pocket.

And then his phone vibrates in his other pocket.

Jamie: OMG dont turn it off
Eric: did you come?
Jamie: yes. dont turn it off.

Eric lowers it down to the second level, just in case, and then pulls out his wallet.

"Sorry guys, Jamie's doing really badly in there, I'm gonna just take our food and get him right out," he says. He pulls out a few bills and slips them to Andy before taking the bag of boxed up food from the returning waiter and heading over to the bathroom and knocking.

"Jamie?"

The door opens, and then he's pulled in, the door shut behind them. Then Jamie is pressing into Eric, kissing him hard and filthy and grinding them together, holding Eric by the ass, and—

"Oh my god, are you still hard?" Eric asks, breathless, as Jamie attacks his neck, kissing and sucking at the pulse point under his jaw.

"Yes," Jamie gasps, muffled by Eric's skin. "Never—never happened before, never come and stayed hard, Eric—"

He keeps grinding into Eric, who has fully joined him in having an aching erection. Eric holds him close and grinds back, reaching up to tilt Jamie's face and pull him into another kiss, all teeth and lips and moans.

"God, we have to get home," Eric moans. "Want—want you—"

"Just—just keep the vibrator on low," Jamie says. "And—god, can we get a cab? Want you to touch me, I feel like—I feel like I could come again, I don't know—"

"Jesus, that's hot," Eric says. "Okay. Come on, let's go."

He pulls open the bathroom door and tugs Jamie out, not even bothering to glance at their friends or pretend they aren't running out to go fuck. Outside, he hails a cab, failing twice before one pulls over and lets them in. He rambles his address quickly and then turns to Jamie as soon as the cab starts moving, pressing his forehead up against Jamie's temple and putting his hand in Jamie's lap.

"God, you're so hot," Eric whispers, pressing down over Jamie's cock and brushing his lips over Jamie's ear. Jamie likes dirty talk, and normally Eric feels silly after a certain amount of it, but it just flows out of him now. "Just want to keep coming, don't you? Keep coming all over the inside of your pants, keep coming til it soaks over my hand. Want that plug to keep fucking into you, you can't even stop moving your hips. God, look at you." He starts jacking the shape of Jamie's cock through his pants, drawing a moan from him—*he is going to tip the driver so much*— "Think you could come again before we got back? If you do, I'll forget the stopwatch—you can do whatever you want to me for however long you want. Do anything you want, anything—but god I want to fuck you so bad—"

"Not yet," Jamie gasps. "Just—just keep doing that, just like that, and just—turn up the vibrations, okay? All the way, just fast, and keep touching me, *fuck*—"

Eric fumbles to keep stroking Jamie with his right hand while his left sneaks into his right pocket. It's awkward and uncomfortable but he finally gets the remote out and hammers the button to full vibrations, and then he drops the remote between their hips and thanks every god in the sky for shitty New York traffic and living far enough away to make this a long enough trip.

Jamie bucks into his hand, head thrown back, shamelessly open in his pleasure, and Eric squeezes tight and that's it—Jamie's body seizes up and his stomach tightens and twitches him forward, hunching over Eric's hand, still pumping him as he climaxes again, breathy, staccato little moans bursting out of him until he slumps, whining uncomfortably and reaching for the remote. Eric reaches it first and turns it off, and Jamie sits slumped and panting.

"Fifty-four minutes," Eric announces, looking at his watch. "Do you want the twenty-six seconds, or what?"

"Nuh uh," Jamie says. "You promised. No timer. Came again."

"That's right, I did." Eric grins at Jamie. "So... what do you plan on doing with me? I believe I heard a "Not yet." Does that mean—"

"Um—"

The cab pulls to a stop, and Eric glances out. They're at his apartment building. He pulls out his wallet and hands the cab driver the fee plus the biggest tip he can reasonably afford, calling out a quick "sorry!" as he pulls Jamie from the cab and lets them into the building.

In his apartment, Jamie turns to him with a weird look.

"Eric, I'd love for you to fuck me," Jamie says. "But... that's one of my limits. I don't want to... to bottom until I'm in a committed relationship, you know? It's just so intense for me. And... you're, like... big." He blushes as he says it. "It'd be too much for me, like physically *and* emotionally. I just... when I do it, my head reacts and I get all emotional and clingy, and we're not—doing that." He runs his hand through his hair and sighs. "So awkward. Sorry. I just. Not yet. Not unless we're gonna really do this."

Oh.

"That's totally fair," Eric says. "And I'm not gonna pressure you, I just—I guess I misunderstood. Or forgot, or something." He grabs Jamie's hands and pulls them to his mouth, then kisses them. "Forget I said anything."

"It's not that I don't want to—"

"Hey, I get it," Eric interrupts. "You don't have to be sorry for having limits, Jamie. That's a huge part of this. I'll stick to your limits. No fucking you until we're officially doing this."

It disappoints him, but Eric feels bad that he's made this into a situation where Jamie can't totally trust him. He could go forever without fucking Jamie; as far as Eric is concerned, that's just a perk, and he's fond of bottoming anyway. But Jamie's trusting him with so much more—he's trusting him to give him pain as well as pleasure, to take care of him, to teach him. And if that's such an intense experience for him, if that requires so much trust, what does that mean for the rest of their play? Could Jamie's fantasies be fulfilled better? Could they be more meaningful to him?

Eric doesn't want to treat Jamie as if he doesn't matter.

"Look," Eric says, pulling Jamie into a hug. "I'm really sorry if—if this was a bad plan. To... to wait. I don't want you to throw away these fantasies with someone you don't trust."

"I do trust you," Jamie says. "I just—let's just call it a precaution. I trust you with everything, but I don't trust my own heart yet."

There's the egg again. Jamie won't hand over the egg around his heart—he's afraid Eric will shatter it. Or maybe it's just really fragile and Eric hasn't learned to be delicate enough to handle it yet.

Yet. Jamie had said not *yet*. He doesn't trust his own heart *yet*. Eric had been firm that this wasn't a death sentence on their relationship—just a testing period. But he's been starting to treat it like that—like a death sentence—anyway. And maybe Jamie's thinking of it like that sometimes, too, but he's saying *yet*. Yet doesn't mean there's an end—yet means there's a future.

Eric can live with that.

"Just promise me, if you're uncomfortable, or if this turns into something that hurts you, you'll tell me," he asks. "I really care about you. I don't want to hurt you in any way."

Jamie looks up at him and sighs. His mouth opens as though he wants to say something, but he doesn't—he just sighs again and then surges in for a kiss.

"Let's go to the bedroom," he suggests, pulling away from Eric. "I believe I've got a whole night to spend on whatever I want."

"You do," Eric agrees breathlessly. Jamie's pulling him along insistently, almost commandingly. Eric's not about to become a sub here—he's never been able to calm down in that position—but he'll let himself be passive, let Jamie take exactly what he wants. Anything, tonight.

There are no words when Jamie gets Eric into the bedroom. He just strips Eric, silently divesting him of all his clothes before shoving him onto the bed, letting him bounce into position on the mattress—on his back, legs hanging off the side. Then he strips himself, pausing to hastily wipe his soft cock and the inside of his thighs and balls with his balled up underwear. He bends and reaches back to remove the plug, dropping it carelessly onto the pile of his own clothes. Finally, he steps up before Eric, their knees brushing, and fidgets for a minute, looking Eric over.

"Okay," Jamie says, as though answering an unspoken query. "Turn over."

Eric does as he's asked—*told*—and shifts himself to lie the right way along the bed, grabbing a pillow to hug beneath his head. Jamie climbs up over him, slotting his knees between Eric's, using them to push Eric's legs further out, further than he really needs to lay himself over Jamie, his lips brushing the back of Eric's neck. His cock rests limp along Eric's balls, a weirdly intimate position when it is becoming clear to Eric that this has nothing to do with sex.

"This—this has been amazing," Jamie says quietly. His hands roam over Eric's sides, warm and dry, leaving goosebumps in their wake. "You're amazing. I never—I never thought I could do this sort of thing. I never thought I'd learn what I wanted, or get it. But you've been teaching me and showing me, and... and I'm really grateful for that."

It sounds like a goodbye. Is this a goodbye? Eric's chest tightens and his eyes burn at the thought—Jamie—Jamie can't be leaving—

"But I have to remember that you're human," Jamie continues. "I guess I forget that, sometimes. You're... you're just a person, no matter how confident a Dom you are. You're still Eric; you still read weird books and wear underwear that totally doesn't match anything else you wear and you still forget your contacts and your glasses and walk around squinting sometimes. And... and you can't read my mind. You can't read my heart, either. You can try and you're pretty fucking good at guessing what my body wants most of the time. But you're kind of in your own little world when it comes to everything else, just like I am."

Eric's trapped in this speech, in Jamie's soft voice, low over the skin of his back, almost unheard beyond the susurration of his palms skimming over Eric's sides, over the gentle burr of his chest hair on Eric's smooth back. Eric holds his breath, breathes as quietly as he can—he can't ask Jamie to repeat any of this. It wouldn't be the same if he had to say it again. It would be less honest, a recital. Eric can't interrupt, not even by breathing.

"And isn't that what this whole thing is about?" Jamie asks, laying his cheek against Eric's spine. "Everyone says so. You have to communicate. And I forgot that we have to do that, because it felt like you just knew how everything was supposed to go. But you don't. And... and I guess I'm realizing that." He falls silent, and for a long moment, Eric wonders if he's falling asleep. But then, Jamie's cheek turns again, and lips drag down his back, moving against his skin and half-muffling the words. "So I'm going to tell you what fantasy I want to do next, and then... we should discuss all of them after this. And keep talking about the whys and wherefores. Because... I think you forgot that I'm still learning. I still don't quite understand what my body and my head are doing to me when we do this, and... and you were right."

"About what?" Eric asks, when Jamie doesn't continue.

Jamie slides back up, and his voice is right in Eric's ear. "You were right about us waiting. Because I can't tell if what I'm feeling now is just... me being a sub, or something else. I don't know if my heart is telling me things because it feels them or because I'm basically drugged whenever you fucking *look* at me like you do when you get all... all Dommy."

Eric can't help but laugh. Now that he knows Jamie isn't planning this as a goodbye, he feels weirdly light and nervous—because they're over a chasm on a tightrope, here. The least bit of miscommunication or dishonesty could tip them off balance, and they're only about halfway across. Eric's only just realizing that there's no net to catch them, not anymore.

What the hell kind of name can he put to them, though? Is it just the intensity of what they're doing, the biochemistry? That's why he wanted to keep this inside a set of boundaries, to avoid this confusion and to avoid pain if they didn't work out together. But they're both swirling in this, and apparently neither of them can tell if it's real. Between that and the tingles and excitement of a new relationship, however casual, it's hard to tell if this might be a real chance for love.

But Eric's becoming more and more certain. And, evidently, Jamie is becoming less certain. They're about to meet in the middle, but if they just cruise on by, Eric will lose Jamie. Jamie will drift farther and farther away, because of the fears that Eric was too scared to assuage.

And he's still scared. Especially now, nakedness against nakedness, with Jamie kissing his neck, having confessed his confusion and his doubt. It's tempting to just blurt out what he feels, to lay it all on the line. But that's not who Eric is, and he doesn't want to get swept up in a vulnerable moment.

He'll sleep on it. He'll think and process. He has to. Impulsiveness is a bad option for Eric, because he is so often terrible at reading people's deeper emotions. He has to be certain of himself and of Jamie before he does or says anything that could disrupt this *something* that he has with Jamie, something he cherishes and wants to keep.

"We can—*oh*." Jamie bites down on Eric's ear, and *that's not helping.* "Just—we can talk about it. We can... we can sort through things. Or you can. I'd—I'd like to help."

"That's the plan," Jamie murmurs, rocking his hips against Eric's ass. "And that's why I'm picking our next fantasy. Because I know what I want you to teach me about next."

"And what's that?" Eric asks, trembling. His body is revving up again, his cock hard beneath him, his skin feeling needy for contact. He wants Jamie so badly, just wants and wants and *wants.*

"I want you to tie me up," Jamie says. "But I didn't—I didn't get to elaborate on that fantasy when I told you. Because you were being a tease, remember?"

Oh, god, he remembers. Such a perfect night. "Yes."

"Well. I want you to tie me up. All the way. Not just my arms and legs, but... all of me. My eyes. My ears. I want—I want everything taken away from me. I—I want to learn more about subspace."

Eric shifts under Jamie, finally managing to wriggle enough room to be able to turn over after an awkward moment when their legs tangle. But finally he settles, smiling at Jamie's breathy little giggles, looking up at Jamie lying over him. He reaches up and flicks a wave of hair off Jamie's forehead.

"We can do that," Eric promises.

Jamie grins. "Thank you."

"You don't need to thank me," Eric says, smirking. "I mean... that's what I'm here for, right?"

"You're here because I like you," Jamie says, kissing Eric's nose. "But I'm not thanking you for that right now. I'm thanking you for saying 'we.' *We* can do that. You're not doing it *to* me."

"No."

"I know how some of my fantasies come off, and the things I like. Sometimes, it seems like I want to be really hurt, you know? One way or another. But I don't, not *really*. And you don't hurt me. No more than I actually want, anyway, and that's just like... you explained why that was normal."

Eric kisses Jamie. "I don't think any of this is normal, Jamie. But it's not wrong."

"Stop doing the perfect thing," Jamie laughs suddenly. "I just gave a whole speech about how you're not perfect."

"I can't help it," Eric protests—the taut string of the moment has gone lax again, and what he really can't help is the grin on his face. "It just *happens*—ah!"

Jamie's got his wrists in a tight grip, and his body weight bears down on Eric, hard. Suddenly, their faces are too close, and Jamie's breath is too warm on Eric's lips.

"I think we've talked enough," Jamie says darkly. "I have a prize to claim."

Eric doesn't reply. Jamie drops kisses down his throat, chest, down his stomach to his cock, hardening again under the attention. Nuzzling along Eric's groin, Jamie smiles and peeks up at Eric as his hands slide under Eric's thighs. He lifts them, spreads them and disappears down, and Eric can only stay connected through the touch of those hands and the press of his tongue as he teases Eric open.

He stays there a long, long time. Licking, stroking, prodding, sucking, *god* he just keeps going, keeps changing it up, never sticking to one move for long. He wrecks Eric apart, into pieces, laid out and quivering and sweating and begging. And he doesn't bother to listen to Eric when he demands to be fucked *right that second*—instead, he pulls out the lube and fingers him patiently, while Eric's patience dies a withered, pleasure-clenched death.

But he doesn't speak. Jamie doesn't say a word, and none of Eric's words seem to matter, so he stops saying them. Jamie goes at his own pace, finally, *finally* rising up and sinking, condom-clad and lube-soaked, down into Eric. Inch by careful inch he slides, pulling back with every bit of progress, drawing it out. Eric writhes and fights against the urge to flail completely out of his own skin.

And as he finally sheathes himself completely, Jamie lifts Eric's legs again, tests every boundary of his body, twists them up around his shoulders, contorting him. And Eric takes it, relaxing and allowing his body to be manipulated, allowing Jamie to press him, limp, into the position he wants. And then—and then Jamie fucks him, gloriously, *splendidly*, perfectly gives Eric exactly what he wants. He lets Eric's body bear him up and pistons his hips, *slap slap slap slap slap*, against Eric's ass.

And then Jamie speaks.

"Want you to tease me when you tie me up," he says, breathless. "Want you to keep my cock out, touch me, keep me on the edge. Want it to be the only thing I feel. Feel your hand around me, over and over, slick and—and tight—*fuck* just like your ass—"

Eric whines, high and constant, shaking apart with Jamie's weight holding him together. The angle is perfect, and Jamie's so hard in him, dragging in and out smooth and steady even with Eric clenching around him, trying to keep him, pull him in *harder* and *faster*. *Fuck* he needs more, needs—needs—

"Touch yourself," Jamie says. "Show me what you'll do when I can't stop you."

Eric slithers his hands down, squeezing between them until he can grasp himself. And that's it. That's all he needs. He holds his hand steady and lets Jamie have him, lets him fuck Eric hard enough that he doesn't have to move his hand at all, his hips slam back and he fucks right into his own fist, and he comes hard, body tightening, legs stretching up, free hand scrabbling for purchase on Jamie's back.

"Oh, yeah," Jamie pants, head dropping, mouth pressing against Eric's throat. "Oh, fuck yeah—"

He bites down, right at the flesh above Eric's collarbone, and sucks, moaning hard as he presses in hard, grinding through his orgasm. And Eric giggles, high on the good sex, flinching.

"Ow," he complains, and Jamie puffs out a breathy laugh.

"Sorry." He lets Eric's legs relax, reaching down to slide free of Eric's body with as little mess as possible. "Ugh. Did I hurt you?" Eric shakes his head, and Jamie grins. He yawns and shifts to the side, curling up against Eric, head dropping to his shoulder. "Good," he says. "Never want to hurt you."

Eric almost says it. He almost says, *I'd never hurt you either.* But the fact is, he just doesn't know. Is he hurting Jamie? He could ask, but Jamie's already breathing slow and even, his body lax in sleep. It's been an exhausting night for him, to be sure—but he sleeps with a little smile on his face.

That's all Eric needs to see. So he doesn't reply, because there's no need for any words at all.

* * *

Only later, when the lights are off and Jamie is long since sound asleep beside him, Eric realizes that, despite how thoroughly Jamie claimed him, despite the bite marks on his skin and the sweat on the tangled bed sheets and the way Jamie so thoroughly took him apart with every tool at his disposal, Eric still has that deep feeling of *want* for Jamie.

It's not satisfied and it's not going away.

SELL THE PLAY

SELL THE PLAY

"I am so tired of waiting for this."

"I know, Jamie, but I'm under some pressure here," Eric protests, hitching the phone back up to match with his ear instead of sliding down his shoulder again as he puts away his groceries. "Sarah's on maternity leave for another two weeks, so I'm covering her job *and* my job, and—"

"I know," Jamie interrupts soothingly. "It's okay. I'm sorry for bitching. You're facing the hallmarks of a shitty patriarchy and a stingy parent company, and here I am complaining about sex. Plus this is partially my fault; I just *had* to take a class—"

"Well, sort of," Eric says. "You didn't *have* to take a culinary course, but you wanted to learn something. And I mean, you have been waiting for something I *promised* you, and you've been looking forward to it, and I don't even know, do you think you need it? I could—"

"Eric, finish up the two weeks until Sarah gets back. We can tie me up then. In the meantime..."

"More quickies?" Eric suggests, laughing. They've barely seen each other for a month, only meeting on weekends and sneaking quick time together while Eric puts in extra time at the office and Jamie takes his new six-week culinary intro course. He'd been bored and had decided to test his horizons and try to find a career again, but all it's really done is double his grocery bill and make his apartment smell like garlic.

"Well... I was thinking maybe taking our time for once..."

"That would be great, but you're about to be late for class if you don't start getting ready, and after my day I'm calling it an early night. By the time you get here or I get there—"

Knockknockknock.

Eric whirls around and faces his door, eyes narrowing. "If that is you right now—"

"Did I play hooky for nothing, or are you going to get your pretty upside-down ass over to unlock this?" Eric can now hear Jamie's voice both on the phone and on the other side of the door.

But he has the opportunity to tease, and he *loves* teasing Jamie. "Are you looking through my peephole? That's really creepy, babe."

"I don't know, I kind of like you like this," Jamie giggles. "Maybe if you open up the door I'll make sure you're in that same position when I go down on you."

Eric hangs up the phone and rushes over to unlock the door. As soon as it's open, Jamie leaps through and pulls Eric into a crushing hug.

"Yay, I missed you," Jamie says. "Now let's make sure your perishables are put away because we aren't coming back out here for anything."

* * *

It still takes almost all of the remaining two weeks for them to get back to each other on a regular basis. Eric finally returns to his own work schedule, and Jamie finishes the cooking class with some pretty useful skills, though with no desire to enter the culinary field.

"I don't think I could take it," he comments one night. They haven't fucked—Jamie came over after his last class and just crawled into bed with Eric, cuddling up and talking. It's late into the night, and they're in boxers and T-shirts, and it's the first time they've had an opportunity for sex that they haven't taken, not even making out. They'd kissed hello when Jamie woke Eric from his light doze, and that was it. They've spent the past three hours just... talking.

"Cooking you mean?" Eric's been wondering and asking whether Jamie had any real interest in cooking, but Jamie's avoided the question until now.

"Yeah. It's so high stress. Like everything is in such a rush, and I can't *not* take my time. I get nervous about getting things right."

"I know you do," Eric says. Jamie's pretty neurotic, actually. His coffee mugs all face in the same direction in his kitchen, which Eric's noticed before, but he also organizes his closet more than anyone Eric's met who wasn't in fashion. And he has to rip condom foils from the very center—little things like that. He manages to exist in everyday chaos, but the constant yelling and disorder of a kitchen with flames flying around and knives and everything out of order—Eric can't imagine Jamie in that space. "So... no Jamie the chef."

"Not professionally. I did like cooking, though."

"You should cook for me," Eric jokes. "I'll hire you. You can cook all my meals."

Jamie pokes Eric in the side. "You want to hire me to be your househusband."

Eric laughs. "If it's a business arrangement, do I still need to buy a ring?"

Jamie goes quiet, and Eric feels himself freezing. He's been feeling himself settle into this relationship more and more as time goes on, especially after they were apart so much over the past six weeks; every doubt he had about Jamie just being in this for the D/s has flown out the window. They've still snuck in dates, and while they've wanted to get back to their scenes and their play, it hasn't been *missing*. It wasn't as though they couldn't exist without it. And Eric had wanted Jamie around so much more than he got him—and he continues to want that. He's not as scared now, not with familiarity creeping up on him. But he's definitely not at the stage where he can act on any thoughts about marriage yet.

"I think it should be part of my job, actually," Jamie says, finally, and Eric breathes again when he sees the playful smirk on his face, hidden beneath days-old stubble that he knows drives Jamie crazy, but that he hasn't attended to for some reason. "You'll know I'm on shift when the ring is on. I take it off and you have to do the dishes after."

"I would see you taking it off all the time, wouldn't I?"

"I don't know; I don't think I trust you to get the dishes actually *clean*."

"I resent that."

Jamie laughs, and leans in for a kiss. "Anyway, I'll keep my job at the flower shop, it seems."

"At least you like it there," Eric says, trying for a silver lining. "Maybe you could take a class in gardening. Agriculture. Something... else, I don't know, what do people in flower shops study? Is there a class for that?"

"Horticulture, maybe?" Jamie suggests. "I don't know, I should probably ask. Maybe I can study flower arranging or something. Move up in the world."

"So you can do the same job you do now, but with paperwork attached?"

"C'est la vie."

Jamie looks so tired when he says it, even though Eric can see that he's trying to be funny. He likes his job at the flower shop, but he doesn't love it. And he doesn't have much else that he really loves. He skips from hobby to hobby and can't seem to find a place to settle. Looking at him now, all Eric sees is that he's floating. He hasn't shaved despite how much he hates having facial hair, he has bags under his eyes, his hair is kind of wild and frizzy and he looks paler than usual. He looks exhausted. And a little bit unhappy.

"Are you okay?" Eric asks. He can't just let this slide, now that he's really seeing it. And he wonders how long it's been going on—they've had so little opportunity to spend time together. Eric feels his stomach writhe with worry.

"I'm fine."

"You look like a wreck," Eric says. "Fine isn't a very good look for you."

Jamie sighs. "Had to be clever about it, huh?"

Eric reaches up and brushes Jamie's hair off his face and then cups his cheek gently. "Is it something I can help with?"

Jamie looks up and *locks* with him, stares right into Eric's eyes and doesn't waver. "I'm wondering that. Because... because I don't want to be *that guy* that like... can't function without..."

"Without submitting?" Eric guesses.

"I don't know. I guess," Jamie says. "You know I've talked to people, and made friends with Leta and some of her other lifestyle friends, and like... I just hear the stories of how reliant people are on it and I didn't want to be that."

"Jamie, you are who you are," Eric says. "And who you are is okay. Wonderful, actually. You're functioning without this, but... it's okay if you need some release. We all have different ways of doing it. Why does this have to be a bad thing?"

"Stop being reasonable," Jamie says. "I'm trying to mope."

Eric laughs and gives Jamie another kiss. "Well, you can mope for as long as you want. Until tomorrow night. Then we're going to explore subspace, remember?"

Jamie bursts out laughing. "I can mope for as long as I want, but not if it's longer than a day?"

Eric grins. He got Jamie to smile, even if he didn't mean to and was just being a dope. He'll take it. "Exactly."

* * *

They wake up in the morning and move around each other as if it's totally natural. Jamie borrows some of Eric's clothes, which fit pretty well despite their height difference, and they pass a smile and some laughter between them when Eric warns Jamie that the socks are his *temporarily*, and they shower and drink coffee and laze around just watching TV and eating ice cream and pizza. Eric wears his glasses instead of his contacts; Jamie doesn't style his hair. They have their feet up on the coffee table, they're slouched down and kind of half-flopped over each other and it's great. They get through most of a season of *Game of Thrones* by the time they are settling down for the evening.

"Never thought I'd like this show," Jamie says. "But I do."

"Told you," Eric says, turning off the TV. "So... are you ready?"

One of the things they did over their six-week hiatus from BDSM was thoroughly establish what would happen during this particular scene. It's planned to its final detail—the first time they have left absolutely no room for divergence.

"Yeah," Jamie says. "Just let me pee first, okay?"

Eric laughs, and gets up off the couch. "Probably a good idea. I'll go get the stuff and bring it right out here."

A few minutes later, they're both back, several things now on the table—leather belts with metal rings riveted intermittently along their lengths, a little box with condoms and lube and a tiny little vibrator sitting on a folded up towel. There's also a fun little sleep mask Eric had made in college—he'd taken a noise-canceling sleep headphones and replaced all the fluff with soft-lined leather that widened into a mask. He has a playlist of endless soothing white noise on his iPod ready to plug into the headphone mask as soon as it is on. There is a huge, soft fleece blanket on the couch. When Jamie sees it all, he takes a deep breath and licks his lips.

"Can we do it now?"

"Of course," Eric says. "Come over here."

Jamie almost bounces over, and Eric laughs, grinning fondly at the little smile on Jamie's face. He can't resist it—he kisses Jamie gently, once, and then he pulls back and gets to work taking off Jamie's clothes.

"I will be binding you up head to toe," Eric explains, going over the plan one more time. "You will always have your voice, though, and I will hear anything you say. I will stay in contact with you at all times. I will ask you to give me a color every fifteen minutes by tapping twice under your chin." Eric demonstrates, and Jamie nods and says *green*. "I will leave your privates out in the open, despite the rest of you being covered and constrained, and I will tease you there for as long as I like, or until you safeword. I will not respond to pleas to stop or slow down or the word *no*. Only your safewords will work. Remind me what they are."

"Red to stop. Yellow to pause. Green to keep going."

"Very good. If at any time I feel like you need a break, I will provide one, and I will not continue until I judge you ready. If at any time I feel like we will stop, I will cease play and tap your nose twice to let you know that you need to start coming out of subspace. I will tap the top of your head twice when we are done." He demonstrates. "You will not be allowed to come during this scene. Once the scene ends, we can discuss further whether you are in need of coming or not. If you are not, you will not come at all tonight. I will decide when and how you come either way. Is all of that what we discussed and do you still agree to everything?"

"Yes," Jamie says. Eric smiles and finishes removing Jamie's clothes. When he's naked, Eric lays the big fleece blanket out over the couch so that Jamie can lie in the center, and when Jamie does so, he wraps it snugly around him. Then, he grabs a belt, and, starting at Jamie's ankles, he wraps a belt just above each joint—ankles, knees, wrists and hips together, elbows and waist together and finally one just beneath his shoulders. He leaves the blanket loosely tucked around his neck; and he shifts the blanket at his groin until his genitals are revealed and then he tucks the blanket back around them.

"How does that feel?" Eric asks.

"Good," Jamie murmurs. His eyes are closed, and he looks totally relaxed except for the slight swelling of his cock.

"Good." Eric slides the sleep mask over Jamie's head, positioning it gingerly until it's comfortably in place. "I'm going to turn on the white noise, now. It's not like *actual* white noise, because I think it's creepy." Eric laughs. "But I put on ocean noises for you. Waves breaking on a beach. Does that sound good? I've also got forest noises and a heartbeat, but the heartbeat one I downloaded might actually be one of those weird *womb sounds* clips, and it's just kinda strange. But it's up to you."

"Ocean sounds great," Jamie hums, smiling. Eric can't help but grin—Jamie can't see him anyway, so he just lets it go. He must look like an idiot, a lovesick fucking idiot.

"Okay," Eric says. "Give me your color and we'll start."

"Green."

Eric plugs in the iPod and sets the ocean noises onto repeat. Jamie sighs deeply and melts into the couch with a throw pillow under his head. His cock is soft, and his breathing evens out as he settles, shifting once or twice to find his comfort zone and then easing right into it.

Eric pulls the box of supplies over to the edge of the coffee table and then sits on the couch, pulling Jamie's feet into his lap. He keeps his hands rested and heavy over the shape of Jamie's feet, cupping them gently and then not moving them except for one grab of the remote to turn on the TV and flip its volume down while he watches a mindless sitcom.

He gets through one episode and then he turns to Jamie, who is breathing deeply and evenly, smiling faintly, as though asleep and dreaming peacefully. As Eric understands it, that's pretty much what subspace is like; it makes the person going under feel dreamy and floaty and as though they're meditating—peaceful and relaxed. At least, that's the hope, so he reaches up and taps Jamie under the chin twice, checking in.

"*Green.*"

Eric laughs. The word is like a whine, drawn out and lilted, and Eric wishes he could kiss Jamie. But part of the plan is to stay removed from anything romantic—not in so many words, but Jamie is supposed to feel suspended, in another world, with only a little point of contact with reality to keep him from panic. So no kissing—not just yet.

But there is something Eric *can* do.

He reaches over and flips open the lid of the little wooden box. He pulls out the bottle of lube and deftly flips the cap with one finger and then flips the bottle in his hand to let it dribble some onto his palm. When he has enough, he tips it quickly to rest on the table, its cap still open—he'll need it again. He spreads the lube between his palm and fingers, and then reaches for Jamie's cock.

He starts with one finger. He draws it lightly up and down the soft shaft and over the head, watching closely as it starts to lengthen and smooth out, growing under his fingertips, which join, first one and then another, tapping out rhythms and drawing wet little patterns over the heating flesh.

Jamie's breathing grows heavier, and his cock twitches whenever Eric touches the head or any other particularly sensitive spot. His hips begin to rock steadily, and he writhes in his binds, stretching the leather and testing its snugness and how firmly it is set in place. Eric did a good job—the belts don't shift, just creak a little when Eric grips the base of Jamie's cock and strokes hard and fast as suddenly as he can.

God, the *sounds* Jamie makes. He gasps and whines and tries to hold back, but all these gorgeous little noises fall from his mouth. Even after Eric pulls his hand back, leaving just the contact point on Jamie's feet, Jamie bucks and moans and offers high, wordless complaints. Eric just smiles and breathes deep—there's no way he can't be aroused, but this isn't about him. He's got to keep control, as tempting as it is to forget it all and let Jamie fuck him instead.

They can do that later. This, now, is for Jamie, and it's not about sex, however erotic it is. It's to test the limits of his mind and body, to send him into a peaceful place beyond that struggle—to allow him to let go of his worries and fears and anxieties and everyday burdens through a careful balance of denying his senses and overloading them.

So Eric waits, and gives Jamie time to float in that state of denial. Then he strikes again, teasing and stroking and tapping and tickling at Jamie's cock and balls, offering any kind of sensation he can, building it up fast and hard. And when he senses it edging too far, he backs away just as suddenly, denying again. Jamie thrusts and wriggles and twists his body around to seek satisfaction, begging shamelessly and whimpering and sobbing as he is edged higher and higher with no real relief. His cock is swollen hard, nearly purple at the head, shiny and straining. His balls are drawn up tight, and he quivers and leaks pre-come onto the blankets around him.

Twice Eric checks his comfort level by tapping under his chin. Both times, he hears a call of *green* that sounds more like a plea and that is actually followed by pleas the second time. By then, Jamie is desperate—it's been well over an hour since this whole thing started, and three quarters of that has been spent torturing him with pleasure that isn't allowed to crest and fall. He's oversensitive, sweating, tense and shaking, and Eric lets him ease down one last time before he decides it's time to take it up to the final notch they'd negotiated.

The vibrator gets a condom on it, to help with cleanup. Eric still wishes he could slide one onto Jamie, but his need is less desperate now, after the time he's spent making Jamie that much *more* desperate. He's settled into his role as Dom, as controller. His body doesn't have needs right now—he's beyond that, in a powerful place that is also so caring and ready to please and provide. It's his job to make this as wonderful for Jamie as possible, and he'll do that job so damn well that Jamie won't be able to stand it. He's living up to that responsibility, as he lubes the vibrator and then turns it on.

He keeps the vibrations on the lower end, because anything could trigger Jamie to come right now, and Jamie wanted to be denied. Eric will provide that—so he's got to be careful.

To that end, he barely touches Jamie with the vibrator. He brushes it up the underside of Jamie's cock, once, and then pulls back. He circles the head with it. He presses it into Jamie's balls. Never more than a few seconds of touch. But Jamie is so hypersensitive that this is enough to make him cry out, body curling up, seizing up in a desire to pull away and push into the sensation at the same time. Eric lets it go on for only ten minutes—it must seem like an eternity to Jamie now. There are tears on Jamie's face, leaking from behind the mask; his voice is hoarse and he's twitching more than usual on the comedown. So one more trick, and then he'll let Jamie float until one of them decides to end the scene.

Eric reaches up with his free hand, the one he'd left as a contact point and he grasps Jamie's cock firmly at the base. Then, he holds the vibrator in his palm and grasps around Jamie's cock from the upper side, pressing the vibrator into it, squeezing them both together, holding it hard right against the head of his dick. Jamie goes almost totally silent, his head thrown back, his breath caught in his throat, except for one high, thin wail that's barely audible above even the gentle buzz of the vibrator. His back arches and his hips are jerking up in sharp little movements, seeking the friction he needs to come. But Eric holds firm for the count of thirty seconds and then he shifts up, kneels over Jamie, and, never letting go of the vibrator or Jamie's cock, he finally leans over and kisses Jamie hard.

It was agreed to be the only time he could kiss Jamie. Right at the end, to help trigger subspace. The intimacy, after being denied physical contact, first through total denial and then through controlled teasing, does its work—Jamie returns the kiss frantically, and Eric lets it go on much longer than he planned to. But Jamie's mouth feels so amazing, so warm and close and intense. The moment passes, though, and as soon as Eric pulls back, Jamie collapses onto the couch, heaving for breath, but otherwise still.

Eric turns off the vibrator and tosses it onto the towel on the coffee table, wiping his own hands as well. Then he replaces his hand on Jamie's feet and breathes.

His own cock is as painfully hard as Jamie's, and now that he's not focused completely on working Jamie up, he realizes just how wrecked he really is. He's thirsty, he's breathing hard, he's aroused almost beyond endurance and he's sweaty. He is desperately in need of physical contact and wants nothing more than to curl up in Jamie's arms. But he'll have to wait until Jamie has come back from his stupor and is okay to be released before he can have that.

It doesn't take as long as Eric expected. There was over an hour of buildup, and all for about ten minutes of Jamie quiet and still beside him. Then, he stirs, and Eric immediately reaches up and taps the top of Jamie's head twice.

"Mmmm," Jamie hums. "Can you, uh. Hi. Just. Um."

Then he bursts out laughing, and Eric joins him. He knows how disorienting returning from a deep subspace can be and so he reaches up and unplugs the iPod to give Jamie back one sense.

"Hello," Eric says softly. "Are you with me?"

"Yes," Jamie says. "Can I have my eyes back too? And... and the rest of me, I'm feeling really restricted right now. Like not in the good way."

"Of course."

Eric removes the mask and lays it on the table with the iPod, smiling when Jamie blinks his eyes open, sniffles and then wiggles his face a little.

"Ugh, I feel gross," he says and then he laughs again. "Sorry. Um."

"The rest of you, yeah," Eric says, catching himself before he just stares dumbly into Jamie's eyes with a dopey smile. But now that he knows he'll be able to touch Jamie, really touch all of him that he really wants to touch, he rushes through the unbuckling, flying through the loosening of the belts before tugging the blanket away. Jamie is flushed and sweaty and his cock is still hard and sticky with dried lube, but he sits up. Eric pulls him into an unbalanced, awkward, wonderful embrace.

"Oh, hi," Jamie giggles, hugging Eric tight and nuzzling his neck, kissing it sweetly. Eric's chest aches.

"Hi," Eric replies, reveling in this moment, relishing it. Jamie is *his*, and who the hell knows if that will ever last, but right now it's happening and it feels so fucking good that Eric can feel his eyes prickling.

This gorgeous, sexy, funny, strange man is all his. And he wants him *so badly*.

"Did you miss me?" Jamie asks playfully, wriggling around to pull back. But Eric holds him fast.

"Yes," he whispers, vulnerable and honest and needy and not thinking it through at all. "I really, really did."

Jamie pauses, his whole body going deadly still for a long moment, but then he melts back into Eric and clings tight.

"I missed you too," he says. And Eric's not sure if he's talking about their six weeks mostly apart, or his time removed during this scene, or if he's like Eric and is talking about both. It doesn't really matter—they're both in this moment together.

Eric leans back just enough to move and ducks his head. Jamie meets him halfway, and their lips slot together, softly but passionately, and just a little bit shy, as if they're kissing for the first time.

A barrier has been cracked, but Eric's not entirely sure what it is or how it happened.

"Please," Jamie whispers, surrendering when Eric kisses down his throat and starts nipping and suckling at the skin there. "Please, I can't—I can't wait till tomorrow, I need you—"

"Okay," Eric gasps, and then Jamie is tugging his shirt off and he's trying to undo his pants with one hand, and finally they collapse into giggles and sort themselves out enough to get Eric out of his clothes properly. Still, Jamie apparently doesn't have enough patience to do that the whole way, because when he pulls Eric in and kisses him again, he only relents enough to pull off Eric's glasses and drop them on the table to get closer to him. Eric still has his underwear and pants caught around one ankle. He doesn't bother to kick them off.

But Jamie is a warm, solid weight beneath him, his arms strong around Eric's back, tugging him closer, and his cock is turgid and hot along the line of Eric's groin, and Eric really can't be fucked to care.

"Come on," Jamie urges, barely above a breath, as though he can't get enough air. "Please come with me, come on—"

Eric reaches out and fumbles on the coffee table until he finds the lube. He shifts it between them and pours a good amount on their cocks, just drizzling it right on them, as cool as it is, and it doesn't matter that they both wince at the temperature on their heated skin; soon enough Eric has a hand around both of them and they're thrusting against each other. It's not perfect for Eric, not what he wants—Jamie's a couple of inches shorter than he is, and while Jamie thrusts right along him harder and harder, Eric can't get the angle and the friction he needs, but he's *so close*—

"Fuck, I'm gonna come," Jamie blurts out, and Eric groans and fucks against him harder. "Keep going, like that, just like—*fuck*, keep going, *yeah*—*unh, unh*—shit, *fuck!*"

Jamie comes, an impressive amount of jism splattering all over the both of them, over and over. Eric lets go of Jamie's cock and focuses on his own, on his hand flying over his cock, on Jamie's thighs hitched up around his hips, on Jamie's nails biting into his ass as it flexes and grinds into Jamie, on Jamie's *mouth*—

"Oh, god, *Jamie*—"

Jamie kisses Eric and swallows down his moans as he comes over his fist, snapping his hips once, twice, before easing himself down and into Jamie's arms, offering and waiting for him when he's finished. He settles down, and Jamie kisses him softly and touches him everywhere, hands all over his body. Eric returns the favor, giggling when he realizes that they're both just basically rubbing sweat and come into each other.

"How do you feel?" Eric asks.

"Oh, god, ask me later," Jamie groans. "I can't think right now."

Eric laughs and then tries to sit up—he has to provide aftercare, get Jamie into a bath, get some liquids and sugars into him, make sure he doesn't crash too hard and go into the ruthless depression that sub drop forces a sub into if aftercare isn't provided sufficiently—but Jamie stops him.

"Not yet," he says. "Just—just a few more minutes? Please? Just—just stay close for a little longer."

Eric blinks and then he returns to Jamie's arms and holds him as close as he wants. Right against him, chest to chest, legs tangled, heads ducked together. Breathing together, hearts beating together. It's every romantic cliché Eric's ever wanted and it's happening every way that he didn't think it could.

Fucking hell.

ACES WIRED

ACES WIRED

Eric feels as if a brick wall has crumbled. And he expected it—bricks have cracks as part of their very layering, and even the strongest mortar can't stand up to too much pressure. But the crumbling of the bricks leaves behind a mess, and Eric feels like an idiot for building it up in the first place if this is what he has to go through.

Eric feels awkward around Jamie, and their dates have been stilted for over a week now, although they've seen each other almost every night. Something about the depth of Jamie's subspace and the intensity of Eric's reaction to it fractured the comfortable idea that they could do this casually, at least in Eric's mind. And now he doesn't know how to do it. He holds Jamie's hand more, but his hand sweats the whole time. He's more tactile, but the touches are stilted and awkward. Their kisses are more lingering, more heated, but Eric has to pull away to breathe, and they haven't had sex. It's as if he's actually started the relationship over—all the half-shy glances and the nervous tiptoes and the testing of boundaries.

Jamie's not on the same page, though. Eric has no idea whether Jamie is still playing, or if he never was, or if he always will be. So they are both confused, and Eric can't help but beat himself up for that. Eric's in a kind of spiral of beating himself up, to be honest—for not realizing, for getting in so deep, for changing things, for falling in love when he hadn't meant to.

He's in love. This isn't a game anymore.

"Can you tell me what's up with you lately? Is this a thing, or—what? Have I done something?" Jamie says one night, thoroughly confused when Eric has backed away from his generous hand cupping Eric through his jeans. He so obviously wants it, but then he backs away, is silent, makes excuses.

"No, god, you're fine. I'm so sorry," Eric says. "I think I just—messed something up in my own head and—I'm trying to readjust."

"And—it was about me," Jamie guesses astutely.

Eric sighs. Communication time. Maybe not total truth time—he's terrified, and he still doesn't know where things stand. "Yes. Just... me realizing that I'm dumb. And too guarded. Now I have to figure out how to be less guarded without being like... all over you."

Jamie grins, and leans in to bite Eric's chin playfully.

"You know what?" he says. "I think I could take you being all over me. I think I might even *like* it."

And that's that. Just like the first time, they fuck on Eric's couch, silly and wild and frantic and close, and Eric is so fucking in love and always has been. It was just a spark back then; sparks are easy to bury, but if they're allowed to grow, they'll eventually start a fire. Now, it's a fucking blaze; his dried-up, semi-cynical, careful, shy little heart was perfect tinder. The last scene they did was a breath of fresh air on that growing flame. Now it's blasting out the windows—cracking the brick walls.

"So what's next, sir?" Jamie asks the next day, quiet as they sit over coffee on their way to their respective jobs. It's risky to talk about it in public, but kind of exciting.

Eric pulls out his phone with an exaggerated flourish, making Jamie laugh his adorable little chuckle, and hits the passcode so he can open his notes.

"Well, how about a fun one?" he asks. "We've got one here about you behind me and unable to move until I've finished a few times..."

Jamie's eyes light up and he nods, biting his lip around a smile. "I like that. Can we?"

"I think we can," Eric says. "Will you need a ring?"

Jamie looks confused for a moment, but then his whole face goes wide and Eric has to giggle.

"Oooh, a—" he looks around quickly, and then mouths at him, *cock ring*.

"Yes, baby," Eric says, just a bit mocking, and Jamie kicks him under the table. "Ow, dammit!"

"Woops. Sorry."

"No you're not."

"No, I'm not."

* * *

One of the most beautiful things about Jamie, to Eric, is how he's grown into his submissive instincts. When Eric met him, he was just realizing them, just finding out what they really were. They've talked about it a little bit—he'd always enjoyed someone else taking control, whether it was planning dates or taking over during sex. He always felt comfortable following someone else's lead. But he wasn't happy there—Jamie is a lively, extroverted person who enjoys *doing* things. By learning what submissiveness really is—achieving comfort and release through the offering of control—he's been able to settle into his submissive tendencies without drowning in them. Some people feel their best when their control is taken away completely, but Eric's never seen that in Jamie. What he sees now is a Jamie who knows how to give up that control through trust and not just through pure need. Then he can take control comfortably in other ways, can feel more confident in himself without unfulfilled urges always dragging him down.

Eric got to be a part of that transformation. And he's lucky enough to be a part of the end result, if he doesn't fuck anything up during their stupid, stupid, dumb, stupid test period.

Could he call it quits? Or should he stick it out? The question is driving him insane. He just wants to make Jamie his, all the time, and he's so in love, but... It still seems fast, as if he'd be making a sudden jump.

He can ease into it. He can *show* Jamie that he's serious, that he's ready for a contract and a serious relationship and everything together. He can show Jamie that he's ready, he can take his time with it, and win Jamie's trust for that next step, because he knows Jamie had doubts about stalling. But maybe Jamie has doubts now about moving along to the next stage.

The possibility remains, the nagging question: Did Eric ruin it? Did his inability to totally trust and throw himself into it headfirst ruin this? Or can he convince Jamie that his caution was the best thing? Does he *need* to convince Jamie?

Clearly, they need to communicate. But Eric doesn't want to ruin the fun scene they have planned for the night. So... this weekend, maybe. He'll plan a date, take Jamie out for a really nice dinner, bring him flowers, the whole nine yards. He will *woo* him. It'll be *amazing*.

But that's for the weekend. Tonight, he'll head to Jamie's apartment after a dinner meeting with his colleagues, and then they'll scene and it'll be fun and lighthearted and wonderful. Tonight he's going to drive Jamie *crazy*.

* * *

He's completely ready for the night when he knocks on Jamie's door.

"Hey you," Jamie says, talking even as he opens the door. "I wasn't —*mmm!*"

Eric's got Jamie's mouth on his, and that's what he uses as impetus to push Jamie back from the door and into the apartment. He kicks the door closed behind him, grabbing Jamie's face and holding him in, kissing him hard and filthy with no break for breath or words. He drops his bag, shucks off his jacket, and then his hands are back, tilting Jamie's face just how he wants it.

Jamie doesn't act beyond kissing back—Eric can tell he's submitting already, knowing the plan. The way Eric simply took over and continues to take what he wants must have been a clue. Good. It gives Eric the control, and he's pulling away from Jamie's mouth only to take off their shirts, while sliding their lips together, tongue sliding into Jamie's mouth, stroking into him, *thrusting* just as he wants Jamie to do once they've really started.

"Safeword?" Eric asks.

"Red to stop, yellow to pause, green to go," Jamie says. "Green, green, green, green—"

Eric pushes Jamie down to his knees and undoes his own belt buckle, leaving it hanging from the loops and popping open his button and fly. A quick tuck, and his cock is out of his pants, settled into the V of the open fly, and he's holding it straight out, lightly stroking at the base with one hand and cupping the back of Jamie's head with the other.

"Suck," he commands. Jamie whimpers, looking up at him from his knees through heavy-lidded eyes, and then opens his mouth, his tongue just past his lips as he leans forward and takes the head into his mouth.

Jamie has a gift for sucking cock. He's enthusiastic about it, a little sloppy, but he loves doing it, loves reducing Eric to a quivering mess. And ever since they had the proper discussions and ditched condoms for oral, Eric's enjoyed the benefit of it fully. Jamie lets Eric's shaft settle into his tongue, curved around his cock like a cradle, sucking hard when Eric pulls up and then relaxing to take him back in. Sometimes he uses his hands, but with Eric controlling everything, one hand still guiding his cock where he wants it. Jamie's got both of his own hands behind his back, holding himself in a simulacrum of bondage. It's gorgeous, his shoulders taut like that, the muscles of his chest presented, his throat slightly back, allowing Eric deeper and deeper, until he can swallow around him.

"Oh, fuck, so good, sweetheart," Eric gasps, rocking his hips as gently as possible, the hand on the back of Jamie's head feeling Jamie's rhythm, pushing him occasionally to go deeper, faster, until Jamie starts to do it of his own accord, bobbing deeply and almost gagging when he pulls a good deal of Eric's cock into his mouth. But not all of it—not yet, anyway. Eric pulls back.

"No, wait," Jamie says, panting.

"And what am I waiting for?" Eric asks, almost snorting when he realizes how imperious he sounds. But Jamie lowers his eyes and shivers, so it has the intended effect.

"I'm sorry, sir," he says, and *fuck* that sounds good, that coy little reminder that Eric's got the reins completely, that Jamie is giving them up so perfectly. "I just—want to suck all of you, don't care how big you are, just—"

He leans in and licks at the head, which is already shiny with his saliva. But Eric pulls it back.

"No, wait until I give it to you," Eric says. God, this is rushing to his head—Jamie willing to do anything, everything for him, even swallow down a cock that's larger than he's used to. Eric's usually self-conscious about it, doesn't want anyone he's with to think he's got an ego over it. It's not as big a boon as his early ventures into porn would have had him believe. But the fact that Jamie is willing to push a boundary to make him feel good, willing to put himself through strain, is *eager* for it and takes pleasure in it—that's incredible. But he's going to make Jamie wait, too. And Jamie will, which is also incredible.

Eric stands before Jamie and strokes himself slowly, watching Jamie watch the movements of his hand, watching him lick his lips and fight the urge to beg for what he wants. But that control is what *Eric* wants. He'll wait as long as he has to.

It only takes about a minute, and all it takes to break the tension is Eric gasping sharply and throwing his head back as he squeezes himself just under the head, tugging there softly but insistently.

"Please—"

"Nnn," Eric says uselessly. Jamie whimpers again. "That sounds good," Eric manages: "Keep going."

He starts to jerk himself harder, with more intent, and Jamie fidgets where he kneels, looking put out.

"Please let me," he says. "Please, I want to suck you. I want to take all of you, want you to fuck my mouth, just take me, *please*—"

"Oh, god, that sounds good," Eric moans. "Tell me more, come on. I might let you."

"Want to choke on it," Jamie continues desperately, urged on by the noises coming from Eric. "Want it filling me up, all the way into my throat. Want to feel you on my tongue, want—want you to bruise my lips, want everyone to see how bad I wanted you to fuck me—"

"Oh shit—"

Eric squeezes at the base of his cock hard, trying to fight off the overwhelming urge to just come all over Jamie's face. But Jamie's been such a good boy, Eric wants to give him what he asked for. So he holds off and thinks for half a minute of copy editing and the work he didn't get done today, and then the sharp edge of orgasm ebbs away and he's settled enough to keep going.

"Okay," he says. "Want you to do it, baby, want you to open up and take it. We'll go slow. Use your hands however you need to."

Jamie brings them up and reaches back to squeeze Eric's ass, pulling the cheeks apart roughly as he swallows him down again, sucking as far as he can before he starts to gag. Eric very pointedly starts to feel empty, and he doesn't know how much longer he can wait to have Jamie inside him if he's going to be doing that.

"Okay," Eric says again. "Just relax. Deep breath in through your nose, throat wide—that's it—" He slips just into Jamie's throat, and then he feels a flutter. He pulls back gently, letting Jamie get another breath before he rocks back in. "God, you're so good to me—"

Jamie whines in his throat and pulls Eric back in, sucking him down greedily, ignoring Eric's slow pace to start bobbing him in and out of his throat. He still doesn't get all the way down, but Eric doesn't care—half an inch left is nothing when Jamie keeps engulfing him like this. He's getting close fast, with that tight wet hot clamp around him—

"Oh god, you keep doing that," Eric says, "and I'm gonna come right down your throat, gonna—gonna—oh, fuck, I'm gonna come, Jamie— I'm gonna come—"

Jamie starts to swallow, and that's it. He comes, rocking up on his toes, legs stretched taut as his torso bows, holding Jamie's head in and grinding into his mouth, twitching when Jamie spreads his ass again as he pulls him in. And then, suddenly, it crashes, and Eric pulls free, flushed and sweaty.

"How's your throat, beautiful?" he asks breathlessly, crouching down and checking Jamie over. He's got drool on his chin and his nose was running a bit and his eyes are teary, but he's smiling as he heaves for breath, looking so pleased with himself.

"Did it," he croaks, and Eric kisses him soundly, gently running the backs of his fingers over Jamie's Adam's apple.

"You did, so fucking well, thank you so much," Eric says, kissing him deeply, happily. Fuck, Jamie just did that for him—something difficult, something so completely and totally submissive, something that required a *huge* amount of trust, and he even swallowed, something he doesn't usually do—usually he finishes Eric off when they're fucking, or jerks him off while they make out.

But not this time. Jamie just rocked his fucking world, and did it while Eric was supposedly completely in control. But Jamie had done all these little things to get what he wanted, and Eric can't help but think fondly, as he smiles back at Jamie's self-satisfied smirk, *you little shit*—

"Good boys get rewards, don't they?" Eric asks offhandedly, and Jamie's eyes go wide as he nods. "Mmm, eager, huh? Well, you can get a reward, my good boy. Made me feel so good. Let me do the same. Let's go get the lube."

He stands and pulls Jamie up by the hand, holding it as he guides them both to the bedroom. When he's there, he kicks off his pants and underwear without looking back to see what Jamie's doing, opening the nightstand to grab the lube before crawling onto the bed and kneeling up near the headboard, facing it.

As though he doesn't even notice Jamie behind him, shuffling out of his own clothes and climbing onto the bed, Eric lubes his fingers and then spreads his knees wide, leaning forward against the headboard before reaching back and rubbing at his own hole.

"Unh, this feels good," Eric says at length, tapping at the tight pucker before pushing at it gently a few times. "Want you to watch me get myself ready for your cock. Think you can have a condom on and ready by the time I'm done so I can take you right in?"

"Yes," Jamie breathes, and Eric slips a finger into himself. The both of them moan, and Eric laughs.

"You like watching, don't you?" he says at length, thrusting his finger in and out. He goes rough and hard, impatient to have Jamie inside him. "You could sit back and watch me fuck myself all day, couldn't you? I might have you do that, you know—at some point." Jamie's breathing heavily, somewhere behind Eric, and Eric grins as he slides in a second finger, and then a third. "See how much I want *you* to fuck me, though? Can't even wait, have to stretch myself too fast because I need your cock in me. You want that? You wanna fuck me?"

"Yes—"

"Too bad," Eric says. "I'm gonna fuck myself, instead. Mind if I use your cock?"

Jamie laughs and groans, and Eric peeks back at him. He's kneeling, holding his cock in his own hand, squeezing the base. "Go right ahead, god—"

"Aren't you supposed to be wearing a cock ring?"

There's a scramble, and Eric laughs again as Jamie hops off the bed to dig into his toy box. When he comes back, he borrows the lube, and Eric hears him fumbling around. Eric pulls out his fingers and drops lower on the bed, sticking his ass back and up, putting both hands on the headboard in front of him.

"Hurry up. I'm all ready over here."

Jamie curses and then crawls up the bed, draping himself over Eric's back and sliding his lubed cock along Eric's crack. "Please let me fuck you, I'm ready, please—"

"Remember what we agreed," Eric says firmly. "I get to come two or three times. That means you have to hold out for at least one more, and if I decide I want another, you'll have to wait for that, too. It could take a long time. Are you ready for that?"

"Yes, yes, please—"

"Good."

Eric rises up on his knees, reaches back, and holds Jamie's cock steady. Slowly, he eases himself back, sitting down until Jamie breaches him, popping past the tight muscle of his rim. Once past that, Eric sinks down quicker, in short little bursts, rocking up and down and going further every time until he's fully seated, legs spread and trembling, Jamie's hands warm on his thighs, helping to hold him open.

"Okay," Eric says. "Sit still."

Eric leans down until he's on his elbows, hands grasped at the edge of the mattress in the gap near the headboard. Jamie shifts only enough to stay comfortably seated inside Eric's ass, wide and hot and spreading him with the sharp, pleasurable sensation of being *filled*.

And then he starts to move.

Eric knows how to work a cock. He's been taking control like this since he learned how—he's always preferred bottoming, the stretch and burn of taking a cock inside him, but he's never considered himself to be submissive in it. So he's adapted, and learned how to control things from a position that seems as if there's no control at all.

Oh, but there is. He moves his hips in undulating circles, up and down and back and forth, taking Jamie to the hilt over and over, drawing groans and cries from Jamie with incredible ease. Jamie stays perfectly still—Eric might as well have tied him up. Because Jamie knows that if he moves, Eric will stop, and probably punish him. And maybe that'll actually make him push Eric at some point, because Jamie is such a sucker for a good spanking. But for now, he's bound up by his need for Eric to keep going, to come again, to get him closer to releasing the cock ring and being able to come himself.

"How's it feel?" Eric asks. "Tell me."

"Oh, keep doing that," Jamie pleads. "Just like that, like that—keep going, fucking please—"

"Oh, *yeah*—"

Jamie's agony spurs Eric on—he's waiting and holding off and letting Eric *use* him, and fuck, Eric *knows* Jamie needs more, knows he needs Eric to come. But Eric needs just a little more before he can even think about going beyond half-hard and back on his way to coming again.

He gives Jamie another minute, and then pauses, reaching up to the top of the headboard, pulling himself up. He shuffles and adjusts, taking Jamie in in little tests until he feels a sharp spike of pleasure up his spine.

"Oh, right there," he breathes, sitting up and then back down on Jamie's cock, letting it brush over that spot again. "Right fucking there."

Within minutes, he's bouncing on Jamie's cock, his own dick fully hard and bobbing between his legs. He can barely catch his breath, his thighs are screaming, but Jamie's hitting him just right, it's so fucking perfect—

"Okay, like that," Eric says, and starts stroking himself again, hand flying over his cock as he takes Jamie's over and over and over. "Yes—yes, yes, yes—*fuck!*"

He comes again, sharper and harder but shorter this time, just a little bit of come flying from his slit before he has to let go and fall back to the bed, tired and unable to keep going.

"Your turn," he gasps out. "You can do whatever you want to keep fucking me. But you're not allowed to take off the ring till I say, okay?"

"Fuck, yes—"

Jamie all but falls over him and starts giving it to him, fucking him hard and fast, in long, steady thrusts, hands digging into Eric's hips. He's driving Eric right into the mattress, and Eric's whole body *burns*, but it's the least he can do—Jamie's pushed himself time and again for both of them, and Eric thinks it's high time he returned the favor. He lets Jamie take what he wants, lets him fuck Eric however he wants. Eric just takes it, lets it happen.

"Fuck, kiss me?" Jamie asks at one point, leaning down over Eric, craning his head over Eric's shoulder. Eric obliges readily, turning his head back and letting Jamie cup his cheek and hold him steady as they kiss, sloppy and off center, not quite as sexy as it seems, but wonderful, connected.

"I need to come," Jamie says. "It's gonna hurt, I don't—I can't—"

Eric nods. "Do it."

Jamie fumbles, not even pulling out of Eric before he unsnaps the cock ring and lets it fall away. Then, with a quick squirt of cool lube over where Eric is stretched around him, Jamie tosses it all away and fucks Eric again, hips hammering into Eric's ass as he starts to babble and lose rhythm.

"Oh shit yeah," he says. "Feels so fucking good, Eric, you just—so good—need you, need to come—just—please, fuck. Please let me come, need to come—"

"Do it, come inside me—"

Jamie makes a strangled noise and stills, holding Eric tight against him, spreading him hard as he comes inside him. Then, slowly, he relaxes, slides from Eric's body and collapses onto the bed.

"How was that?" Eric asks, lying on Jamie's chest and rubbing his hand over Jamie's chest and stomach, giving him all the contact he might need.

Jamie looks down at him very seriously. "I think my cock might fall off." And then he bursts out laughing.

Eric can't help but join, head falling to Jamie's shoulder and shaking as he says, "God, I love you."

Jamie freezes. "... What?"

Oh, shit. *I didn't mean to say that— I know we're not ready— I had a momentary lapse of judgment— How does one develop amnesia—* "Um."

Jamie sits up, and Eric bolts up next to him, knowing he looks as though he saw a ghost. Jamie stares at him steadily, almost in awe, and then his face breaks out into a tentative smile.

"Did you mean it?"

The hope, the nerves, the happiness all fight to break free of Eric's chest like little torpedoes trying to blow him up. And the moment he sees the same thing in Jamie, *pop—pop—pop—* the explosions aren't so bad after all. More like fireworks.

God I'm a fucking sap—

"Yes. I mean it."

Jamie's face crumples and he hits Eric on the shoulder.

"Ow!"

"You fucking—*asshole*," Jamie laughs, sniffling and wiping away tears. "All this time I thought I was counting down the days—"

He launches into Eric's arms, clinging and crying, and Eric feels as if he's been hit with a deadly explosive after all. "Jamie, I'm so sorry—"

"Do *not* apologize," Jamie scolds, sitting back and hitting him again. "You're an asshole. I can't believe I'm in love with you, you're such a—"

"Asshole?" Eric laughs, and Jamie kisses him, frantic little pecks on his lips.

"That was improper grammar and terrible manners," Jamie says, "interrupting me—"

"Say it again," Eric says. It's addictive, he wants to say it again himself, but he needs Jamie to do it first—

"I love you," Jamie says, with a grin, and Eric leans in and kisses Jamie again, pulling them down to lie next to each other. And it's as if they're physically closer, as if Eric's arms just automatically hold Jamie a little tighter, as if his chest seeks contact with Jamie's, as if his legs twine themselves tighter around Jamie's. The heaviness of the barrier between them is gone, and Eric feels as though an elephant just got up from its seat on his chest and Jamie replaced it, light and warm and a welcome weight. It's the weight of commitment and promise, rather than the trap of uncertainty, which had been mostly Eric's doing in the first place. He set the trap, and now he has to defuse it, and he can't do it fast enough. He craves as much closeness to Jamie as he can get.

"I am sorry though," Eric says. "Not for saying it—don't hit me! Just. For being dumb."

"Well, you told me something changed in your head," Jamie says. "It was either this, or realizing you wanted to stop. I'm glad it's this."

"I couldn't stop with you," Eric admits. "I'm in this. Unless you want to stop—"

"No," Jamie says. "You were right. If you'd forced your feelings with me, you might resent me. I was okay waiting until you were ready."

"That's what this was, wasn't it?" Eric muses. "I was going slow."

"I'm okay with that," Jamie says. "I always was. I was just afraid that so much time would make you realize you didn't want me—"

"How could I not want you?" Eric asks. "You're—you're everything, Jamie."

Jamie's face twists again and he sniffs as he bends to kiss Eric once, then pulls back and says "I don't want to get snot on you."

"I don't even care," Eric says. "But where does this leave us? You said you don't want to stop."

"No, I still think this is a good idea," Jamie says. "For both of us. We're obviously compatible—I mean, for this lifestyle. Outside it, too. But I think we should finish up the fantasies before we write up a contract or do any repeats or try new stuff. I want a solid foundation if we're going to—to do anything permanent."

Permanent. It settles heavily in Eric's chest, but the weight is warm and welcome. Forever with Jamie—he likes that idea, and Jamie's right. It's important to get that right. "Okay. So we finish up the fantasy list. What's next, then? We've got... some pretty heavy stuff coming up."

Jamie nods. "But—I'm ready for it. I don't know if I would've been, if—if we hadn't gotten this far, you know?"

"I know. Some of these scenes require a lot of trust."

"And vulnerability," Jamie says. "It's one thing to trust you with my body. My heart..."

"I think that's what happened when—when we did the bondage, to get you into deep subspace," Eric admits. "I think that's how I finally realized what I was feeling. Because you did trust me like that, and because... because I trusted you, too, and you didn't break it. My egg."

Jamie stares at him blankly. "Your heart is an egg?"

"No!" Eric laughs. "Never mind. I'll tell you the story sometime. It's all fucked up in my head right now."

Jamie chuckles and cuddles into Eric's arms, kissing his jaw. "Can I request our next scene, then? And... and something else?"

"Sure," Eric says. "Request away."

"I want to do the roleplay of Master and slave," Jamie says. "I want to plan a whole day like that, come up with what we'll do all ahead of time and—and just see how it goes. And... I want to forget condoms. Like, totally."

"For good, you mean?" Eric asks, eyebrows high.

"Maybe not entirely," Jamie says. "They're useful. But I mean... for the scene, and maybe when we feel like it, after? If you like it, I mean. I—I'm ready to consider feeling that myself."

Eric blinks. "You mean—"

"I maybe want to bottom?" Jamie says uncertainly. "I mean, I won't lie, part of me has been nervous because of this." He taps Eric's cock, soft and damp. "I've only done it a couple times, and never that—much. And it was weird every time, and so intense, and I just... I want to build up to it, okay? Because it really affects me, like... inside. And not just inside my ass," he adds, laughing self-consciously. "And... the last time I did it, I had a hook-up before I met my last boyfriend, and... it was just bad. But... can I tell you more about that another time, maybe?"

"Of course," Eric says. "We'll take as much time as you need."

"Okay," Jamie says. "So... some time this week, we can plan a day for the next scene, and then... we'll keep going until we're done."

"And then we'll keep going after that," Eric says.

Jamie grins, and then settles down, yawning. "Tired me out."

"Tired *me* out."

Jamie laughs sleepily, and a few minutes later, he's slipped into sleep. Eric smiles and kisses his hair. "I love you."

"—m'too."

Eric laughs quietly. Right now, he doesn't care that Jamie's still got on a soiled condom, or that he's lying in a wet spot, or that the light is still on. He'll get the light and clean up later. Right now, he's holding his man.

His man, with whom he's planning to continue keeping up a boundary. They're in love, they're together, so—why continue? Eric doesn't doubt anymore, not their compatibility, not their potential for a real future. So why keep holding off?

Jamie wants to. Jamie needs to be sure. And Eric can see how it's a good idea, even if a big part of him would rather just throw the caution away and have Jamie as *his,* undeniably, officially, *forever.* But Jamie needs this. So Eric can do it.

"Good night, Jamie."

NULLIFY THE CUT

NULLIFY THE CUT

Eric knows that if this scene is going to work, he's going to have to let go of any lingering shame at liking things that are out of the ordinary. He's been doing sex on the atypical side for *years* of his life, but there's always a little voice that wonders, *Why do you even like this?* Especially when they were building up to *this*, such a specialized scene.

But he's not having any trouble letting go of that now that it's happening, not with Jamie clad in only knee pads, elbow pads, and a collar—all a deep brown leather that looks incredible next to his skin—and crawling around Eric's apartment. He looks *stunning*, and Eric's been hard since they woke up an hour ago and started the scene by putting the non-outfit on Jamie and going over the rules.

Obey all orders. Do nothing without permission. Stay on all fours unless instructed otherwise. Use 'Master' at all times. Expect punishment for violations. Serve. Safeword if necessary. Master is in charge.

Eric can't help it. He *likes* playing the part of Master. This is the extreme of their play with dominance and submission. If nothing else, it's an interesting study in how they handle those roles when the role is all there is. But it's also exciting. They're taking things to the highest level, and it's *really fucking hot*, especially because Jamie is specifically trusting Eric to push his boundaries a little, too—he's supposed to be unmerciful.

"Come here, baby," Eric says. Jamie stops straightening the coffee table and crawls over, kneeling at Eric's feet. "Do you want to make your Master come?"

Jamie sighs blissfully and nods. "Yes, please."

"So polite," Eric murmurs approvingly. "Did you finish the living room?"

He knows perfectly well Jamie has cleaned the living room. It took him most of the hour to sweep the floor and dust, and Eric had been watching from his armchair the whole time. But this is the role—Jamie asked for a Master who is demanding but indulgent, who gives lots of praise but isn't afraid to punish. Someone who would treat him like a prized pet or servant rather than an equal human. That's the fantasy, the roleplay. They're both roiled up, their instincts being acted upon and then some, and it's going so much better than Eric expected.

"Yes, Master," Jamie replies, eyes cast downward.

"Good boy," Eric says and smiles as Jamie preens. "Good boys deserve rewards, don't they?"

"Whatever my Master wants."

Eric almost breaks to remind Jamie that of *course* it's about what Jamie wants and that *matters* and—but that's not what this is about. He's not teaching Jamie anything. Jamie's not his student right now. He's his sub, acting the part of a slave, and the whole *point* of this is to make it all about Eric. Jamie might be getting a thrill out of it, some fulfillment, but it's about Eric's pleasure alone. Eric would be lying if he said he didn't like that—anyone would.

"That's right, baby," Eric says, reaching out and cupping Jamie's chin, rubbing his thumb over his bottom lip. "Go ahead and bring that pretty mouth over here."

With his free hand, he wiggles his pajama pants down over his cock, pulling it out and stroking it as he guides Jamie's head in. Then he just sits back, relaxes, and watches as Jamie sucks him down, pulling him in as far as he can, bobbing fast and hard as if Eric's orgasm is all he wants and he wants it *urgently*.

"That's it," Eric urges. "Make your Master come, go on."

Jamie moans, and it's enough—Eric comes almost casually, smoothly tensing up, cresting and going lax again as Jamie swallows around him and licks him clean.

"Thank you, Master," Jamie says, and Eric leans down and kisses him softly.

"Thank *you*, my good boy." Eric pets Jamie's hair and smiles down at him. "So good for me, such a sweet boy. Are you mine, sweetheart?"

"Yes, Master."

Eric grins and kisses Jamie again. "Good. Now. Why don't you get up off those pretty knees and bring breakfast out here for us? Coffee and croissants."

"Yes, Master," Jamie says, and then he crawls out of the room before rising up to his feet and going about his business in the kitchen. Eric picks up a book off the coffee table and starts to read, not particularly interested in doing anything besides watching Jamie and kissing Jamie and loving Jamie. But Jamie's playing his role, so Eric should do his best to play his and not get distracted, as nice as it would be.

A few minutes later, Jamie comes out with a tray. He sets it on the coffee table and then immediately kneels.

"Breakfast, Master," he says. "Coffee, with your coconut creamer and three sugars. And a glazed croissant. I made the glaze myself—it's banana."

Somehow, Jamie had managed to keep this a secret. And they are *in Eric's apartment.* "Sneaky boy," Eric says, genuinely impressed. "Look at you, spoiling me. If you keep this up, I might let you come later."

Jamie bites his lip and lets his head fall to Eric's knee with a groan. Eric laughs and pets Jamie's hair—and it's amazing, how they can still be *them,* even when they're playing at being something else.

And then they eat breakfast. Eric puts the tray on the thick arm of the chair and rips off little pieces of croissant to feed to Jamie and himself. It's delicious—the banana glaze is good; Eric can't help but be grateful to the cooking classes Jamie took. And the coffee is just how he likes it. Eric loves the way Jamie takes the bites from him, letting his lips close around Eric's fingers as he feeds him, smiling up at him from his knees, so open and trusting and beautiful and unashamed of his position.

When they finish, Eric sets the tray on the coffee table. "I'm going to take a shower now. Clean up in here and then run the water for me. I expect you to wash me, do you understand?"

Jamie's eyes develop a distinct twinkle. "Yes, Master."

"Good boy." He leans down and kisses Jamie. "I'm going to get undressed and then I'll be in the shower. You can stand up."

He takes his time going to the bedroom to take off his pajamas, which he hadn't actually worn to bed the night before. Usually he does wear them, feels more comfortable wearing *something* to bed. But he and Jamie had had an energetic night, and his sweaty skin had protested being covered up, so he'd fallen asleep naked. But he's the Master, and Jamie was supposed to be put in a position of subservience and vulnerability; both of them naked wouldn't serve that purpose. Eric takes off the pajamas and tosses them aside, grimacing at the croissant crumbs that fall from the folds. Then he waits a minute to give Jamie time to comply.

When he hears the water running, he counts to ten and then heads to the bathroom.

God, Jamie is *good* at this. He's already kneeling beside the tub by the time Eric gets there and, as soon as Eric walks in, he looks up, smiles and then reaches out to be ready to pull the shower curtain aside. Towels are piled on the toilet seat so they're closer than the rack, and the room is pleasantly steamy. Jamie's elbow pads and knee pads are off and piled carefully on the counter next to the sink, but his collar is still on.

"You're all ready," Eric notes. "Except you didn't take off your collar."

"Only my Master has the right to remove my collar," Jamie says.

Eric nods approvingly, a little shocked. They hadn't put that down as a rule. Jamie had probably done a little research on the topic of collars, because they had never really discussed one. Collars could be a big deal. Today's was a simple thing, nothing special, and Eric would never make Jamie wear it regularly, even if he wanted to. It wasn't the right shape, the leather was a little too stiff—no, this wasn't a collar for commitment, this was a collar for casual play. But if Jamie was researching...

Another thought for another day. For now, Eric smiles and steps forward, removing the collar with a simple slip of leather and nickel buckle. He puts it aside and then turns, letting Jamie hold the curtain open for him before rising and following him in.

It's not the biggest tub, but they make it work with some huddling and careful footwork. Jamie washes Eric thoroughly and keeps it as perfunctory as he can, even with his hands all over Eric's naked slippery body—after all, he doesn't have permission to tease Eric. But as Eric rinses off, he remembers that he is not bound by that rule.

"Now I'm going to wash you," he announces, and then he switches places with Jamie, letting him go under the hot spray.

And he's true to his word. He does wash Jamie. But that's obviously not his primary goal. He lets his hands linger in all the spots he knows drives Jamie wild—his throat, his nipples, the V of his hipbones, the curve under his ass—not to mention the copious attention he pays to Jamie's cock, which is steel-hard and hot and curving up to his belly as if it's trying to escape the torture and curl into it at the same time.

"Please, Master," Jamie gasps after several minutes of this, after Eric has washed the rest of him and returned quite a few times.

"Too much for you?" Eric asks. "Very well. Let's get you rinsed off, then."

Eric steps back, all the way to the back of the tub, and leans back against the cool tile wall, allowing Jamie plenty of space to rinse himself off—and watch. Eric reaches down his own body, as obviously as he can, and when he catches Jamie's eye, he stares right at him as he starts to stroke himself slowly.

"Go ahead," Eric says, trying not to laugh at Jamie frozen, bug-eyed at Eric shamelessly touching himself and clearly using the sight of Jamie as fodder for it. "Rinse off. Thoroughly."

Jamie hesitates a beat and then starts to rinse himself off, letting the water cascade over him, following its paths with his hands, sluicing away leftover soap. He caresses himself from neck to thighs, slow and sensual, peeking up shyly at Eric, who continues masturbating easily, watching closely, until Jamie is obviously clean and free of soap.

"Step out of the shower and dry off," Eric says suddenly, struck with an idea and feeling wicked. "I'll be out in a minute."

Jamie doesn't even lift an eyebrow. He just steps out as gracefully as he can, flicks the curtain closed again and, as far as Eric can tell from the vague outline of his shadow, does exactly as he's told.

Eric smirks, leans against the wall under the spray and takes himself in hand again, adding just a little bit of soap to make it slide easier. And then he goes for it, his arm pumping fast, his hips pistoning as he fucks his own hand.

"Oh, fuck," he moans loudly. "Unnnnh, *yeah*."

On the other side of the curtain, all movement is very suddenly still. Eric can't help but smile as he pants heavily, working himself up quickly, deliberately not holding back the whines that build up in his throat and explode out in short, high bursts as he jerks himself fast, reaching down with his other hand to cup and caress his balls, squeezing lightly.

"Oh, Jamie," he whimpers, his bicep burning, wrist too tight, but he's *so close*. "God, *yes*. Just like that—just like—ah, *ah!*"

He comes, just a little dribble of it, having come so recently before. But it served its purpose—after he turns off the water, he shoves open the curtain to see Jamie standing stiffly, towel held out awkwardly in front of him, waiting, careful not to brush his own erection.

"Mmm, thank you," Eric says lazily, milking it. Jamie looks wrecked, his breathing jagged, his thighs trembling and tensed. Good, so perfect. "Dry me off."

Eric stands still, holding his arms out and letting Jamie get to work. He stands perfectly still, eyes closed, letting his thoughts be as placid as possible. It works—by the time Jamie dries him below the waist, his dick is already soft again, limp over his balls, a clear sign that he'd finished himself off in the shower while Jamie had been out here, listening, denied.

"Thank you," Eric says when he's finished, leaning in and pecking him on the lips. "Now—let me put on your collar. You can put on your pads again, and then we can go to the bedroom so you can dress me."

* * *

Eric makes Jamie do a lot of waiting over the next twenty minutes. He goes through his closet musingly, though he's hardly ever that picky about what he wears on a casual day. Jamie looks as though he's going insane as he kneels and watches Eric holding clothes up again and again, asking Jamie to tell him how they look and showing off his naked body by twisting and turning and posing.

But it's time to move on. Teasing Jamie is fun, but he'll reach his limit eventually.

"Okay," Eric says. "These jeans, this shirt. Do you like them, baby?"

"Yes, Master," Jamie says, eagerly shuffling forward on his knees. "You'll look incredible."

Eric hums, flattered. "Well, stand up and dress me so we can see. Grab me some briefs, too, from the top drawer."

Jamie does as he's requested and then helps Eric into them, sliding the thin briefs slowly up Eric's legs before stretching them around his ass and cock. He takes time to arrange the fabric, too, making sure it's comfortable before twitching back as if he's almost beyond self-control.

Jamie grabs the pants.

This time, when he kneels to help Eric step into them, he doesn't rise for several seconds, breathing deeply and steadily. When he stands, pulling up the jeans, it's quicker this time, and Jamie holds back and keeps his hands as far from Eric's skin as he can. When he stands all the way and does up the fly, Eric grabs him around his waist and hauls him in.

"Are you having trouble, sweetheart?" Eric asks. "Or can you take a little more teasing?"

"I—I can take it, Master," Jamie says. Eric smirks. He sounds determined, but Eric keeps thinking of one of the qualities Jamie asked for in his Master—*unmerciful.*

"Good," Eric says, voice husky, one finger trailing slowly down Jamie's back, barely touching. Jamie's pressed right against him, and Eric can feel how hard he is through the jeans. When Eric's finger reaches his ass, he slips it gently down the sacrum, and then between his cheeks. Finally, he rocks forward, and stops teasing and presses hard against Jamie's hole.

"Fuck—"

And Eric feels something warm dribble on his stomach. He looks down—Jamie's cock is twitching, and Jamie is half-sobbing in his ear, body bowed down. And there's a white splatter dripping down the hair trailing beneath his jeans, pooling at the waistband.

"Oh, Jamie, that wasn't very good, was it?" Eric says, trying to stay as calm as possible. In reality, that was *so hot*, he was barely touched and he just *came,* and *fuck* if that kind of power isn't the sexiest thing Eric's ever felt. But Jamie just disobeyed.

"I'm sorry, I'm so sorry Master—"

"Go stand in the corner," Eric says firmly. Jamie jerks into movement, shuffling ashamedly to the far corner of the bedroom, where there is room. He faces the corner, tight shoulders and stance. Eric follows, crouches, and takes hold of Jamie's knees and spreads them wide, settling his feet where he wants them. Jamie is exposed this way, vulnerable, his balls dangling heavily between his legs. Eric moves his hands up and places them flat on either wall at shoulder-height, giving him a little support. "Now. You will stand here, and think about what you did. When I come back, I want you to be able to tell me *exactly* why what you did was wrong."

And then Eric leaves the room. He doesn't go far. Just to the bathroom, and quietly, so Jamie doesn't hear him leave and think he's been totally abandoned. Once he's wiped the come off his stomach and stripped the soiled jeans, he returns right away.

He dresses himself quickly. He knows that Jamie knows what he's done and why it was wrong—it's time to get the answer and dole out the punishment.

He also grabs a belt, but he doesn't put it on.

"All right, Jamie," Eric says, keeping his voice displeased. "Tell me what you did wrong."

He folds the belt, holding the hard buckle and the tail end in his hand tightly, and tests the flexibility of it. It's a relatively soft belt, old and used, but it's still in good shape, supple and strong. It's wide, and it'll leave a good stinging mark, He'll be careful not to hit hard enough to leave too much bruising. But Jamie doesn't know that yet.

"Master, I came without permission," Jamie says, as though reciting. "I disobeyed, directly against your order, which was not to come. I disrespected you by disregarding your order and I also told you I could take it and couldn't, so I lied. I'm sorry, Master; it won't happen again."

Eric drags the folded end of the belt loosely down Jamie's spine. Jamie jumps, and then whimpers, writhing as much as he can with his wide, rigid stance.

"You are correct," Eric says. "You know now that I have to punish you for it."

"Yes, Master," Jamie says. "I deserve it, please punish me."

"Look at you, greedy for it," Eric hums. "Can't wait to get all bruised up. Where do you think I should do it, Jamie? I reserve the right to disagree with you, but—" he lets the belt drop from his back and flicks it up gently between Jamie's legs, tapping his balls ever so lightly. "What about here? Should I leave a couple reminders here, since this is what couldn't stop itself?"

Jamie arches, whining. "Master, please—"

"Yes or no."

"—no."

"Thank you for being honest," Eric says. "How about we stick to that beautiful ass of yours, huh? I like the look of it when it's all red—"

"Please, please Master—"

"Is this a treat for you?" Eric asks, very obviously teasing. "Maybe I should pick something else—"

"No, please—"

"I won't," Eric assures. "It's okay, baby, you can trust me. It's just so hard to pick with you. So many options. Such a good sub, when you follow orders. So why don't we do this spanking now so it can be done and forgotten, hmm?"

"Yes. Yes, please, Master, do it."

"All right," Eric says, sidling up next to Jamie. He places his left hand on Jamie's arm as an anchor, and then tests the swing of the belt very, very lightly, swinging slowly to tap Jamie's ass with the barest contact. "Ten hits. You are allowed your safewords if you need."

"Thank you, Master."

"Count."

The first hit lands solid across his ass with a satisfying *thwack*. Jamie hisses, his back tensing.

"One," he says, exhaling shakily. Eric swings again, *thwack*. "Two."

This isn't a spanking for pleasure. Even though it's still play, it's a punishment. So Eric doesn't stop to please Jamie in between, or praise him. He just does his job and gives the punishment. He lets Jamie count his way through the belting so he can focus on laying the strikes, ensuring that they don't all land in one spot or hit too hard toward the loose tip (which can bruise heavily), or hit with the edge (which can split skin).

"Ten," Jamie gasps, and Eric immediately drops the belt and turns Jamie from the corner and pulls him into his arms.

"All done, baby," he whispers, petting Jamie's hair and holding him tightly as he sniffles into Eric's shoulder. "You're forgiven. It's all forgotten now. You're such a good boy for me."

"'Mm sorry," Jamie mumbles, and Eric pulls back and tilts Jamie's chin up with one finger.

"No apologies," Eric says. "You took your punishment, so you've made up for it, and the slate is clean, okay? And you're not doing anything to apologize for right now."

Jamie nods, and then buries himself back in Eric's arms.

* * *

The city is too hot for a walk, but Eric takes one anyway, to retrieve a late lunch for them from a weird sandwich shop/juice bar combo a couple blocks away. Their food is really good if he avoids the vegan options, which are great in some places, but not this one. And it has what he wants for Jamie, as well—a protein smoothie that tastes really good and is fairly filling, which will help with their afternoon plans.

When he has the food, he takes his time ambling back. Jamie had been worn out after his punishment, and Eric had tucked him in for a nap before heading out, telling him lunch would be back when he woke up. He wants Jamie to have time to rest and relax, even if he does wake up before Eric gets back—take off some of the pressure of the roleplay. It's been intense, as light-hearted as their play has been, and Eric can't imagine this being his lifestyle. It's got fun parts, and it's really hot, but he's sure he'd be exhausted by it within a day or two, and Jamie would be tired of it long before then. Jamie is a sweet man, helpful and kind, but this roleplay has been holding him back. Eric kind of misses him, misses his banter and his insightful pleasantries and his silly jokes and the way he makes fun of Eric sometimes—all the things he's so comfortable with even when he's subbing. He's still himself when he subs—he's always *Jamie*. Eric's not sure that *he's* always exactly who he is at all times. Sometimes he feels vaguely like a fraud, as if he's living someone else's life. But the feeling has been less and less so with Jamie, who always looks at him the same way, no matter what he's doing.

Eric hurries the last half a block to his building. He misses Jamie; he aches for him after such a short time. Maybe leaving him alone wasn't the best idea—

But when he finally gets up to his apartment and peeks into the bedroom, Jamie is still asleep. He's sprawled out on his stomach, mouth a little bit open, ass still shiny with the Lidocaine Eric had applied. The leather pads and collar are off, and his hair is in total disarray. Eric bites his lips to stifle a giggle—he's adorable and he's all Eric's.

Eric is a lucky son of a bitch. That much he knows for sure.

"Eric?"

Eric looks up from Jamie's ass and sees Jamie rubbing his eyes and yawning.

"How did you even wake up?" he half-whispers, slipping into the room and perching on the edge of the bed. "I was quiet."

"Mmmm, physically, yes," Jamie says, scooting so that his head in on Eric's lap. "But I could feel you looking at me. At my ass, actually."

Eric lets out the giggle this time. "I was actually noting that it was shiny from the Lidocaine gel. Speaking of which, I should probably check you over and apply some more."

"Fine, but I'm not moving," Jamie says bluntly, sliding off Eric's lap.

Eric laughs. "What happened to you being the slave, huh? Is this you saying you're done for the day?"

"Not done," Jamie says as Eric shifts down the bed and checks over Jamie's ass carefully for any cuts or bruises. "Maybe... can we renegotiate the boundaries a little bit?"

"Sure, if that's what you want," Eric says. Everything looks good; Jamie's red and obviously sore, but he's not injured or complaining of any undue pain. Eric grabs the Lidocaine from the bedside table and starts to apply it. "Is there something I'm doing wrong that you want me to change?"

Jamie considers for a moment. "It's not that you're doing it wrong. I mean, you're giving me what I asked for. And it it's really hot. But I guess... it's just making me a little anxious? Like. I don't feel like *us*. I don't feel like we're a couple who's in love, you know?"

Eric nods. "Yeah, I know what you mean. I've kind of missed how we usually are."

"Yes!" Jamie says. "So... how about we keep going as we were, except... except we can talk like we usually do? Like I want to keep crawling and I like serving you and I think it's fun that you're totally in control—that's what I want. But I don't want to feel afraid to talk to you."

"I understand," Eric says. "I'm sorry what we've been doing wasn't totally perfect for you—"

"Hey, we've had an awesome track record," Jamie says. "I've loved everything so far. And this isn't a total bust; I'm not safewording. We're just...playing ourselves instead of different people who are kinda like us."

"I like that," Eric says, rubbing in the last of the gel before pulling his hand away, sticky with the gel left between his fingers and faintly tingly. "I'm gonna wash my hands; I've got some leftovers. How are you, need any clean up?"

"I'll wipe up in the bathroom after you get back," Jamie says. "Then we continue?"

"Deal."

* * *

Jamie happily sits next to Eric's chair at the table, sipping his smoothie.

"I love whatever this is," he says at length. "But am I going to get a bite of that wrap? It looks really good."

"It is," Eric says, chewing his last bite. It's roast beef with some kind of creamy herbal sauce and enough veggies to fall out every other bite and it's pretty amazing. "But I got you some non-solid for a reason."

Jamie's eyebrows shoot up. "And... that is..."

"Do you remember our dinner out with Andy and Leta and the others?"

Jamie smiles. "You mean the one where I came in my pants."

Eric smiles right back. "Mmm. Except you're not wearing pants today. And you'll be enduring what you did then for a much longer period of time, so... I don't want you to need to take it out."

"Oh, okay," Jamie says. "That would be gross, so good idea."

"I thought so, too."

When lunch is finished, Eric turns and smirks at Jamie.

"I want you to go kneel on the coffee table," he says. "I'll clean up here, so don't worry about that. Just get up on the table and get on all fours. I want you waiting that way for me. And then we'll play."

"Okay," Jamie says.

Eric stands up and starts cleaning as Jamie crawls around the armchair that separates the little dining area from the living room. Eric brings everything to the kitchen, takes a few minutes to make sure everything's cleared, and then heads back in.

Jamie looks incredible. He's facing away from Eric, away from Eric's armchair, ass up in the air, back bowed, arms tight as he holds himself up. His knees are spread as widely as he can on the narrow table, and his head is hung. When Eric gets closer, he sees that Jamie is half-hard again, and he smiles and walks right past him to the bedroom.

The lube and the plug are where he left them in the bedside table, and he grabs them and returns to Jamie, casually walking by with them in hand. He sits in his armchair, sets the lube and the plug between Jamie's feet, and then sits back and *looks*.

"Eric?" Jamie says at length, sounding nervous.

"Shhh," Eric admonishes. "I'm right here, baby. I'm just admiring the view."

Jamie laughs, head hanging, shoulders shaking, and it does some really interesting things to Jamie's body, kind of *bounces* it. Eric smiles and enjoys the view for a moment longer before rising, putting one hand low on Jamie's back for stability and using the other, in combination with his foot, to shift the coffee table back.

"Whoa!" Jamie laughs, steadying himself. Eric sits back down, on the edge of the seat, and it's perfect—with his knees wide, the table is right below him and it puts Jamie's ass at just below eye level and easily within reach.

He allows Jamie enough time to draw a breath and then he leans forward and takes two handfuls of Jamie's plump rear, squeezing the muscles and spreading them apart. Jamie lets out a loud gust of air and drops to his elbows, stretching him out and tilting his hips so he's even better presented. Eric moans and shifts uncomfortably—he's already come twice today, so it's going to be a little longer before he can manage it again, but if Jamie keeps this up, he might set a record.

"So pretty," Eric says, too focused to bother thinking about it. It just *is* right now. "Look at you, just—so eager. So willing. And you trust me, and—god, Jamie, that feels better than anything. You know I'm going to do truly *filthy* things with you, and you still just offer yourself up, just—keep saying yes to me. And I love that." He stands up, leans over, plants a tiny kiss right at the top of Jamie's sacrum. "I love you."

"I love you too," Jamie coos back, and Eric laughs.

"You sound like you're joking," he teases back.

Jamie sighs, and says, in all seriousness, "I'm not. I really do love you, Eric—*oh wow*, okay—"

Eric kisses Jamie, down there in a private place, intimate and close. It's different now—being in a scene with Jamie, exchanging that trust; it makes him feel *more*. More important, more cherished, more as if he matters and that this matters between them. It feels *beautiful*, as if they're creating something together.

Creation, and even love, can be a lot of things. Right now, in his giddy happiness with the man lying spread and open for him, Eric thinks it should be *fun*.

Eric smirks as he prods at Jamie's hole with his tongue again, quick and insistent. He spreads Jamie's cheeks wide and presses his face in, working in his lips, sucking and kissing and licking, hard prods at the wrinkled muscle of his rim, surrounded by soft kitten licks, swirls and Xs and crosses and dots. And Jamie moans loudly above him, progressing to babbling and begging when Eric has relaxed the rim enough to breach it, slipping inside, a quick dart in and pulling back once, again, again, *again*.

"God, Eric, more," Jamie pleads. "More, more, please more—"

"What do you mean by more?" Eric asks, slipping the tip of his finger in, out, in, out. "More of the same, or more in general?"

"*More*," Jamie says. "Fingers."

"I can manage that," Eric chuckles.

A squirt of lube, and then he slides his finger all the way in. Jamie's eager enough that there's not much resistance for the single finger, but he's tight, and Eric knows building him up to bottoming is probably a good idea. It'll be easier if he's used to it—Eric himself enjoys it much more when he does it regularly, and he vaguely remembers a not-entirely-pleasant first time.

This isn't a case of virginity with Jamie; Jamie's done it before, but not in a very long time. He'd finally admitted to Eric, in the late hours of the night after their last scene, that the last time he'd bottomed, he hadn't wanted to—had just gone along with it, and that afterwards he'd felt dirty and used. He hadn't bottomed with his last ex at all, which had lead to their breakup. Eric would never leave Jamie for that—he'd happily go as a total bottom if Jamie never wanted to. But Jamie does want to; he just needs the trust to do it. And now that the trust is strengthening, he needs the buildup. Not only as a physical experience, but as an emotional one. A plug, a crop handle, a finger, a tongue—that can provide the physical. Those have been providing the physical buildup for some time, actually. But they will have to increase the amount to get Jamie comfortable enough for Eric's size, which has been more of a bane than a boon. The emotional buildup, now that it's a certainty, is going to take even more care.

Eric's willing to provide that care. Anything Jamie needs for this to be a good experience.

When Jamie's rocking back onto his finger, Eric lubes and sets up a second finger, lining it up and letting Jamie rock back onto it at his own pace. He takes it quickly—first one knuckle, then the next and finally down to the root, parting around them with gentle pushes out as he sits back, keening louder when he pauses, the fingers all the way inside him.

"More," Jamie insists, voice shaking. "Please, more."

"You want three?" Eric asks, breathless. He leans forward and pets Jamie's flank as he lays a kiss on the crease at the apex of his thigh. "You've only just got two."

"I—I don't like prep too much," Jamie confesses. "It just feels—too much, I just get anxious. I'd rather just take whatever I'm going to. I don't like a lot of buildup—"

"Shhh, it's okay," Eric says. "I'll give you three. But this doesn't have to be about prepping, okay? Let yourself enjoy it for what it is. If you feel the least bit anxious, we'll back off. You never have to power through anything, okay?"

"Okay," Jamie says. "Just—it feels good, I just feel the need to get it over with."

Eric very carefully removes his fingers, and having forgotten a washcloth or baby wipes, wipes them on his pants. He can change them later, it's just lube.

"Wait, why—"

"I want to try another way for this," Eric says. "Come on, I want to be able to help you calm down and enjoy it and see your reactions."

He lies down on the couch, and opens his arms. Jamie slides off the table and turns to lie in Eric's arms, burying his face in Eric's neck. Eric holds him close and soothes him, petting his hair and wrapping him up with arms and legs.

"It's okay," he says. "Whatever you need, it's okay. Do you want to stop?"

Jamie shakes his head. "No. This—this is better. Keep touching me."

Eric reaches out and pull the table closer so he can grab the lube, which he spreads on his fingers again. This time, he keeps Jamie close and reaches down between them and back, stroking Jamie's hole gently before sliding a finger in. The angle is a little more difficult, but Jamie's not a big man. Eric easily shifts him up a little bit and manages to get just the right angle.

"Oh, um—just—"

"Yeah, baby?" Eric asks softly, crooking his finger. Jamie jumps, gasping.

"No, no—just—oh god, wow," Jamie babbles, and Eric giggles.

"What do you need?" he asks, keeping his finger away from the hypersensitive nerves of his prostate.

"Give me—give me three," Jamie says. "Do it, I want it—"

He rubs against Eric as best he can with Eric's arm between them, but both of them are hard and they manage to find an angle that presses them lightly together. It feels amazing, having Jamie cradled against his body, rocking against him in one direction, just a tease of their cocks pressing together through Eric's pants, and back onto his fingers in the other, taking the bundle of fingers with quick little jerks that steadily grow into long, steady thrusts back and forth, his mouth open against Eric's neck, breathing hot and wet against his pulse.

"Does that feel good?" Eric asks, lips against Jamie's temple.

"Nnn-yesss," Jaime groans, breath jagged. "Just—keep going."

"That's right, baby," Eric says. "I won't stop. Go ahead and come, let yourself feel good. I'm right here."

Jamie speeds up, thrusts back harder, clutching hard to Eric's shoulders, muffling his cries against his throat. Eric whispers encouragements, endearments, urging Jamie on until he finally sits back *hard*, throwing his head back and gasping as he comes, sluggish spurts dribbling over his cock and onto Eric's pants.

"God, look at you," Eric whispers, overcome. "You're so beautiful, Jamie. I love you so much."

"Love you too," Jamie breathes, falling into Eric, who lets his fingers slip away and holds Jamie in a tight embrace, shaking as he tries to get hold of the strength of his feelings in that moment. Jamie gives him what he needs, though, saying, "Want you to come, too. Come on me?"

"You want that?" Eric asks, laughing out of sheer shock—that's a new request, and not anything Eric expected, though certainly not unwelcome. Jamie nods, smiling mischievously.

"Yeah," he says, pulling back, laying himself out on the other end of the couch, legs spread with one up to the back of the couch. He reaches down behind himself and holds himself open. "Right here."

Eric stares for a long moment before he reaches frantically for his fly, fumbling. "Oh my god."

He doesn't even get them down his thighs. He just pulls out his cock, launches forward onto his knees, and leans over Jamie as he starts fisting his cock, no teasing, no finesse, just trying to come as fast as possible.

"Soon you get to come inside me," Jamie says. "I can't wait for that. Can't wait to let you fuck me."

"Oh, fuck, don't stop talking," Eric begs.

"Can I request the threesome fantasy as our last one?" Jamie asks. "I want to watch you fucking another sub, want to *ache* for it to be me. And then he'll leave and it will be me, you'll fuck me and come inside me and—"

Eric comes. He comes *hard*, hips stuttering as he shoots white over Jamie's ass. Jamie hisses and spreads wider, tilting up, catching it. Eric smiles and grabs the plug from the table, lubing it.

"Do you want the come inside?" he asks.

Jamie looks up at him with mischief in his eyes. "Yes, I do."

Eric smiles at him and obliges, sliding what he can into Jamie with a finger before sliding the plug in. It pops in easily enough, the widest part sliding inside and then disappearing as Jamie closes up around the thin neck of it. Eric settles the long base along the path of his perineum and between his cheeks and then pats Jamie's ass lightly.

"Feel okay?"

"Feels great," Jamie says. "Except for the messy feeling. Not so much there."

"I'll go get a washcloth," Eric says. "Then we'll clean you up and see how we're feeling."

* * *

The plug vibrates on low for the rest of the day. They make dinner together, Eric standing behind Jamie and vaguely pretending to help while Jamie does the brunt of the work. They eat at the table, and Jamie kneels beside Eric and lets Eric feed him lovingly. They cuddle on the couch, watching two really terrible movies on Netflix and poking fun at them the whole time. Eric keeps full contact with Jamie, running his hands over Jamie's bare body, kissing the side of his neck, his temple, his shoulder, his cheek, grazing his lips over the sides of him that he can reach, as if Jamie's a piece of art and Eric is trying to frame him, show him his edges and maybe make him feel a little more beautiful in the process.

Finally, when the sun is down, the movies are over, and Jamie is yawning into his own shoulder (a habit that makes Eric want to squeeze him, it's so cute and strange—why he doesn't just cover his mouth with his hand, Eric could never tell), Eric slings Jamie over his shoulder and carries him laughing into the bedroom.

When Eric lays him on the bed, Jamie looks up and sighs, almost as though regretting something. Eric can feel it too—the scene is over. It feels as though something has clicked, shifted into another place. Eric turns off the vibrator before reaching down and wiggling it out slowly.

"Thank you," Jamie says.

"You're welcome." Eric lies beside him and leans in for a kiss, but Jamie pulls back. "What's wrong? Did I hurt you?"

"No," Jamie says, smiling reassuringly. "Um... could I go take a shower? Alone? I just want to... clean up and... process everything. There's just a lot going on in my head and I want to sort it out for a minute."

"Of course."

Jamie kisses Eric before he goes, but Eric still worries once he's in the shower. So he cleans, makes sure the bed has fresh sheets and that they're taut and smooth. Usually he'd just make sure the sheets were covering the bed and not worry about wrinkles or presentation—he's just gonna get back into bed and mess it up at some point, in his own view—but Jamie likes everything neat. Jamie of the perfectly lined-up coffee mugs and rolled-up socks lined up in his drawer, and who has to have an even number of drinks in his fridge. Eric can put some effort into making his damn bed in order to make Jamie more comfortable.

Maybe he can do a lot more to make Jamie more comfortable. He wants Jamie around a lot more often and for a much longer timer, and—and maybe if they eventually lived together—

That's where he wants to go, isn't it? He wants Jamie to move in with him. Or he wants progression, anyway, because it's not feeling like *enough*. They've gone deeper and deeper into this together, they've exchanged their love and entrusted their hearts. It's been more intimate, and more precarious because of that. Because they're still seeing this through, these last few scenes; they're finishing what they started.

Does Eric still want to go through with it? Yes, he does. He sees the reasons for it. But it still feels like distance. He's eager for it to be over, for it to be finished. He wants to make the bed like this every day; he wants to surprise Jamie with little things—a made bed, clean dishes, a nice dinner, extra closet space. He wants to see Jamie's face light up every day. And he wants to see it *now*.

But it's only just a little longer. And it's only if Jamie still wants it, *god*, please still want it.

"All done—oh, wow." Jamie enters and walks over to the bed and runs a hand over the smooth sheets, smiling. "You made the bed. For me?"

"Don't change the subject," Eric says, beckoning him over. "Come on, let's lie down and talk?"

"Sure." Once they're carefully on top of the sheets, lying on their sides, facing each other, Jamie smiles. "I'm sorry I needed time to myself. I just—wanted to think about the day. Without you giving me a lesson," he adds, poking Eric's stomach.

Eric covers his face. "I do that, don't I?"

"Yes, you do," Jamie laughs. "I normally like it, I like learning things and I like figuring them out with you. But I was a little too jittery and overwhelmed just then. So. Shower."

"You don't have to explain or apologize," Eric says. "I get it."

Jamie looks at him frankly. "No lesson on why I might need alone time sometimes?"

Eric pokes Jamie this time, pouting. "You already know the science side of stuff. Don't pretend you didn't look it up after I explained it the first time. So if you feel it, I'm not going to tell you you're *wrong*—"

"I am teasing you, love," Jamie says.

Eric grins. "I like you calling me *love*."

"I like calling you that, too. But we're getting off topic," Jamie says. "I was thinking in the shower, remember?"

"Yes. Go ahead."

He takes a minute to gather himself, and then says, "I think today was... kinda fun. Especially after we figured out that the total slave thing was not working. But."

Eric smiles when Jamie hesitates. "Go ahead. No judgment, remember?"

"Yes," Jamie agrees. "Okay. I just—don't think this is as much of a kink as I thought? I liked it enough, it was hot, but it was exhausting. I don't think I'd ever be able to do it as a lifestyle, or even a full day. Maybe a quicker scene."

"Then we'll just do it once in a while, when you feel like it, and… that's that," Eric says. "I liked it enough, myself, but not enough that I want to ask for it again if you're not thrilled about it. You know?"

"Yes. Good." Jamie scoots forward into Eric, snuggling into him. "That's better. Okay. I liked making today about you feeling good, though. And it made me wonder—what about your fantasies? We did one once, but… the rest of the time it's been just mine."

"True," Eric says. "Well… this has just been so interesting, I guess? I haven't thought about my own fantasies."

"Why don't we try to do one," Jamie says. "You pick the next fantasy. It can be one of mine, or one of yours, or both. And you let me know when you figure it out."

"It won't be long, trust me," Eric says, burying his nose in Jamie's hair. "I'm all out of stamina or this would be a good time to fuck again."

"Mmmm. But we could still make out?"

"You have the best ideas."

Jamie grins up at him. "But first—thank you for making the bed."

"Who said I did it for you?" Eric teases.

Jamie raises an eyebrow. "You don't even roll up your socks."

A memory hits Eric, and he smirks. "Of course not. I don't want to give you the opportunity to steal two at once."

Jamie stares at him blankly for three or four seconds that feel much longer—Eric feels stupid—and then he shakes his head. "I can't believe you remember that stupid joke."

Eric rolls his eyes. "Don't even give me hell. You're the one who made it in the first place—"

"Shut up and make out with me."

And at that point, Eric can't really think of any reason not to do as Jamie says. So he does.

DOWN TO THE FELT

DOWN TO THE FELT

"I miss you."

Seeing Jamie's face from two feet away really isn't that satisfying when it's on a screen, and in actuality he's over two hundred miles away from Eric.

"I miss you too," Jamie says. "But... a week? Then there'll be an opening at that home, the one Grandma likes."

"That's good," Eric replies, trying to sound and look sympathetic enough to translate across an Internet connection, when he'd otherwise show it physically with a hand on an arm, or a hug, or brushing Jamie's increasingly long hair off of his face. "She excited about it?"

"As much as someone can be excited about being put in a home," Jamie says with a shrug. He looks distracted and tired, and Eric's heart aches for him. "Abandoned by her family—"

"You're not abandoning her," Eric insists. "You know you're not. She *asked* you to find a permanent place with full-time care. And it's a retirement home, not a nursing home; she'll have a lot more independence—"

"I still feel like shit."

"I know." Eric grimaces. Jamie's been torn up about this since his grandmother brought it up, when the second month of his stay was beginning and she realized he was planning to become her caretaker. She's called Eric of her own accord and asked for his help. Jamie had thrown a fit over that conversation, not speaking to Eric for a whole week. Finally, Eric bought train tickets and went to D.C. to see Jamie in person. But that was two weeks ago, and it's been almost a full two months since Jamie had been in New York, and that day or two together wasn't really enough.

"How's her hip?" Eric asks at length, trying to change the subject at least a little bit.

"She's fine," Jamie says. "She hates her walker; she says it makes her look old."

Eric laughs. "I love your grandma."

"Wanna say hi?" Jamie asks. "She's around here somewhere."

He picks up the laptop without waiting for an answer, because he knows Eric wants to say hi. Eric isn't kidding—he really loves Jamie's grandmother, who's a no-nonsense type of woman with a killer sense of humor and a huge smile. She adores Eric right back and insists on talking to Eric on the phone when he and Jamie start their nightly call.

Eric takes that minute to wipe his eyes. He doesn't want to pressure Jamie with anything, or burden him with how badly he's missed, so he doesn't want Jamie seeing him cry. It's been a special kind of hell without him. It's the way it was before they met—long hours of work and, yeah, an occasional drink out with Andy. But Eric's been avoiding those meetings, because Andy and Leta parted ways, and Andy has a new pet she's all over. Eric wishes he could drag Jamie around again; he vows that they'll go out more when Jamie gets back.

And they haven't scened. It's been hard on Jamie, finally getting a consistent source of the comfort and release he needs, and then losing it almost completely and all at once. His grandmother had fallen, and he'd been her next of kin—the call had been insanity, tears and demands and gasps. Then Jamie was rushing to pack and Eric was calling to check flights and train tickets alike until they'd found a train leaving for D.C. two hours later. And then they were in a cab, and then Eric was seeing Jamie off. It had been so sudden, so chaotic. And then Eric just felt empty. Jamie had called him four times from the train and another three times from the hospital, unable to stay off the line with him for long. Eventually, he's become able to go through a day without Eric, but they still try to text throughout the day, and the nightly calls are a must for both of them. They video chat when they can as well, when Eric's not swamped with work, and when Jamie's not busy taking care of his grandmother's slowly improving health.

Jamie's unraveling, a little bit. Forgetting to eat, not taking any time for himself. Eric's had to do some long-distance Domming, helping Jamie stick to a schedule and take care of himself, but he thinks Jamie really needs a scene, and Jamie has been asking about the one they'll have next. It was only when Jamie and his grandmother had agreed on a retirement home and gotten the paperwork started that Eric started planning it, knowing that Jamie would be home soon. He'll tell Jamie more about it when they can talk in private. For now, he just waits for Jamie to find his grandmother in her big house.

Eric knows he's found her when he hears a string of words he doesn't know the meaning of at all. Jamie's grandmother can speak perfectly clear English, but she'd taught Jamie his passable Vietnamese when he'd moved in with her, and it's what she prefers to speak at home.

"Hello Eric!"

"Hi, Mrs. Tran," Eric says, waving at the tiny older woman. She's petite—not even five feet tall, thin, her posture only just bending under her age. But she's still forceful; her eyes are clear, her silvery hair pulled back into a long, wispy braid from a lively, wrinkled face that's marked with all the sunny days she's seen and the smiles she's given. She wears what Jamie called *áo bà ba,* traditional Vietnamese clothing of loose silk pants and a long buttoned shirt with slits up the side, all in bright colors decorated with embroidered flowers. "How are you feeling today?"

"Impatient," she says matter-of-factly. "I want my nice new room and freshly cooked meals."

"I cook for you," Jamie protests.

"You're a good boy, but I don't like hearing you clean up."

She winks at Eric, and he laughs. She's great; He decides he'll have to convince her nurses to set up video chatting for her when she gets to the home—she refuses to do it herself.

"I like hearing you clean up, Jamie," Eric adds, and Jamie gives him an unamused look.

"Yes, go clean for your boyfriend," Mrs. Tran says. "I get around with the damn walker; you're not needed."

"Thanks, Grandma," Jamie says. "But I have to be here at least until—"

"Eric, I will give you my card," she interrupts. "You should buy him a plane ticket. For now."

"I'll buy it with my own card if it gets him back to me, ma'am, but your safety is important, too."

Jamie does smile at him then, and it's worth the clucking of Mrs. Tran's tongue as she waves him off.

"I cannot talk to idiots," she says. "Go have your alone time; I need my rest."

"Goodnight, Grandma," Jamie says, kissing her cheek.

"Goodnight, Mrs. Tran," Eric says, and she waves, before the image of her is replaced with the darkness up against Jamie's chest as he cradles the laptop and leaves the room.

When Eric can see again, Jamie is adjusting his seat on his bed, still exactly as he'd left it in high school. Eric smiles at Jamie as he finally seats himself and balances the laptop on his knees, giving Eric a good view of him relaxing.

"Hi," Eric says, leaning back on the couch and generally looking like a lovesick idiot in the little preview window.

"Hi," Jamie echoes. "So my grandma was teasing more than usual when she told you to get me home soon. Everything's been finalized; she goes to the home on Friday, and I just have to make sure some paperwork gets to her lawyer for safekeeping. And then my job is done. I should be home Saturday night."

The news is spectacular—it's Tuesday, and that leaves only four more days. Eric claps and can't help but say *yaaaay* in the most obnoxious little voice, but Jamie laughs and blushes.

"Yes, I—I wanted to be in private before I told you."

"I wanted to be in private too, but for a different conversation," Eric says. "That's actually quicker than I thought you would be home, so... I have to tell you my part now, so we can begin."

"Oh yeah?"

"Yes," Eric says. "I figured... when you get back, we can do a scene. A fantasy."

Jamie perks up. "I had ideas about that, too. But tell me yours first."

"Okay." Eric clears his throat and settles. "Okay. So. I figured we could do your fantasy about the wax play? And I can get in a fantasy with that one, too."

"Ooooh, what's that?"

"Photography?" Eric suggests. Seeing Jamie's eyes widen, he quickly adds, "Not like super raunchy porn stuff! That would be awesome, but I would actually just love to do some artistic shots. Use colored waxes, drip them over your back, then photograph it? Your face wouldn't even be in the shots, just a nice non-graphic nude—"

"That sounds perfect," Jamie says, breathy and eager. "That's—that's good, I like that."

"Oh? You want to be photographed? Want to pose for me, make me want to put the camera down?"

Jamie bites his lip, eyes dark, but he shrugs. "I actually thought I could start a modeling career."

Eric laughs. "I could see that. Do some headshots, no one will know that below the frame I've tied you up and tortured you for hours. You'd look gorgeous, no one could resist you—"

"How about my idea, now that you've mentioned tying me up and torturing me?"

Eric's immediately intrigued. There are only two other fantasies after the wax—the pushing of the safeword boundary, and Jamie tied up and watching Eric fuck another sub. It sounds like the latter— "Do tell."

"You know... my fantasy about you... spanking me? Or... or paddling, or whatever. And... you keep going even though I safeword?"

Oh. That one. "Yes, I know that one."

"How about we combine it?" Jamie says. "We can do the wax, and the photography... that can be a sort of... build up? And then... then we transition. Like... when you peel off the wax, you—you can flog the fresh skin. That would—my skin would be more tender, right?"

"It would be very tender," Eric says. "And the blood would be near the surface, so we'd have to be very careful not to break the skin. It would be a lot more delicate—"

"I—I wouldn't mind if you broke the skin?" Jamie says.

Eric shakes his head. "I—I wish I could give that to you, Jamie, but I'm uncomfortable with it. I'll—I'll bruise you if you want. If you like that feeling and the look of it, that's okay, I can give that. But I don't know if I could actually see you bleed because of me—"

"No, no, that's fine," Jamie says. "Never mind, I didn't—I won't do it if you're uncomfortable, of course. You've always respected my limits; of course I'll respect yours."

"Thank you."

Frankly, Eric is panicked about the mere idea of any bloodplay. He's not *afraid* of blood, per se, but the line for his own comfort is drawn before that. If Jamie wants to be hurt a little bit, Eric will do his best to do so safely and enjoyably, but he would never want to *harm* Jamie. There's a big difference, and any breaking of the skin, any blood, feels too much like harm. But thankfully, it doesn't appear to be a big deal for Jamie. They can move on from that.

"I can do something, though," Eric says. "Give you some sensation. You want really intense, right?"

"As intense as you can go."

"Maybe we can try a soft flogger," Eric says. "I'll do a little research and pick something out, okay? And I'll show you before we—"

"No." Jamie shakes his head and gives him a little breathy smile. "Don't show me. Just—just do it. And—and don't warn me? Like when we're in the scene. I don't want you to tell me before you do anything."

"Jamie—"

"I know that's—but I looked this up."

"And you realize it's not SSC, right? Jamie, play *needs* to be Safe, Sane, and Consensual, and I'm not sure this fits that—"

"But it *is* RACK."

Risk Aware Consensual Kink. Something Eric's never touched in his time in the scene. It's a grey area, a hard end of BDSM, and it works stupendously for a lot of people who like the hardcore element, who like the thrill and the pain. Eric's not very good at doing anything that doesn't feel caring to him. He can pretend to be rough, but when he actually goes there, it unsettles him. And this is edging that line.

"Are you aware of the risks?"

"Yes," Jamie says. "From my end, I am informed and I am ready. I want this. If you don't, that's okay—we can figure something else out—"

"No, I just... I want to be careful," Eric says. "I'll do it for you. All right? We have to agree on how it's going to go completely, though. No surprises."

"Done."

* * *

They do talk about it. And most of the talking is Jamie putting his trust so completely in Eric that he just doesn't want to know anything outside of his own instructions to shave his body completely and moisturize heavily for a few days before the scene.

"I know I can trust you," he insists, at least ten times. Eric knows he's trustworthy, but that doesn't mean he's not nervous for this. So he does what he does best—he prepares.

The bedroom is where they'll do it, for maximum comfort. He buys an all-purpose fabric tarpaulin—not the most comfortable thing, but it's not canvas or the plastic-y blue things. This is brown and green, simple and utilitarian. Then he buys thick, special candles that will burn fast and at low heat, in all kinds of vibrant, oil-based colors (so they won't alter the melting temperature), and some mineral oil. Finally, he stocks up on his aftercare items, and adds a few more things—namely, a first aid kit. He had a basic one before this, but he picks up a much larger one. It's probably not going to give him anything more usable than what he already has, but it calms him a little to be so totally prepared for anything.

And then he sets up his bedroom. Tarp on the bed. First aid kit under the bed. Aftercare items—Lidocaine gel, baby wipes, juice box, ibuprofen and a chocolate bar—on the nightstand. Also on the nightstand is some soft black silk rope. He's wearing his soft belt. The candles are laid out on one side of the bed, and his lighter is nearby. He has his camera sitting on the dresser—nothing fancy or special, just a regular digital camera.

And that's it. It's not nearly the most complicated scene he's done, or even that they've done together, but it might be the most difficult.

By Jamie's request, they're going to do it the moment he gets home. They've both missed it, Jamie especially—he desperately wants subspace, and Eric will give him what he needs to the best of his ability. He'd do anything for Jamie.

So when he stands in the airport, waiting, he forgets his nerves and his heart takes over. The anxious buzz is replaced with anticipatory thumping, excitement he can't suppress as he watches the arrivals board and stands next to baggage claim. It only grows when he sees Jamie's flight has arrived. Five minutes, ten minutes. And he's waiting.

And then, seventeen minutes after the plane arrives, Eric spots Jamie rushing down from the direction of the gates, approaching with a strange half-run, half-walk, all-waddle that looks as though he wants to just run but is too nervous to do so, and god it's *him* and Eric's *missed* him so much and *fuck* he is so in love with this man—

"Jamie!"

Jamie spots him, grins, and then he speeds up his waddle-run. Eric waits for him, unable to stop watching and laughing, but before he knows it he has his arms full of his boyfriend. Everything washes over Eric at once, as if his senses are amped up and he can feel everything ten times as strongly—the way he smells, the sound of his breath and laughter, the solidity of his body, the strength of his arms—all of it is so *real*, more real than it ever has been, and Eric buries his face against Jamie's shoulder and tries to hold back tears and feels *so stupid* about it, but he just *missed* this man so much and he has never, in his entire life, felt happier than *right this second*.

"Kiss me," Jamie says eventually, when it's clear Eric won't be releasing him anytime soon. "Please, please kiss me, missed it, missed you—"

Eric lifts right up, and finds Jamie's mouth with his. And it's as though the taste of him is stronger, too—he'd forgotten, even after just over two months. And he'll get to discover it again, get used to it again, get used to the soft drag of Jamie's lips, the warmth of his mouth when he opens and closes it in tandem with Eric, the slide of his tongue in between, the way he holds the sides of Eric's neck and puts his thumbs up behind Eric's jaw. He'll forget what *this* moment is like soon, this intense moment of reconnection—maybe. It's pretty strong, and he'd like to remember it.

But all too soon Jamie pulls back—they're still in a public place, and they have plans.

"Take me home."

"Okay."

* * *

Outside of the door to Eric's apartment, Eric stops them.

"When we go inside, we can head straight to the bedroom and start the scene," Eric says. "When that happens… you're giving up any control, right?"

"Yes," Jamie says.

"And based on what you want, I will not listen to anything you say. I won't listen to *no*, I won't listen to *stop*, and I won't listen to our safe-words. You realize that this means that I won't know if you actually stop consenting to what's happening."

"I trust you," Jamie says. "I trust you to know what I want, what I need, my body—all of it. I want to give everything up to you."

Eric has a brief suspicion that Jamie sees this as romantic, the ultimate display of trust, and it might be that, but Eric's not feeling romantic. He's just feeling uncertain again. But then, that's the point of the easy buildup—he can get into the Dom role with the wax play, and when the time comes, he can do what Jamie wants, and maybe he'll want it, too. He's bruised subs up before—hell, he's bruised Jamie on several occasions. There's an appeal, when it's totally consensual, and the subs want it so much, want the release that comes with it, the reminder, the ache and tenderness and even the visuals. When it's done *safely*, when participants are *sane*, and when they *consent*, it's beautiful. But Eric's still just so unsure of removing that last factor. He's always felt that removing one fractures the others. It's like taking a leg out from a three-legged table—it might balance, but the slightest upset can topple it.

Jamie's trusting Eric to keep everything in balance. And he'll do his damn fucking best, he really will. He wants to give Jamie everything he's ever dreamed about.

"Okay. So you consent to this scene, knowing all the risks, knowing that you could be very hurt, knowing that you have absolutely no power, no say, no way of communicating with me truthfully from now until the scene is over?"

"I consent," Jamie says softly, smiling. Eric nods.

"Okay."

He opens the door, and lets Jamie walk through first. Then, he follows Jamie to the bedroom.

Jamie stops just inside the room, eyes darting between all the various effects of their upcoming play. He licks his lips, and Eric can't tell from the gesture if he's nervous or excited. Either way, they're in the bedroom—their scene has begun.

"Leave your bag outside the door." When it's set down, and Jamie is back inside the room, Eric shuts the door. "Strip and then kneel."

Jamie takes off his clothes hastily, efficiently. When he's naked and kneeling—and, Eric notes, unaroused, so Jamie's probably nervous rather than excited after all—Eric walks over to the bed and picks up the candles. He sets them up in a row, in rainbow order, on the dresser next to the door, parallel to the bed a couple feet away, and lights them one by one. They burn bright, and by the time he lights the purple one at the end, the red one at the beginning already has a small pool of liquid wax at the center of the pillar, around the base of the wick. Eric smiles at them—they're pretty colors, jewel toned, and they'll look amazing against the cool, light brown of Jamie's skin.

"Go lie face down on the bed," Eric says. "Wait there."

He doesn't watch Jamie follow the order—he goes to get the remaining supplies. In the kitchen, he opens the freezer and pulls out a bag of ice and empties it into a big bowl. He carries that to the bathroom, where he grabs several towels. Then, it's back to the bedroom.

Jamie is lying face down on the bed, as instructed. Eric sets the bowl of ice and towels on the dresser near the candles, and then heads to the bed, grabbing the black silk ropes from the nightstand.

"I want you to stay as still as possible," Eric says, adjusting Jamie until he's spread-eagle, starting with one wrist, tying it with the rope and then tying the loose end to the headboard. Then, moving to an ankle, he says,

"This will hurt. I don't care what noises you make. So feel free to beg, to cry, to scream. It won't matter."

Jamie shudders, his breathing deepening—it was the right thing to say. And when he's tied completely, he rocks against the bed just once, just a little bit—finally turned on, it seems, and that's a good thing. Despite his assurances that he doesn't care, Eric *does* care. He's not totally into his role yet, and he'd rather Jamie enjoy this at the moment. But he can try to get into the headspace—it'll be a little easier with the sensual experiences that are coming up.

He grabs the mineral oil and twists off the cap. It's so smooth in his hands that it's almost as if it's not even there, but when he starts rubbing it on Jamie's dutifully hairless back, his palms start to tingle with its spread. Jamie relaxes completely under his hands, groaning as Eric kneads his muscles, treating him to a full massage. He starts out with knots in his muscles, probably from the lengthy stress of dealing with his grandmother's injury and the pain of admitting her to a home. Then Eric moves down, massaging Jamie from shoulders and arms all the way down to his calves, until the entire back of his body is shiny and practically melting under his fingers.

Of course, he's about to face another kind of melting. The silly thought makes Eric smile and he's glad Jamie can't see him. He's supposed to be stern and unshakable right now, not making dumb puns in his head.

He gets up and heads to the candles. The pools of wax are ample and the right size for what he wants to do. He picks up the red candle and carefully carries it over to the bed, blowing out the flame so that the wax doesn't burn too much or catch fire on its way to Jamie's skin. This also gives the wax time to cool just a little bit before he pours—the candles are Japanese wax and can burn too hot over time. He sits next to Jamie on the bed, leans over him and carefully poises the candle where he wants it, just between Jamie's shoulder blades.

There are several ways he could do this, but he has an agenda. He could splatter the wax widely, which would create a lot of sensation, but spread out, so it would be less intense. He could go slowly, paint it around with his fingers or a brush. He could've even gotten a wax melter and ladled a large amount of wax over him at once, thickly, which is his intended effect, but too quickly over. No, he's going to pour a thick layer of wax over Jamie a little bit at a time. The thicker layer will keep the heat in the skin, too, even as it dries, keep the blood close to the skin, keep it sensitive. It takes a while, and he might have to freshen up some spots, but Jamie is oiled and sweating slightly already; his body heat will help with keeping things as warm as Eric wants them to be for the duration of this part of the play.

He tips the candle close to Jamie's skin, drawing it diagonally down from near his spine to his side. Jamie tenses and hisses, but within seconds the wax is setting, slowly but surely. It's a line about three inches long, maybe an inch thick, the color rich as it sets. Eric blows cool on it, and then rises and heads to the dresser again, lighting the red candle again and picking up the orange.

He repeats the process, blowing out the flame, leaning over Jamie, pouring the wax, putting it right along the red, just a little closer to his side. It's roughly the same size, roughly the same shape. He cools it, relights the orange candle and grabs the yellow. And it goes on and on, cycling through the rainbow colors, to green to blue to purple, six colors repeated over and over, patterned over one side and then the other, drawing hisses and pained groans out of Jamie again and again, until most of his back is covered in what looks like a multicolored houndstooth pattern, wide up near his shoulders, tapering unsteadily down to his tailbone, a single line of wax dripping to his sacrum. Finally, Eric covers bare spots and draws a multicolored swirl of lines down his spine, letting the wax drip thin this time, over and over, until it's all twisted together in a beautiful rope of colors.

And then finally it's over. Eric dips a towel in the ice to collect any water, and then runs it lightly over the wax, hardening it further. Jamie's legs twitch as though he wants to move, probably uncomfortable with the tightening on his skin, but he stays obediently still.

"Photo time," Eric says.

He picks up the camera and turns it on. The lighting in the room is dim but good—the candles are still burning to the side, and the bedside lamps are on, so there's a warm glow. Eric straddles Jamie's thighs, kneeling up and keeping his weight off of Jamie, and aims the camera.

"Gorgeous." And it is. The pictures aren't in any way professional—Eric likes to think he's got an artistic eye, but his hands are never quite steady enough and he can't seem to translate the images in his head into images on a camera or a piece of paper. But these pictures of Jamie are probably his best. It's cheesy, it's cliché, and Eric usually gets a little embarrassed for himself when he thinks things like this, but he thinks these are beautiful simply because it's Jamie, and Eric loves him. He doesn't have to have the perfect angle or the best lighting or the best frame of the shot, because in every angle and every frame and in every light, Jamie is utterly stunning to him.

When he's finished taking the photos, he sets the camera aside. He stands and he looks and he lets the moment settle over him. The play has been wonderful—he's turned on, he's excited, and the scene has settled into him. And Jamie appears to be fine—he's flexed into the bed a few times, clearly aroused now, and his forehead is buried against the bed, cutting off his sight. He's probably seeking subspace, if he isn't there already, knowing what's to come and what he'll have to endure.

Eric takes the ice and grabs a big piece of it. He brings it over and rubs it over the wax directly, making it as hard as possible. Then, with the edge of the ice, he taps hard on the wax, weakening it a little bit, putting little cracks in it—it's not that hard, but any advantage he can get, he'll take.

He tosses the ice carelessly into the corner of the room. Then, he undoes his belt and slides it from its loops. He wraps it around his hand, buckle in his palm, until just a little tail is left, six inches long, hanging from his fist, steady under his thumb.

He doesn't say anything. Jamie doesn't, either. The moment stretches, tenses, like a rubber band. It could snap back into shape, it could break entirely. Either way, Eric gets to decide when to stop this. Jamie doesn't have a say anymore.

He reaches to a piece of wax low on Jamie's back. With his nail, he digs under it, and when he has a decent hold on it, he tugs sharply. A chunk of about two and a half colors tears from Jamie's skin easily, aided by the oil he'd applied before and the fact that he'd cooled and hardened the wax beforehand. And as soon as that skin is revealed, pink and warm, Eric snaps the belt, letting the tip of the thick leather strike the skin hard.

"Oh, fuck!" Jamie cries, tensing, breath catching in his throat. "Ow, ow—"

Eric does it again, another chunk, this one further up his back, on the other side. He peels away some wax, just a couple inches of free skin, and then snaps the leather. And then again, and again, four, five, six times. Each time, Jamie cries out, body writhing uncontrollably, cracking the wax further, giving Eric easier grips and peels so he can strike again.

But the more this happens, the more unsettled Eric becomes. It starts as just a spark of concern as he sees the first place he struck turn dark red, obviously the start of a bruise. Jamie likes bruises—as long as they are consensually placed, he really loves the sight and feel of them, from Eric leaving hickeys across his chest to the deeper bruises of a good spanking. And Eric likes them too—not just on Jamie, but on himself, when Jamie fucks him rough and leaves fingerprints bruised into his hips, bite marks on the backs of his shoulders. They're reminders, little aches to carry around and remind him of what they've done.

But these are different, somehow. Jamie is in actual pain, uncomfortable pain that he *can't* consent to. He gave blanket consent at the beginning, of course, that's the point of this. But Eric knows that Jamie is going to safeword. He knows Jamie is going to stop consenting, but also that Jamie wants to give up that consent and have it violated. He wants Eric to do that, to take that trust and claim it completely and keep it only by not *permanently damaging* him. That's the only line.

Eric freezes, just after the seventh strike. He can't do this. He can't cross this line; he *knows* Jamie is going to safeword, and he can't face that. He can't *force* the man he loves in any way, even if they agreed upon it; it's a line and it's getting closer and clearer and Eric knows he can't—

"Red."

He drops the belt as soon as the word is out of his own mouth. He holds his breath, and he grabs a towel, rushing to the bathroom to run hot water over it before rushing back and applying it, peeling away the softened wax with as little pain as he can, scraping it rather than tugging it, letting it slide away. When it's done, he dabs at Jamie's back with the towel, pulls over the aftercare kit, and pulls out the Lidocaine. The towel is on the floor, the wax is everywhere, and Eric doesn't care. Jamie might be talking, too, but Eric's ears are rushing, his body is shaking, and he *needs* to get Jamie taken care of before he can let go. So the Lidocaine is applied, thick to the forming bruises and then gently and thinly over the rest, just in case. Finally, he tugs at the ropes, trying to loosen them with slippery hands, finally letting out a sob and wiping his hands, feeling like an utter failure at *all* of this. He tugs the ropes dry this time, and they're loose, all of them, and finally he just sinks to the floor, back against the side of the bed, and buries his face in his hands.

"Eric—Eric, please talk to me—"

It feels *wrong*. He couldn't do it. He just couldn't keep going. The spark of concern had just grown and grown so fast, roiling in his gut until he was shaking with anxiety. He knew that he was about to violate something he never wanted to violate, something that just couldn't mesh with the identity he'd settled into as an entire person, his role as Dom included. Blanket consent wasn't enough—it might be for someone else, but Eric doesn't want to do anything that might fall outside of complete and total consent at all times, always given.

Jamie's arms wrap around him. He feels the warmth and the strength and he breaks. Sobs tear out of him, tears leaking despite his hands pressed over his face, his body huddling in on itself. He crossed a line in himself and hurt himself in the process. And god, he must've hurt Jamie too, pulled him out of subspace, harmed him, exactly what he didn't want to do. But Jamie had *wanted* it, and Eric couldn't, and—

"Sorry—" Eric sobs again, cutting his own words off. "S-so sorry, sorry, I'm so sorry, Jamie—"

"Sshhh," Jamie whispers, cradling Eric close. "It's okay. I'm okay. I'm fine, you didn't hurt me. Focus on you—can you try to breathe with me?"

Jamie's got a hand on his chest, which is fluttering and jerking in shallow, panicked breaths. He presses hard, steadily, and Eric exhales everything as best he can. When Jamie pulls his hand back, he tries to follow it with an inhale to match. It takes a few times to succeed, his lungs screaming and demanding quicker breaths, but after a minute or two he's breathing steadily, his tears falling in a quiet, quavering drip rather than the frantic, panicked bursts of shame that had been cascading out of him.

"I'm going to help you up," Jamie says, his voice calm and gentle and even. "We're going to head into the bathroom, and we're going to take a bath. And then when you're ready, we'll talk about this, okay?"

Eric nods, wipes his face, and follows Jamie up to their feet as best he can. He follows Jamie around the bed, watches him grab the aftercare kit, and then lets himself be led from the bedroom and into the bathroom. Jamie sits him on the toilet, pulls the juice box from the kit and sticks the straw in before handing it to Eric.

"Drink that," he says, and then he turns to the toilet and starts running the bath.

Eric does as he's told. It's easier, and he doesn't have to think or question. He just has to trust Jamie, let him take over while he's like *this*, broken down and *weak* and—

"Come on, let's get in."

Jamie sits down first, letting Eric lie between his legs. It's a clumsy, tight fit, and one of Jamie's legs ends up out of the tub completely, lying along its side. Eric lets himself be held, lets the water pool around them. And after a few minutes of lying there, Jamie's lips brushing behind his ear, he takes a breath.

"I couldn't do it," he says. "I knew you were going to safeword, I knew it was coming. And I just kept seeing you bruised, like *bad* bruises, and I knew you couldn't stop it if you wanted, and—and that just ruined the consent for me. I'm really sorry, I know you wanted this—"

"Hey, it's okay," Jamie says. "Eric, that was a fantasy. That's it. I know I was eager, and I am really, really sorry if I pushed. But I don't care about a fantasy, not like I care about you."

"I just—maybe I shouldn't have pretended I could do this—"

"If you didn't want to at all, I agree that we should've talked about it more and that I wish I'd known more of your concerns," Jamie says. "I like to *think* I would've listened, but now that I'm thinking about it, it's like... you were hesitant, and I still insisted—"

"No, you were—" Eric stops himself, and sighs. "I guess we should both make sure we're always communicating as well as we can."

"I agree," Jamie says. "I'm sorry, okay?"

"I'm sorry, too."

"Not for safewording—"

"No. For not trusting myself and speaking up." Jamie just nods, nose pressed against his ear, and Eric relaxes. "So we can take RACK off the list. If—if you still want a list."

Jamie reaches around, cups Eric's cheek, and turns him so they face each other over Eric's shoulder.

"I want everything with you," he says deliberately. "And the reason I pushed so hard was to get the fantasies over with—I'm ready to be yours, I'm ready for a contract. I want that."

Eric turns over and kneels over Jamie, leaning in to kiss him. "So we're done with the stupidest idea I ever had? We're doing this, committing, et cetera—"

Jamie laughs. "I've *been* committed, but I guess we can call it that." He leans their foreheads together. "Serious talk time?"

"Sure."

"We've been throwing around some weird definitions about 'together,'" Jamie says. "We decided to take it slow, and then it was about getting the fantasies done, and... and I feel like we should've just said fuck it the whole time, you know? Like, why are we doing this?"

"We had good reasons, I think," Eric says. "At some point, anyway."

"Yeah, I mean—it all made sense at the time," Jamie says. "And I feel like—after tonight, why continue? Why not take this as the sign that maybe fantasies don't always work? Because—because I don't want us to be fantasy, Eric. I don't want this relationship to have turned out to be just some *thing*, just a... I don't know, an *experiment*. I don't care what fantasies I fulfill from here on out, I haven't for a while. I just want you."

Eric nods, holding his jaw tight. He doesn't want to cry again. "I love you."

"I love you, too," Jamie says, a laugh on the edge of his voice. "So—do you want to skip the next fantasy?"

"What is it?" Eric asks. "It's the threesome, right?"

"Yes."

Eric sits back, looks down at Jamie seriously. "Do you—do you still want that to be your first time bottoming with me?" he asks carefully. "I understand if you don't, I don't care if you never want to—"

"No, I do," Jamie says. "I trust you with it, with myself."

Eric smiles. Jamie just took care of him after he used a safeword, after he had a *panic attack*. He just so smoothly stepped in, and knew Eric well enough to know what he needed; if Eric can't trust him now, he's got serious issues. And he does trust him—that much is true. So he understands, he wants to be close to Jamie, to take care of him. That vulnerability is appealing, especially now that he feels... *closer* to Jamie, somehow. Probably his brain is pouring out its chemicals, but for once, Eric could not give a shit about what his chemicals are doing or why.

"Do you want to do it that way, then?" Eric asks. "You wanted it for a reason, if I remember correctly."

Jamie had only mentioned it a couple times, but he nods now, and says it outright. "I want to see you with someone else first—I guess to see it can be really good. And to make me wait, and to build up anticipation in a good way. It'll be really hot, I think. But if you aren't comfortable—"

Eric takes Jamie's hands. "I'm not worried about being jealous—I trust you, and I know that I couldn't want anyone else the way I want you. But if you are—"

"I'm not," Jamie says. "The idea of you fucking someone else doesn't bother me. It's just sex, you know? Just your body. I know you're mine."

Eric smiles and leans down for a kiss. "Yes, I am." He kisses Jamie as sweetly as he can manage. "So are we doing this? One more fantasy?"

"One more," Jamie agrees. "And then it's just us, no more holding back because of any lists we need to complete, okay?"

Eric smiles and nods. "I like the sound of that."

HITTING THE JACKPOT

HITTING THE JACKPOT

Exploring Jamie, exploring with Jamie, has been Eric's favorite way to spend his time over the past seven months. Work no longer consumes his every day. He doesn't spend every free second wallowing in bad TV and bad food. He doesn't end his nights lonely and missing that little spark in his chest that comes with the satisfaction of sharing himself with someone.

Seven months they've been doing this—seven months since Eric snagged a room card, lucky number seven, and found Jamie waiting for him inside. Seven months since he broke the rules and got Jamie in return. And that moment, that night—it was like pulling the lever on a slot machine. Seven months, the reels spun, and going into this last fantasy, planning it with Jamie, knowing that after this they can take it one lifetime at a time in any way they want—it's landed on all sevens. A jackpot.

But no, not really—that metaphor doesn't feel right. Because Eric's seen the sevens a few times. It's less like slots, it's as if he threw some dice and landed sevens every time—seven always wins. A few times he hit another number, felt as if he lost a little bit, but really, it's just been win after win after win. One big win, with loaded dice. And he couldn't care less that all of this happened because he cheated. He'd do far worse to win someone like Jamie in his life.

Jamie has ended up being everything Eric wants. If Eric were younger, more naive, he'd probably have seen it exactly the way he sometimes suspects Jamie does—the meeting of two kindred spirits. And he has felt it in pieces—when they're deep in a scene, when Jamie goes under and gives himself over to Eric with total abandon, Eric feels it rise inside him. Jamie's trust is like baking soda and vinegar, welling up into something explosive and passionate that overwhelms him, changing his very makeup into something that is purer. He turns into someone who believes that he and Jamie are really meant for each other. Feeling that, having Jamie precious and vulnerable in his hands, accepting him and all that he believes and somehow knows to be true—it's something Eric has wanted, and has tried to deserve. And now that they're almost finished, it's as though he's succeeded. They're going to write up a contract. They're going to stop the game and just *live*.

Eric's ready for it. So the planning goes as fast as he can make it go.

"Okay," Eric says one night. "I know someone who'd be interested, an old friend from college. He introduced me to my first boyfriend in the scene, and he and I hooked up once, but it never went anywhere. And I haven't really spoken to him in a couple years, just some social media nods back and forth, you know? I can talk to him, introduce you two—"

"If he's hot, and can take your cock, I don't even care," Jamie says, frisky again even though they just had sex, hurried and clumsy after not seeing each other for three days due to conflicting work schedules. "Just want this—"

"I want you to be comfortable, Jamie," Eric insists, and Jamie shakes his head.

"I am, I'm comfortable with whatever you want," Jamie pushes back, rocking on Eric's thigh, reaching down and stroking him with frantic fingers. "If you think he's attractive, I'll know. You show it all over your face, it's so hot—"

Eric laughs and flips Jamie onto his stomach, rocking into his ass suggestively, ready to tease Jamie into wanting to be filled the whole week over. He won't do it until it's time—but he can make his beautiful sub beg for it—

"I'll give him a call, then."

* * *

His name is Phillip Miles, but back in college he was Lip. Eric can't shake the habit of calling him that, but Lip doesn't seem to mind when he gets

Eric's call. He and Eric had been in the same group of friends back in college. He'd also been Eric's introduction into the scene. He'd introduced him to Stanley, who'd been Eric's boyfriend and then encouraged him to explore being a Dom. Then when the relationship with Stanley had bitten the dust, Lip had introduced Eric around a little more, shown him the ropes. They'd hooked up once—a drunken shenanigan after a failed night of dancing, agreed never to be repeated. But Lip seems more than happy to oblige Eric's request, despite the fact that it would technically be a repeat. Ropes and all, even if they weren't going on Lip himself this time.

"So let me get this straight," Lip says, voice a little rougher than it was back in college; Eric can hear his pretty little grin over the phone. "You want me to come over to your boyfriend's place, let you fuck me until I actually cannot anymore, and then I get to either lay around and watch you with him or go home, no strings attached."

"Yeah, pretty much," Eric corroborates, and Lip laughs.

"Well, count me in," he says. "You wanna text me the details?"

And it's that simple. Four days later, Eric grabs Jamie around the waist after supper and kisses his neck.

"Lip will be here at eight," he says. "What do you say we shower up, get pretty, and then I'll tie you up while we wait?"

They fool around in the shower, and Eric makes sure to let Jamie come at least once, because they'll both be waiting a long time once Lip gets here. So Eric kneels, takes Jamie's cock in his mouth, and sucks him eagerly, letting Jamie fuck his mouth while he reaches back and fingers Jamie open, moaning when he can grab a breath. He jerks himself roughly with his free hand, coming long before Jamie does.

With that done, they wash each other thoroughly, soap slippery between them, giggling and groping each other happily until they're finally clean. Drying off is a similar affair, until finally they end up on the bed, still charged and turned on. Eric buries his face in Jamie's ass and eats him out vigorously around two fingers thrusting in and out of him hard.

But he doesn't let him come that time. Instead, he gets Jamie up on his knees near the headboard and takes the ropes and ties him up thoroughly, adding decorative knots around his torso simply for the joy of it. And then he kisses Jamie deeply, tongue fucking his mouth until Jamie is whimpering. He then pulls away and ties a gag around his mouth.

"Lip will be here soon," Eric says. "You wait here. And think about how later tonight, I'm going to fuck my cock right into your tight little ass."

Jamie groans even as Eric shuts the door, smiling to himself and ready to wait around for the next ten minutes for eight o'clock to arrive.

And it does. Lip shows up at the appointed time to Jamie's apartment, and he and Eric sit down in the living room with a glass of wine each to talk before they get started.

"Where's your sub?" Lip asks, and Eric smirks into his wine.

"He's already tied up," Eric says impishly. "I'm really not planning on making this easy for him."

"God, this is going to be fun." Lip sips his wine and smiles playfully at Eric. "So let's go over this again—and what are the limits?"

Eric swallows his mouthful of wine. He usually prefers other drinks, but he remembered Lip likes wine. Jamie had indulged in a glass before their shower, so he'll enjoy it this once. "Well. We're going to go in. He's tied up, like I said. He wants to watch me fuck you, and if you can still manage to come two or three times in a row, that would be great," Eric says. "But whatever way it goes, he wants to watch and be unable to do anything. You and I are going to keep it sexual, he doesn't want to see us pretend romance or anything. And then when you and I are done, he asked that you come sit out here. This is big for him—he changed his mind on letting you watch—or you can go home, up to you. But if you do stick around, you can have some pizza with us. And just—nothing too hardcore, I don't think it should be an issue. Just fucking."

"So... I'm not banned from touching your boy?" Lip asks, eyebrows raised. "I ask because... if you want me to... I could always make things a little more fun."

"Like how?"

Lip grins.

* * *

With a small addition to their plan in place, Eric leads Lip into the bedroom. Jamie is kneeling at the head of the bed, tied to the headboard, trussed up in silky ropes from his shoulders to his thighs. His cock hangs heavy and swollen between his legs, and he's panting around the simple fabric gag.

He moans when Eric guides Lip in, and the subs both give each other once-overs. Jamie looks wrecked—Lip is a handsome man, tall and ropey, his skin dark and smooth. He's always got a smile, and it only grows when he sees Jamie and nods appreciatively.

"Where do you want me... Master?"

Jamie whimpers, cock bobbing as he tenses and fights his binds, and Lip's grin lights up. Eric settles into his role for this and nods to the bed.

"Strip. Lie sideways across the bed, parallel to the footboard, on your stomach."

Eric stands and watches, arms crossed, as Lip does what he instructs. Eric can see him relaxing into it, the game turning into something much less playful as it begins, something darker and harder. Both Lip and Jamie focus totally on Eric, eyes darting to him periodically, and he stands firm, watching with a practiced cool gaze as Lip finally lays himself over the bed, head resting on his arms, slender body naked all the way down to where his feet lie dangling off the edge of the bed.

Eric nods approvingly, and then begins to undress, one piece at a time, slow and steady. Two pairs of eyes are on him, watching every revelation of skin until he's completely bare. He folds up his clothes with his back turned, laying everything carefully on Jamie's low dresser across from the foot of the bed. Then, completely bare and unashamed, he walks over to the side of the bed where Jamie keeps his toy box, and roots through it to find their cock ring.

It's leather, and Eric's grateful for its pliability as he wraps it carefully but tightly around his cock and balls, softened with just a touch of lubrication to ease potential chafing. He finds himself aching to see how long he can stand it, how long he can use it for the fulfillment of his sub, how much he can make him take. It's not as though they've never used one— Jamie knows, and Eric can see it in the way Jamie stares right at his cock, too hard, jutting out and hanging slightly with its weight.

One of these days, he's going to do to Jamie what he plans to do to Lip—he wants to fuck Jamie until Jamie can literally no longer take it. But for now, he can have a little practice and make Jamie watch what's in store for him.

He turns to Jamie, smiling. "Nod for green, shrug for yellow, shake for red," he instructs, and Jamie instantly nods, biting around the gag. "Color," he says, turning to Lip.

"Green," Lip provides, and Eric smiles.

"Such good boys."

He crawls onto the bed, straddling Lip's thighs before bending over, hovering over his back, his lips pecking a light trail from the top of his spine.

"Mmm," he says, making sure his voice is loud enough to carry. "Why don't you turn your head over and tell Jamie how this feels, Lip?"

Lip obeys, sighing as Eric digs his fingers into the muscles of his back, licking into the dips in his flesh that appear when he tenses and relaxes.

"Good," he breathes, head now facing up toward Jamie. "His lips are—warm. Soft. Strong hands," he says with a laugh, when Eric digs into his sides.

"Where do you want my mouth and hands, Lip?"

Lip shivers at the sure tone in his voice, as though Eric knows exactly where he's going and the question is a formality. And for all intents and purposes, that's true—but Lip can't be sure of it, and Eric relishes his anticipation.

"Lower," he says. "Please, Master. Lower."

Eric very nearly laughs. "You mean... here?" Eric slips off the edge of the bed and starts stroking at Lip's thighs and calves, digging into the tanned flesh there. Lip wriggles.

"Higher," he whines, and Eric inches just a little bit upwards, hands skirting underneath the crease of his ass and thigh, barely touching. Lip pushes back hopefully. "Higher, Master. Touch my ass."

Eric hums and obliges.

"Good boy, asking for what you want," he says encouragingly. He sits over Lip's thighs again, hands grasping at his cheeks, spreading them and squeezing them firmly. Lip arches his back into it, responsive and eager. "Jamie, do good boys get rewards?"

He raises an eyebrow at Jamie, watching as he heaves for breath and nods frantically, high noises escaping his clenched teeth. He's hunched over as much as he can, his hips twitching with the need to get friction for his poor cock, still hanging untouched. Eric licks his lips deliberately.

"If you're a good boy, Jamie, I might be persuaded to ease some of your discomfort," Eric offers. "But for now, I want you to keep your eyes on me; and try to stay quiet."

Jamie nods, swallowing his noises, and Eric smiles widely at him. But he offers no words, instead slithering down until he's half off the bed, awkward but necessary as he spreads Lip's legs. He hovers over the bed and allows one leg to take his weight on the floor, the other bent up to kneel on the bed as he bends over, giving Jamie a nice view of his ass perked up into the air, his cock throbbing hard out of its little leather cage.

He dives into his work with all eagerness—he has always loved rimming, and Lip is gorgeous, and so responsive and vocal. It's one of Eric's biggest turn-ons—something he loves very much about Jamie, and something that he appreciates in any sub. And Lip really doesn't disappoint. At the first touch of Eric's tongue to where he's spread open between Eric's thumbs tugging at the wrinkled skin of his hole, he groans, his voice rough and broken as it rings out wordlessly for several moments. But then, Eric stiffens his tongue and starts to prod at him in earnest, licking and sucking him loose, and the words leave Lip in a steady string.

"Oh, fuck, yes," he gasps. "Master, please, more—fuck me with your tongue, please, yes—"

Jamie stays quiet. His beautiful boyfriend. Eric looks over periodically, and he can see him shining with sweat and straining in his binds, but he makes no noise aside from the harsh hissing of his breath around the gag, which is dark with his spit. Eric is so, so proud, and he makes it a good show for his boy, making Lip thrash and writhe and beg, palming his own cock when the pressure grows too strong, staring hard at Jamie as he does so, his mouth still working on Lip's spit-slick hole, poking and wriggling and stroking and sucking with every trick he knows.

"Please fuck me," Lip finally begs. "Please, please use your cock, I need it, need it to fill me up, fuck me right into the bed, please—"

"God, both of you are so good to me," Eric breathes, working his jaw and smiling at Jamie with his chin shining with saliva. Jamie's face is twisted up in serious desperation right now. He looks down at Lip, who's turned to peek over his shoulder, and a brief moment passes between them.

"Please let me," Lip begs. "Please, Master, let me suck his cock."

Jamie gasps high and hard, and Eric smiles over at him. "Do you want that, my beautiful boy?" he asks. "Want Lip to give you a little relief?"

Jamie nods, and Eric instantly shuffles up the bed, cupping Jamie's face in his hands. His cheeks are faintly wet, from tears and spit and sweat, and Eric strokes them clean, kissing the corners of his eyes.

"You've been so good," he whispers. Then, raising his voice. "Lip, please come up here?"

Lip crawls up, and Eric lifts Jamie up to a better posture, massaging his skin beneath the ropes, his fingers just able to slip in and give his body some stimulation after being pulled so tight. Lip nuzzles at Jamie's thighs, and Jamie bites hard on the gag.

"No, baby," Eric says suddenly. "I want to hear you. And I need you to tell me when you're too close, okay? This is just for a little feeling, you won't be coming yet. Okay? Give me a color."

He loosens the gag and drops it down to hang loose around Jamie's neck, and Jamie pants out, "Green, green, please—please—please sir—"

Eric glances down at Lip, who looks like some intensely sexual cat rubbing and licking at the thin skin of Jamie's thighs, just next to his heavy balls.

"Go ahead."

Lip doesn't play around. In one swallow, he's got Jamie in the back of his mouth, his throat working and opening, his neck twitching with it, and Jamie's crying out, almost slumping over again until Eric catches him and helps hold him up.

"Oh, yes, how does it feel baby—"

"God, Eric, *fuck*—so good, *unh*—"

"That's right, let me hear you," Eric urges, and Jamie complies so wonderfully. He doesn't use as many words as Lip—the occasional curse or plead is all he needs. The rest are wordless cries and exclamations and high keens, his beautiful face twisted up and desperate as he tries not to look down and watch Lip sucking him off enthusiastically.

"Are you getting close, baby?" Eric asks, stroking Jamie's hair and letting him rest his head on Eric's shoulder. "I can feel you shaking, tell me now—"

"Y-yeah, close, I'm close—"

"Lip, stop." Lip pulls off and wipes his chin, and Eric nods back toward the foot of the bed. "Back to position," he says. He turns to Jamie, wiping his face again. "Are you okay, honey?"

"Yeah," Jamie rasps. "Yeah, please—just—wanna watch, wanna see—"

"Want to see what?"

"Fuck him," Jamie whines. "Please, fuck him."

"Yes," Lip agrees emphatically, arching his back and offering up his ass for Eric's use. Eric wants to spank it raw, actually, seeing the glint in Lip's eye. "Please, Master—"

"Very well, baby," Eric whispers to Jamie, kissing his cheek. "Do you want the gag back on, or can I leave it off? Can I hear you talk about how we look?"

"Yes," Jamie agrees, and Eric takes the gag off completely, dropping it to the side and kissing Jamie sweetly, rubbing his arms as best he can with the rope crossing over them to keep them against his body.

"I love you."

He leaves the bed, and returns with a condom and a bottle of lube. He slips on the condom, lubes up, and then traces his slick fingers up Lip's crack, brushing over his spit-wet rim, still soft and loose the way Eric left it. Lip's totally relaxed—in the perfect space to give it to him, just the way Eric wants to—hard and fast, the first round. After that, he can draw it out.

"Are you ready?" Eric asks, slipping two fingers inside him. He eases past the resistance and stretches him easily after just the briefest tension, and then gives him three fingers with almost as much ease. Lip is wonderful that way—he so easily gives himself up, just goes along with everything that happens. And he knows what's coming— his body was half the reason Eric chose him and not any number of other acquaintances from the scene. He's a friend and a cool guy, but the most important part in the equation is his ability to keep going again and again. Eric looks forward to it, and Lip does too, judging by the willingness with which he opens up for Eric.

"Yeah, yeah I'm ready," he breathes. "Fuck me, Master."

Almost before Lip's done speaking, Eric spreads him open and sinks into him, replacing his fingers in a smooth plunge.

"Uhhh, yeah," Lip groans. "Do it, come on—"

Eric happily obliges. Once he's fully sheathed, he adjusts his legs, straddling on either side of Lip's legs and pushing them together, tightening the grip around his cock. Lip follows his guiding hands, raising his ass up and pushing his shoulders down, his head perfectly settled down on the bed, his eyes locking right onto Jamie and hazing over as Eric bends over him, holding him under his chest and up to his shoulders. He thrusts once, slow and easy, to check the fit of their bodies and the comfort of it. Once he's satisfied, he starts a hard pace, hips pistoning hard as he holds firm on Lip's shoulders.

"Oh, fuck," Lip says, mouth dropping open, eyes drifting closed. "Oh, fuck, yes, fuck me—"

Eric doesn't pause. His cock is throbbing and oversensitive, the blood trapped beyond the leather, keeping him heavily tumescent as his balls try to draw up and his nerves scream their protests, their need to reach peak and come. But Eric won't, and can't—he has two beautiful subs to service, and one of them is tense and crying out beneath him, impaled again and again as Eric's hips work furiously, the friction sweet as he's swallowed up with every jerk down.

Lip's quick to reach his climax. Eric's pushing his hips right down into the bed, sliding him against the bedsheets, and his cock is trapped under his stomach, surrounded and thrusting between all of that weight with Eric's frantic pace. Within just a few minutes, he grips the edge of the bed above his head hard, biting his arm and pushing back with that leverage, his cries hoarse and muffled into his bicep. A few seconds later, he's lax, limp as Eric continues to fuck him, high-pitched whines leaving him as he takes it, wriggling with a touch of discomfort.

But he takes it—his refractory period is so blessedly short; after some uncomfortable tension, he starts rocking with Eric again, moaning loudly.

"Oh my god, oh my god—" Jamie is babbling, and Eric slows down his movements, rocking slowly, long pulls out and hard pushes in, looking over at his sub with a smile.

"You wanted to watch me fuck him a few times, right honey?" Eric asks teasingly, and Jamie almost sobs, writhing and sending a string of pre-come off the tip of his cock onto the bed between his thighs.

"So hot," Lip pants. "Jamie, watch—he feels so *good*—*nnn*, his cock is—*fuck* it's big—"

Jamie's eyes widen; Eric knows he's been nervous about Eric's size. He stares at where Eric disappears inside of Lip, and Lip's arousal at being filled so much seems to seep into him as well. He licks his lips and whimpers, straining toward them, and Eric pulls slowly from Lip, letting Jamie watch as Lip gapes around nothing as he withdraws.

"No, come back—"

Eric lays a hard smack on Lip's ass, and Lip bites back his words, burying his head down into the bed.

"I think it's time we showed Jamie a different angle, don't you?"

"Yes—yes Master—"

Eric pulls back and goes up to Jamie, half-lying back and settling his head back on Jamie's shoulder, propping himself up against Jamie's torso and resting his arms over Jamie's trembling thighs. Jamie's cock pokes him in the back, leaving a smear, and Eric turns to nuzzle under Jamie's jaw.

"Lip, face the footboard. Show Jamie what it looks like."

Lip obeys, putting some more lube on Eric's cock before straddling him, holding himself up with hands on Eric's stretched out legs, his knees bent slightly, sinking back with Eric's steadying help to take Eric to the hilt again before sliding up, holding his weight forward and letting Eric and Jamie both catch a perfect view of Eric's dick disappearing between his cheeks, his rim stretched wide and swollen around its girth.

Jamie's breath is heavy and harsh in Eric's ear; he periodically drags his lips over Eric's ear and temple, high noises cracking from his throat as Lip bounces, straining to keep Eric inside him, never lifting much before he slams back down, hips rocking back and forth as he draws up and down, his whole back undulating in the low light of the bedroom, wide and sweaty and a deep brown color that looks stunning next to Eric's pale, flushed skin.

"Doesn't he look so good?" Eric asks quietly, letting Jamie's cock catch along his spine.

"Yessss," Jamie whines. He can't seem to keep himself in control, heaving breaths into Eric's ear. "Yes, so good—want to be him right now—"

"Oh, baby," Eric gasps, thrusting up into Lip, hands flying down to hold his hips down so he can grind up hard. It's torture, not being able to come when everything above the knees and below the waist seems to be burning with the need.

"I'm—*uh*, gonna come," Lip grunts, reaching back and spreading his cheeks for them, and Jamie cries out, pulling his hips back from Eric and biting down on Eric's shoulder. Eric grabs Lip's wrists and brings them together, tugging him down and fucking up, and Lip bows and cries out and sits back hard, bucking and spilling onto Eric's thigh.

"Think you can come one more time for me, Lip?" Eric asks, and Lip peeks back, slumped over and leaning heavily on Eric's legs.

"Y-yeah," Lip gasps. "I—I might. I just need—um—"

"Tell me," he orders, and Lip slips off of him and kneels next to Jamie.

"Uh—I need something for my cock," Lip says. "I can't come just from—just from your cock again. Getting kind of numb."

"That's okay," Eric says. "Jamie—do you think you could help Lip out?"

"Yes—yes please—"

"Um—can you just use—fingers?" Lip asks. "I'm—I can't stretch anymore, too big—"

"Okay, okay," Eric says. "Are you sure you can take more? We can stop now—"

"No," Lip insists. "Green. Green, green, green. One more."

Eric lays him down, and turns to Jamie. "I know you wanted to stay tied—do you want to? I can take care of Lip myself." Jamie looks torn, and Eric instantly strokes his face. "I'll leave you right here if you want. Want to watch me suck him off? Swallow his cock right down?"

Jamie nods. "Yeah—yeah, I'm sorry, I—"

"Never apologize," Eric says, kissing him. "This is for you, Jamie. Your fantasy. You think you can handle this? I'll untie you right after."

"Yeah, green," Jamie says, taking a deep breath. "Go ahead. Please, Eric."

"Okay."

Eric leans down over Lip, spreading his legs and plunging in one finger after slicking it heavily with more lube. Lip groans, and Eric strokes until Lip thrashes. Once his target is found, he strokes around it, bending down to suck around Lip's half-hard cock.

"Go—go fast," Lip says. "I can't make it if you don't just do it—"

"Are you too sensitive?"

"No, do it. I can take it."

Eric does as he's asked, sucking hard and pressing a stroke over his prostate. Lip tenses and shouts, overcome with sensitivity, but Eric trusts him to know his body. Again, it only takes a few minutes of playing him as hard as possible before Eric flicks his tongue into Lip's slit and tastes a quick spurt of salty come.

"I'm—I'm done, oh god," Lip moans. "Can't—oh fuck—"

"It's okay, you were so good," Eric says, pulling away from his ass and cock and stroking his neck and shoulders. "Very good boy, thank you so much—"

"You don't need to soothe me, okay?" Lip whispers. "I didn't—didn't go under or anything. Just—take care of your boy."

"Okay. Thanks for all this—and if you wanna stick around—"

"I'll go wait out in the living room, have some more wine," Lip says. "Recover a little. Use your shower, raid your fridge. You owe me pizza, too, remember?"

Eric laughs and kisses Lip's temple softly.

"Just give me my time with him, and we'll order," he says. "Use whatever you want—and if you need me, just let me know—"

"Go be Jamie's Dom," Lip urges. "I can take care of myself; I'll let you know if I can't."

He slips from the bed and hobbles to the door, winking at Jamie on the way out.

"Is he—" Jamie starts, watching the door shut.

"He'll be okay," Eric says. "He does this all the time, trust me."

"I resent that," Lip calls from the other side of the door, and Eric snickers turning back to Jamie.

"If he needs me, he'll let me know, okay?" Eric assures. "My job now is to take care of you. What do you need, Jamie?"

"Untie me," Jamie says. "Just—need you inside me, please—can you?"

"I can," Eric says. "I can't say how long I'll last, but I'll give you everything I can."

"We can work up to more later, just *please*—"

Eric works swiftly to undo the knots and unwind them from Jamie's body. Once he's free, Eric lays him gently out, propping him up with pillows and massaging his poor muscles. Jamie groans through it, relaxing down and down and down until Eric's sure he's on the edge of sleep but for his purpling cock standing turgid above his tight balls.

"Let me open you up, baby," Eric murmurs, grabbing the lube and parting Jamie's legs, stroking over his hole gently, far different from the treatment Lip had requested. Jamie allows it, accepts it happily, sighing and offering himself with bared throat and lax limbs.

"Take off the condom?" Jamie requests, when Eric is thrusting three fingers loosely, spreading Jamie easily in his relaxed state. "Don't forget, want you bare—"

Eric pulls his fingers free slowly, and he smiles down at Jamie, sudden tightness and tingling in his eyes. This man—god, he's *everything*. His trust, his generosity, his sweetness. Eric is so far gone.

Why did he ever fight this? Fear is the worst reason to keep himself from someone so perfect for him.

"Yes," Eric agrees. "Yes, Jamie."

He pulls the condom free and tosses it aside. He'll clean it all up later. Nothing matters now but Jamie beneath him, spread and wanting.

"Are you ready?" Eric asks, lubing himself and lying between Jamie's legs, drawing the head of his cock in short stripes along Jamie's perineum, following the tight little seam there with his aching slit. "We'll go slow—"

"I'm not worried," Jamie whispers, stroking Eric's face with weak hands. "I trust you to take care of me."

Eric kisses him deeply, and when Jamie's arms wrap around his shoulders, he pushes in. Jamie grunts as Eric breaches the rings of muscle, one and then the next. His eyes close tightly, and Eric strokes his thighs and kisses him again.

"Relax baby," he says. "Relax, you can do it."

"So—so much—more than I thought—"

"I know, I'm sorry—"

"No, s'good," Jamie pants. "God, Eric, it's so good, please—"

Eric slides further, and Jamie gradually opens around him, rocking in little movements until Eric settles inside him. Here, he lets out a little cry, fingernails digging into Eric's shoulders.

"Just—just hold on a sec," he says, voice tight. Eric hushes him and nods, kissing every inch his lips can reach, hands stroking over Jamie's trembling thighs, drawing sweat along the twitching muscles, the softest caress. As long as Jamie needs—any amount of time, Eric will wait.

After a long moment, Jamie opens his eyes and looks up at Eric, tears quivering on the edge of his eyelids.

"Are you okay, Jamie—"

"I'm great," he quavers. "I'm—Eric, I'm so good, you have no idea—"

Worried, Eric says, "Tell me."

Jamie laughs, wiping his tears away, and he shakes his head.

"I just—this is always a big deal to me," he says. "I've told you before. Always want it to mean something—not just another thing to do, you know?"

"I know, baby—"

"And it does mean something," Jamie whispers. "It means everything, Eric. Feeling you like this, letting you in. I just—I never thought I'd be lucky enough to have someone like you, and here you are, and you're just—you're everywhere, inside me—"

"Jamie—"

"I'm just—so full," he giggles, kissing Eric sweetly. "I feel like you're taking over everything—I'll never stop feeling you like this. And I just looked up, and all I could think was, *finally*. It's so dumb but I finally feel like I just—belong to you, Eric. The way you're looking at me, and how hard you're trying to make this good—you're everything I've ever wanted—"

"I love you," Eric gasps out, and out of his control, his hips thrust just the tiniest bit. Jamie gasps and returns the movement, and before either of them can question it they're moving together, barely parting, struggling with each other to stay close and whisper their breaths between them, only them. "Love you, Jamie, have for so long—"

"Love you too," Jamie says, hitch in his voice, face drawing up, tears leaking from his eyes. "Eric—"

Words fail. They clutch and move and cling and breathe, inhale, exhale, inhale, exhale to and from each other's lips, sharing everything their bodies can handle. There are no words in this place, no expression but the give and take of their bodies, Eric opening Jamie so wide around him, Jamie whimpering and sobbing and taking it, babbling nonsense, lifting his legs around Eric's waist and pulling him in, in, in.

Eric can barely catch his breath. Jamie is sweating and biting his lips, holding back so hard, and he can barely last any longer himself. He hurts with the need to come, and he bends down to suck a mark into Jamie's collarbone.

"Need to come," Eric says. "Tell me what you need, what—"

"Just—just tilt up a little—"

Eric does as requested, adjusting a few times before Jamie scrabbles at his back, leaving sharp lines of pain behind that have him arching into his thrusts.

"Yes, there, right there, don't stop—"

Eric cries out, sharp and staccato with his desperate need to catch his breath, his inability to do more than fuck Jamie and let his body do the work, his mind swirling into nothingness, a vortex of sensation and pleasure as Jamie shouts his name, stretching his legs up and pumping his ass up to meet Eric's hips, tossing his head and digging his fingers in hard, clutching too much, too much—

"Come, Jamie, please—"

"Keep going, *keep going*, don't stop—fuck, Eric, *fuckfuckfuck*—"

Jamie cries out, a broken wail, and shoots several long ropes of white up his stomach, painting him. Eric fumbles down around his cock, unsnapping the leather and pulling it free roughly. Two more thrusts and he seizes; the muscles in his stomach and back and thighs spasm wildly as he comes hard into Jamie's ass, grinding deep and making uncontrolled noises into Jamie's neck, kissing his pulse slowly as he comes down.

Jamie is totally gone. Drifting, eyes fluttering under closed lids, eyelashes wet and sticking together, mouth open and drawing in deep, gasping breaths that slow with every second. Eric doesn't move—lets Jamie hold onto him, lets himself grow soft inside, holds himself up just enough to keep his full weight from Jamie, enough to keep him totally in contact, skin to skin, sweat to sweat, heartbeat to heartbeat. Eric thinks his heart might have filled all the free space available in the room, actually, hammering hard and needy in his chest.

"Love you."

Eric pulls free from Jamie—falls free, slipping easily from him—and kisses him, letting Jamie turn into him as he settles on the bed. "I love you too," Eric hums, holding Jamie close.

Jamie smiles up at him. "Let's make that contract," he says, as if he'd do it right this second. And Eric would, too. And he will. He'll fall into the clichés and the fairytales and he'll let himself believe—because he can't deny it anymore. Not after that.

"Okay," Eric says. "We'll pick out a collar tomorrow. Something fit for a fairytale prince," he adds facetiously, giggling at his own joke.

Jamie grins and buries himself in Eric's arms, and settles into Eric. He made the right choice.

And then all of a sudden, Jamie laughs. "I wonder how many fairytales end with a BDSM contract."

Eric laughs too, but he doesn't really care. What he knows is that they'll lie here and cuddle until they finally remember that Lip is out in the living room, probably ordering way too much pizza without them. They'll go out there, they'll eat, they'll cuddle on the couch and when Lip leaves, they'll stay up way too late and eat more pizza and then they'll probably pass out on the couch without cleaning up. They'll scramble to get ready in the morning before they remember that it's a Sunday and they don't work. They'll get breakfast, they'll relax, they'll talk about their contract.

They'll draw it up, they'll shop for a collar, they'll sign it all up and it'll mean something to them. Then they'll make love and fall asleep and start another day. They'll start a lot of days. Over and over again.

Their fairytale ends that way. He can cash in his chips, ride off into the sunset, whatever. It ends with Eric and Jamie together.

That's all he needs.

FARO SHUFFLE

FARO SHUFFLE

A collar is a symbol. The one Eric has picked out for Jamie isn't for casual play, and it's not quite a wedding ring. It is, in his estimation about three quarters of the way to the latter.

It's got a ring *on* it. But it's not going to be used for fingers, unless Eric decides to drag Jamie around by it.

"Can I see it?" Jamie asks every night in the two weeks from its purchase to the date of their party, their *ceremony*.

"See what?" Eric replies every night, with a small smile on his face. The collar is in a box on the otherwise unused top of Jamie's kitchen cabinets. Eric knows Jamie would sweep everything in Eric's apartment, regardless of how unlikely the spot, but his own apartment would never be a suspected hiding place; it has high shelves and even Eric, at over six feet tall, can't reach that high usually. Some creative balancing on the counters while Jamie showered, though, and the collar had remained hidden despite Jamie's best efforts.

Eric isn't really a fan of Jamie's apartment. Not lately. It's been out of his way, inconveniently far from his own home. But it's useful, for now. For these past two weeks.

But now they're in Eric's apartment, lying on the floor of the kitchen, covered in stray splashes of vinegar and sweat, and Eric is glad it's in his own place, because he wouldn't have wanted to expend the effort of cleaning for nothing.

"I smell like a salad," Eric says vaguely. He's low on caffeine, but dirtying the coffee pot after just having cleaning it—and everything around it— seems like a bad idea.

"Better than smelling like a pool," Jamie says. "Or... chemicals. Vinegar works great for cleaning and stain removing and deodorizing, and it's natural—"

"Baby," Eric laughs. "You told me this about five times before we even started."

Jamie rolls over onto his side, props himself up on his elbow, and raises an eyebrow at Eric. "I am passionate about vinegar."

"I know," Eric says mildly. "That's why I smell like a salad and have a clean kitchen."

Jamie grins. "You're going to let me reorganize everything in here, too, right?"

Eric bursts out laughing and rolls into Jamie, burying his face against Jamie's sticky shoulder. He smells pretty good—the way Jamie does, pepper and man smell, but now with the added layer of distilled white vinegar lingering around the edges.

He kisses Jamie's neck. "Yeah. Knock yourself out. Just—expect a lot of having to remind me where shit is."

Jamie giggles and rolls away, rising to his feet. "Yes! I'm gonna start. You go start rubbing down the bathroom."

Eric groans. "Why, though?"

"Because A, you decided to go nuts and redecorate everything and you can't do that in a dirty place, and B, we are having a party," Jamie says. "And I don't care if it's only a few people, we're going to have a clean apartment."

We. Eric likes the sound of that.

He stands up and kisses Jamie's cheek quickly. "Fine, have it your way," he teases, and then dodges the answering swat and heads for his next cleaning duties.

* * *

The apartment is clean and magically doesn't smell a bit like vinegar by the time their guests arrive Saturday evening. There's a gentle scent of rosewood and jasmine from some oil concoction Jamie had been boiling on the stove the past couple of nights, and it feels right with the *new look* of Eric's apartment, graciously provided by Jamie himself at Eric's expense.

Andy whistles when she walks in, arms laden with bags, clearly impressed. "Well shit. What happened to your stuff?"

She looks really weird in a mustard yellow button-up with a kind of ugly long collar, and Eric goes ahead and says so, accepting the hard poke to his shoulder in retaliation. "This is fashion. Which you should know about, because your place is following it for once."

Eric looks back into his apartment, the living room spread out before him, now comprised of squares. The couch is made up of square shapes, the coffee table is now three cubes with open sides, and Eric's overstuffed armchair now has a cover over it so it's white with black square-ish block letters scattered over it that don't spell anything. Jamie had wanted to get rid of it completely, but Eric had put his foot down on that—the only thing he hadn't been willing to change. But he'd conceded to the cover, because it's still just as comfortable no matter how it looks.

"Well, you have to move with the times, you know?" Eric says casually, but Andy's been his friend for years, and she pokes him again.

"You let Jamie do everything," she says. "Are you going to—"

"Shut up?" Eric interrupts, too loud out of panic. "Yes. I am, and you too. Come on, drinks."

"My girlfriend should be up soon," she says. "Different one from last time, this one's name is Ayana." She grins wickedly. "She's Ethiopian and she's a gymnast—"

"Please don't give me details," Eric says, leading her to the kitchen. There, Jamie is chatting with Leta and Jeremy, the guy Leta brought to the dinner at the restaurant, when Jamie came in his pants. Jamie glances up, catches Eric's eye, and grins.

"Do you want a drink *now*?" he asks, wiggling his own. "And you, Andy?"

"What have you got?"

"Wine, beer. We're all drinking tequila sunsets." He holds up his glass again, half-full of a reddish orange drink.

"What is a tequila sunset?" Andy asks, as Jamie pours two more from the gigantic pitcher he'd made.

"It's a tequila sunrise that I was too lazy to mix individually, so it doesn't have layers," he says. Andy chuckles appreciatively as she takes the drink and sips it. "Mmm, that's good, thanks." She looks over at Leta, smiles, and then turns and starts talking to Jeremy as Jamie ambles over to Eric.

"Here you go," Jamie says, handing Eric his with a kiss. "Who are we waiting on now?"

"Andy's new girl, and Lip," Eric says. "And then we can do the ceremony, and then they can go, right?"

Jamie leans in close, pressing his torso against Eric's side, and smiles. "You're the one who suggested a party. With people."

"I wanted to do this one thing right," Eric says.

"You're a slow learner," Jamie sighs. "It's right if it's us, okay?"

Eric nudges Jamie in the cheek with his nose. "Yes, sir."

"Oh, very funny—"

"Hi, guys!"

Eric breaks away, and then is gathered up into a hug by Lip. "Whoa, when did you get here?"

"The door was broken down while you two were in your lovey-dovey world," Andy says. "My girl's here, too; come say hi."

Eric looks over at Jamie as Lip pulls him into a hug, mouths *I love you*, and heads over. Might as well get the host duties out of the way—there will be plenty of time ahead to be wrapped up in Jamie. And besides, Lip is rattling the box with the collar at him, along with a large white ribbon bow—they're all that's left to be ready for the ceremony.

* * *

Andy, Ayana, and Leta are seated on the couch. Lip is in the armchair, and Jeremy is perched on its arm, feet crossed against Lip's thigh. Before them, between them and the door, with the kitchen behind him and the hallway behind Jamie, Eric stands, holding the box with their collar, Jamie kneeling before him at his feet with a smaller box in his hands.

He's thought about these words for weeks. They'd agreed to keep things casual, because the contract they'd come up with was casual. It was just a paper form of their relationship, their boundaries and their hopes. Nothing restrictive, nothing binding, just something they could use as a tool for their scenes—just like the collar. But this ceremony feels important, and it's the one semi-formal part of their night. This is a promise to each other, to be with only each other, to commit. An extra step in the classic relationship progression that Eric had always been so hopeful for, but now so grateful that he didn't stick to.

"Jamie Kader," Eric says, smiling down at Jamie and opening the box. "I offer you this collar to wear when we are together as Dom and sub, to act as a symbol of our bond, to remind you that I'm always with you even in the deepest of subspace, and to show that I've promised myself to you by putting it on you, however you need me, however I need you."

Jamie tilts his head back, baring his neck in acceptance. Eric reaches down and fastens the collar around him—fitted, warm brown leather with a magnetic T-clasp in the back and a D-ring at the front, both copper plated to give them a gorgeous color. It looks stunning next to Jamie's slightly lighter skin, and with his eyes, which match the colors closely.

When it's clasped and carefully centered over the dip of Jamie's collarbone, Jamie grins.

"I'm gonna steal what you said," he says. "My ideas all sucked."

Eric laughs. "Go for it."

"Eric Yates," he says. "I offer you this cuff to wear when we are together as Dom and sub—and when it matches your outfit—to act as a symbol of our bond, to remind you that I'm with you even when I pass out on you, and to promise myself to you for whatever you need and—I'm pretty sure I said that wrong—"

"Close enough," Eric says, holding out his left wrist. Jamie picked out a simple cuff—the same color as the collar, because they'd coordinated that much; Eric appreciates its simplicity. It's just a cuff with two tiered layers, strapping together on the inside of his wrist.

"I'm gonna get that buckle in copper," Jamie says. "I like the copper, I want it to match."

"We'll get it done," Eric says. "In the meantime, get up here."

He pulls Jamie to his feet, and then Jamie's in his arms, kissing him as their friends whoop and catcall and applaud.

"Gifts!" Andy calls. "Come on, make out later, I have shit to give you!"

They pull away from the kiss, but not from each other. Eric feels too clingy, too needy for Jamie's body against his; by the way Jamie clutches at his back and presses his head against Eric's neck, he clearly feels the same way.

"Where are we supposed to sit?" Eric asks. The couch and the chair are all taken—

"Floor," Jamie says. "Come on, you can do it, old man."

"I'm less than a year older than you are," Eric protests, but he sinks down with Jamie before the coffee table, reaching for one of the gift bags their friends are pulling out and tossing haphazardly onto the coffee table. "All right, what's the swag?"

The swag turns out to be a whole lot of sex toys. Several dildos, paddles, cuffs for wrists and ankles and one that attaches both to a collar. Different kinds of lubricant, massage oils, three different kinds of rope. Eric particularly likes the gift from Ayana.

"It is a chastity cage," she says as soon as it's pulled out of the bag, her low voice lilting prettily. It looks like a leather jock strap with a metal sheath in the shape of a limp penis attached to the front. "You put yourself inside and you cannot get hard or orgasm."

"God, please look up how to use that before you put it on, by the way," Andy says.

"No worries there," Eric says, putting the thing back in the bag for safekeeping. "Education first."

Jamie leans in, biting his lip. "Educate fast, okay?"

Eric smiles at him sidelong, but before he can respond, Jamie stands.

"Okay," he says. "I have a gift for you."

He heads into the bathroom, and Eric looks around at his friends. Out of all of them, only Leta doesn't look confused.

"What did you hide in my bathroom?" he asks.

Leta shrugs and then breaks out into snickering just as Jamie returns. "Ta-da!"

He's carrying a big glass vase filled with green leaves topped by anthuriums. As soon as Eric sees their heart shapes, the spadices sticking out, he bursts into laughter, hands flying up to cover his face.

"Oh my god," he says, voice muffled behind his hands. "Are you serious?"

Jamie is clearly delighted with himself, his grin splitting his face, dark eyes sparkling. "I am very serious. I think it is only fitting that we start how we began. And I have a special reason for getting these."

"To make me die?" Eric asks. His face feels hot and tight from holding back laughter and tears alike; *god* he loves this man so much.

"No," Jamie says. "I got them because I looked up the meaning after I gave you that first one. And there's a bunch of stuff about hospitality, but it *also* stands for letting your desires be irresistible. And they're for celebration when you get those desires. So... you were always pretty irresistible to me, and now that I have you... I want to celebrate."

He holds out the flowers, and Eric takes them and holds them up to his nose automatically.

"These don't smell like anything," he says. And everyone is instantly laughing at him, he is an *idiot*. "I—thought they'd smell like something. They don't."

Jamie takes the flowers out of his hands and puts them on the coffee table before falling into his arms, laughing. "I love you."

"I love you, too," Eric says. Over Jamie's head, Lip catches his eye, making a wild gesture that Eric only understands because he knows himself that it's time. It means *go for it*.

"I have a gift for you, too," he says. "It's funny that those flowers mean hospitality, too, because... so does my gift to you."

Jamie looks up at him, confused. "Okay? Please tell me you didn't get me the same thing—"

"No, but... I mean, you got it for yourself, by extension," Eric says. The anxiety roils in his gut—this is technically too soon in his own mind, but it feels *right, fuck* does it feel right. "I mean... if you want. You don't have to accept, but... I'd like very much if you did."

"Okay," Jamie says, looking around. "What is it."

Eric kisses him gently, and then whispers, "Look up."

Jamie looks up. There, in the center of the ceiling, is the white bow.

"There's a bow on your ceiling," he says. Eric bites back laughter, and waits for Jamie to get it. And within a minute, he does. His eyes widen, and he looks down at Eric, mouth hanging open.

"Eric?"

Eric kisses him again, smiling.

"Um. I'd like to give you... this, as your gift. This place. A home."

"Oh my god," Jamie says, smiling wide. "Are you serious? Say it, say it so I know—"

"Move in with me," Eric says.

Jamie squeals and throws his arms around Eric's neck. "Oh my god, this is why we cleaned—"

Eric laughs, and holds Jamie tightly. "Yes. Yes it is."

"So you don't clean otherwise?" Andy asks, but Eric just flips her off.

"Honey, people don't clean like I clean," Jamie says. "I am on a whole other *level* of clean—"

"I kind of like it when you're dirty, personally," Eric says, pulling Jamie close to him.

"Oh my god, I think that's our cue," Andy says, standing up and pulling Ayana with her. "We're out of here."

"Same," Leta says, stopping to peck them both on the cheek. "Have fun, boys!"

"We're gonna head out, too," Lip says, smiling in a mischievous way. Eric notices Jeremy lingering, waiting for him.

"Ooooh, nice," Eric says. "Thanks for coming, Lip."

"Anytime," Lip says, clapping them both on the back with each of his big hands. "Except for the next... two hours."

"Ambitious," Eric says.

"Not nearly enough," Lip chuckles. "Let me know if you need help moving, Jamie. I can show off my muscles."

And then, with a wave, the apartment is empty but for them.

"What now?" Jamie asks, holding Eric tightly, nosing at his jaw. "Should we plan out how we're going to move my stuff? What I'll need and everything—or we can finish writing up our contract; we were supposed to have that done for the ceremony—"

"I think that can wait," Eric says, glancing down at their laden coffee table and then snaking a hand up to Jamie's throat. He bends a finger into the D-ring at the front of the collar. "I think we should try out a few of our gifts."

Jamie looks down, and then back up Eric. "Should we make a list?"

Eric smiles. "I think we can wing it, this time."

THE END

ACKNOWLEDGMENTS

First and foremost I want to thank the team at Interlude Press for finding this story and believing in it. Candy, Annie and Lex, especially, you guys are amazing and the work you do is special. I'm grateful to be a part of it.

Special thanks to Jude for the continual help and encouragement during the craziest month ever. Further thanks to my husband, for his support and love even though this isn't his thing, and my family, who were cheerful about the whole process. Also thank you to all my friends and followers who adored this story from its humble beginnings to what it's become now, and who have supported me unequivocally.

About the Author

Moriah Gemel has a dedicated following for her realistic, sexually-charged stories developed over twelve years in online fan communities. Passionate about sex education and the realistic portrayal of BDSM, she has the goal of both entertaining and educating readers.

Load the Dice originated as a short fan work, written in three parts. For her first work of professional fiction, she has turned it into a serialized novel in ten parts, now complete. Moriah is hard at work on her second novel, as evidenced by all the empty coffee cups in her home.

She is married and has a young son.

Find Moriah at <u>moriahgemel.com</u>.

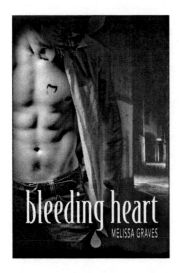

Also from interlude press

interlude ✦ press

One Story Can Change Everything.

interludepress.com

Twitter: @interludepress * * * Facebook: Interlude Press
Google+: +interludepress * * * Pinterest: interludepress
Instagram: InterludePress

CPSIA information can be obtained at www.ICGtesting.com
Printed in the USA
LVOW07s0136230115

423969LV00001B/26/P